Praise for *Trebl*

"A pleasing read with a thoughtf
rings, and some foodie tips."

—*Kirkus Reviews*

"A lighthearted and amusing story with the added bonus of several yummy recipes."

—*Mystery Scene*

"*Treble at the Jam Fest* has all the necessary elements to satisfy cozy mystery lovers: likeable, believable characters, a fast-moving plot, and a logical ending. Great fun!"

—*Suspense Magazine*

"A delicious mystery as richly constructed as the layers of a buttery pastry. Wine, enchiladas, and song make for a gourmet treat in the coziest town in Montana!"

—Krista Davis, *New York Times* bestselling author of the Domestic Diva Mysteries

"Leslie is a fellow foodie who loves a good mystery and it shows in this delightful tale!"

—Cleo Coyle, *New York Times* bestselling author of the Coffeehouse Mysteries

"Music, food, scenery and a cast of appealing characters weave together in perfect harmony in Leslie Budewitz's latest book."

—Sheila Connolly, author of the Orchard Mysteries and the County Cork Mysteries

AS THE

CHRISTMAS COOKIE CRUMBLES

Other Books by Leslie Budewitz

AS THE

CHRISTMAS COOKIE CRUMBLES

A FOOD LOVERS' VILLAGE MYSTERY

LESLIE BUDEWITZ

MIDNIGHT INK
WOODBURY, MINNESOTA

FIRST EDITION
First Printing, 2018

Book format by Cassie Willett
Cover art by Ben Perini
Cover design by Shira Atakpu
Editing by Nicole Nugent

Midnight Ink, an imprint of Llewellyn Worldwide Ltd.

Library of Congress Cataloging-in-Publication Data
Names: Budewitz, Leslie, author.
Title: As the Christmas cookie crumbles: a food lovers' village mystery / by Leslie Budewitz.
Description: First edition. | Woodbury, Minnesota: Midnight Ink, [2018] | Series: A food lovers' village mystery; #5
Identifiers: LCCN 2017051233 (print) | LCCN 2017054898 (ebook) | ISBN 9780738755335 | ISBN 9780738752419 (alk. paper)
Subjects: | GSAFD: Mystery fiction.
Classification: LCC PS3602.U334 (ebook) | LCC PS3602.U334 A92 2018 (print) | DDC 813/.6—dc23
LC record available at https://lccn.loc.gov/2017051233

Midnight Ink
Llewellyn Worldwide Ltd.
2143 Wooddale Drive
Woodbury, MN 55125-2989
www.midnightinkbooks.com

Printed in the United States of America

For the villagers, who make this place home.

Acknowledgments

I'm grateful to my friends and neighbors for their support, and for tolerating the changes I've made to our community on the page. Although the Playhouse is real, its history as the Bijou is not. But Decorating Day is great fun—if you find yourself in Northwestern Montana in the season, come on by and lend a hand!

It takes a village to catch a killer—and to write a book. Thanks to the retailers—booksellers, kitchen shops, galleries, and gift shops—who have championed my books, especially those in western Montana. I've also learned a lot by watching retailers in action. Thanks to Cathi Spence of Think Local for the story of the surprise at the back door, and Jeannie Ulrick of Roma's Kitchen Shop, who dealt so graciously with the man puzzled by shopping bags.

Once again, my sister-in-law, Kathy Jensen Budewitz, lent me her name and her love of dragonflies and fabric. Jordonna Dores shared tales of running a Christmas shop, and regularly saves my backside during the Bigfork Festival of the Arts.

A trusted critique partner is worth her weight in double chocolate truffles. Thank you, Debbie Burke. Thanks to independent editor Ramona DeFelice Long for the insights and questions that made me dig deeper into my characters and their motivations.

The national board members and staff of Sisters in Crime have been my close friends and companions these last few years, and I love you all.

It's unbelievably useful for a mystery writer to be married to a doctor. Thanks to Don Beans for the medical details, although as always, I can't promise that I correctly understood everything. I also deeply appreciate the male perspective, so important here and in *Treble at the Jam Fest*.

Thanks to Terri Bischoff, Nicole Nugent, and the rest of the Midnight Ink crew, and to cover artist Ben Perini, for bringing the village of Jewel Bay to life.

And thanks to you, readers, for welcoming Erin and the villagers into your hearts.

Live in the moment.
Unless it's unpleasant.
Then, eat a cookie.
—Cookie Monster

THE CAST

Merry Christmas from the Murphy Clan:

Erin Murphy, manager of Murphy's Glacier Mercantile, aka the Merc

Adam Zimmerman, Erin's fiancé

Francesca "Fresca" Conti Murphy Schmidt, Erin's mother, the Merc's manager emeritus

Chiara and Jason Phillips, Erin's artist sister and her computer whiz husband

Landon Phillips, their son, age six

Happy Holidays from the Merc:

Tracy McCann, Creative Director and Chocolatier

Lou Mary Williams Crawford Vogel, sales clerk extraordinaire

Season's Greetings from the Thorntons:

Merrily Thornton, back in town, hoping for a second chance

Walt and Taya Thornton, antiques dealers obsessed with Christmas

Holly Thornton Muir, the local veterinarian

Ashley Larson, Merrily's unsuspecting daughter

Brad Larson, Merrily's estranged husband

Happy New Year from Villagers and Friends:

Sally Grimes, Puddle Jumpers Toys and Clothing for Children

Greg Taylor, Jewel Bay Building Supply

Ned Redaway, Red's Bar, Head Elf

Wendy Taylor Fontaine, Le Panier Bakery

Kathy Jensen, Dragonfly Dry Goods

Candy Divine, Sugarplums and More

Best Wishes for a Safe Holiday:
Deputy Kim Caldwell, newly appointed Detective Commander

Undersheriff Ike Hoover, soon to be sheriff

Deputy Oliver Bello, the new guy

Deputy Oakland, solid as they come

Dreaming of Mice and Catnip:
Mr. Sandburg, a sable Burmese, king of Erin's roost

Pumpkin, a full-figured orange tabby, challenger for the throne

One

"Oh, pooh." I pointed at the label on the big gray tub of Christmas lights at my feet. "This box goes to Jewel Bay Antiques. 'Spose they got ours instead?"

"Does it matter?" Adam, my sweetie, asked.

"Yeah. We have a wider storefront than they do. Plus ours are the new LEDs. How about you get the ladder and stretch out the garland, and I'll go swap them for our lights." Instinctively, I rubbed the colored stars tattooed inside my wrist for luck.

"I'll go along to see their window," my mother said. "Taya creates the best displays in town."

"Don't let Tracy hear you say that," I replied and picked up the rubber tub.

We wound our way through clusters of Elves—the villagers of Jewel Bay, Montana, in disguise—working the magic that transforms our town every December. Elves had gathered last weekend for Bulb Turning Day to unkink strings of lights, check bulbs, and tie new red bows to replace those inevitably lost to wind and weather. Tree Elves had cut saplings to be lashed to every post and pole. This morning, volunteers ran power lifts to hoist garland up to second-story eaves and decorate our old one-lane bridge, while on the streets, each business added its own festive touches to the Christmas Village theme. Fresh-cut pine scented the air.

"Hey, Erin. Good morning, Fresca," merchants and volunteers called as we passed by. Nearly everyone calls Francesca Conti Murphy Schmidt "Fresca," although I sometimes mess up and call her Mom at work. At sixty-two, six months remarried after a long widowhood, she rocks a Santa hat.

In the next block, Walt and Taya Thornton stood outside Jewel Bay Antiques and Christmas Shop, studying their window. A big tub of lights stood on the sidewalk next to a pile of garland.

I set my tub down next to theirs, happy to be rid of the weight. Actually, I set their tub down next to ours—they hadn't yet noticed *Murphy's Mercantile* written on the lid.

"Oh, Taya," my mother said, taking the elfin woman's arm. "It's perfect."

She was right. Inside the Thorntons' big front window stood an antique Father Christmas, nearly five feet tall. He wore a flowing maroon velvet robe and a fur cap so luxurious it could have been mink, trimmed with a sprig of fresh holly. Around him were gathered miniature creatures of the woodland, from a mischievous red fox and a white ermine to a pair of majestic reindeer, each so realistic I half expected them to glance up at me. Last year, my first Christmas back home in Jewel Bay, the Village Merchants' Association had debated starting a window decorating contest, but in the end, we'd happily agreed that the Thorntons would always win, so why bother? And this display proved us right.

Tracy, my shop assistant and design expert—I've dubbed her Creative Director—would make sure the Merc's double windows brimmed with good cheer. They would be bright and fun and make shoppers smile. But this—this was the display everyone would remember.

"Isn't zee village zee most beautiful?" Our local French chef appeared on the sidewalk, bearing a tray of pastries.

"So is that," I said, my mouth watering at the sight of a fruit-topped lemon cream tart. I am on close personal terms with all the pastries from Le Panier, my closest village neighbor. The chef's wife, baker Wendy Taylor Fontaine, approached, the new baby in her arms sporting a tiny knitted elf hat and a green sleeper trimmed in red fleece. "Oh, that outfit is adorable."

"A gift from Sally Grimes," Wendy replied. Even Sally Sourpuss, owner of the children's shop across the street, could be sweet when it came to babies.

"*Ah, la bébé. Elle est si belle, quand elle dort,*" her husband said. Ever since the little one's arrival a few weeks ago, his excitement at fatherhood had increased his occasional lapses into French. But the beauty of a sleeping baby, I understood.

A shout behind me drew my attention from the pastry tray.

"Go away," Taya Thornton yelled. "You've shamed us enough."

My mouth dropped open. I hardly recognized the woman who'd been my beloved kindergarten teacher, her skin now flushed, her lips twisted. Behind her and half a head taller, her husband Walt looked confused, his kind eyes uncertain whether to focus on his wife or the fair-skinned blonde in the cherry-red ski jacket and Santa hat who stood a few feet away.

Merrily Thornton. Their daughter, a few years older than I. "I came to help you decorate."

"We don't want your help," Taya snapped.

"Taya." My mother reached out, but the other woman shook her off.

"Surely we can work this out." Walt's voice was thin and strained. He took off his Santa hat and ran a hand over his nearly bald head. "It's Christmas."

"We gave you everything, and how did you repay us?" Taya shouted. "Why couldn't you be more like your sister?"

I felt as if I'd been slapped, and the words weren't even directed at me. Merrily's shoulders sank and her round cheeks fell, her eyes small behind her tortoiseshell glasses.

Fresca slipped an arm around Taya's narrow shoulders and turned her toward the door of the antique shop. My mother is slender and unfailingly gracious, but she can be quite forceful.

Walt took a step toward his daughter, hand outstretched, palm down. "It's best, for now, if you stay away." He dropped his hand and shuffled after his wife.

Only then did I notice the villagers who'd stopped their decorating to watch, silent and horrified. Across the street and half a block down, Sally stood, coatless, on the sidewalk in front of Puddle Jumpers, one hand over her mouth.

I turned toward Merrily, the good cheer gone from her face, and looped my arm through hers. "Come decorate the Merc. I never say no to a good Elf."

∞

Merrily helped me haul our tub of lights down the street. Her mother's outburst had me rattled and I fumbled with the twine as we tied the string of lights onto the fragrant pine garland. But Merrily showed no distress as she worked beside me.

When we finished attaching the lights, Adam grabbed one end of the garland and climbed up the ladder, Merrily at the foot, ready to feed him more garland. I stepped backward into the street and flipped the pompom of my Santa hat out of my eyes. "Left, about six inches."

My beloved, who'd stuffed his Santa hat in his hip pocket, nicely accentuating his backside, looped the wire over the first hook and moved to the second. He missed on the first try; the haphazard way the hooks had been screwed into the Merc's soffits prevented him from actually seeing what he was doing, always a handicap in Christmas decorating.

On the next try, the wire snared the hook. For a moment, it held, then came a splintering sound and the soffit gave way. High in the air, Adam swayed. I darted forward to keep the ladder from tottering over and smashing my fiancé in the street three weeks before our wedding.

In one graceful movement, Adam let go of the garland and jumped, bending his knees and landing on his feet in one piece.

A chunk of plywood landed beside him.

He wiped his forehead with the back of one ungloved hand. "Sorry, little darlin'. I broke your building."

I gulped down the breath I'd been holding. "Thank God you didn't break your neck. I'll see if my brother can patch it."

"Are you okay?" Merrily asked. For a moment, I'd forgotten she was there.

"Yeah, thanks," Adam replied. "Those hooks are so rusted and bent—if they hold through the season, I'll eat a reindeer."

"Don't even say it." My double great-grandfather had built this sandstone fortress in 1910. Murphy's Mercantile had been open for business ever since, although the Merc had long outlived its days as a full-service grocery. Keeping up the structure was every bit as big a challenge as running the specialty local foods market my mother and I had created.

Owning an antique building is like playing one continuous game of pick-up sticks.

With Merrily and me holding the ladder, Adam finished attaching the garland to what remained of the soffit. I didn't breathe easy until the job was done and his feet were safely back on earth.

Merrily scanned the bustling scene. "My daughter would love this," she said, and I turned to her in surprise.

"Your daughter? How old is she? Where is she?"

Before she could answer, Lou Mary, my star sales clerk, emerged from the Merc bearing a tray of steaming paper cups. "I just *adore* Decorating Day. It's magical, the way the whole village transforms. Cocoa, anyone?"

I handed cups to Adam and Merrily, the scent of chocolate tickling my nose. The interruption had changed the mood, and the time to quiz Merrily had passed. For now. I gave her shoulder a reassuring pat, and she gave me an appreciative look, her eyes bright.

As surely as you can count on holidays sparking family crises, you can count on cocoa.

"You want to plug it in and make sure we don't blow the place up?" Adam asked, his tone teasing, his dark eyes dancing.

"Go ahead," I said. It's hard to cross your fingers in gloves, though I tried. This Decorating Day, always the first Saturday in December, was chilly, but at least we weren't trimming the town in a snowstorm.

Adam plugged in the lights and the colors shone through the thick greenery.

I clapped my hands together, my fleece gloves making a soft thumping sound. Beside me, Merrily beamed. Across the street, my nephew, Landon, let out a shriek of glee. He bounced up and down, smacking his red mittens together. My sister, Chiara—said with a hard *C* and rhymed with *tiara*—rested a hand on his shoulder, the other on her very pregnant belly. Her husband battled his own balky stretch of garland, and Adam carried our ladder across the street to give him a hand. The other artists in Snowberry, her co-op gallery, busily tied bows on trees and set up Mexican luminaria beneath the gallery's bay window.

Lou Mary had it right: Jewel Bay's transformation was truly magical. But magic takes a lot of work.

"Let's get a warm-up," I said after Merrily had swept up the pine needles and I'd set the empty tub on the sidewalk for the Storage Elves to collect.

Merrily followed me inside. "I always liked this building," she said, glancing around at the high tin ceilings, lit by the original milk glass pendants, and the shelves brimming with the best food and drink our food-loving village had to offer. "Town's changed so much—great to see this place thriving."

I stepped into the commercial kitchen where Fresca, Tracy, and other vendors cook up the products the Merc depends on, and grabbed two heavy white mugs. Filled them from the vacuum pot sitting on the stainless steel counter that separates the kitchen from the shop floor. Slid a mug across the counter to Merrily, who settled on one of the red-topped chrome bar stools Fresca had scavenged from an old drugstore in Pondera—said *Pon-duh-RAY*, the big town, all of thirty thousand people, thirty miles away.

At the front of the store, Lou Mary watched Tracy work on the window display.

"You're calmer than I would have been. Want to talk about it?" I asked Merrily.

She cradled her cocoa, a strand of pale hair falling across her face. "Forgiveness has never been my mother's strong suit. Even though it's been twenty years."

I didn't have to ask what "it" meant. I knew—everyone knew—she'd spent several months in prison as a young woman. She'd been upfront about it last fall when she came back to Jewel Bay and started job-hunting. "So, why'd you come back? I mean, this is a small town and your parents are fixtures."

"It was time. My marriage had ended. The dog died. And I hoped..." She eyed me over the rim of her mug. "My daughter just started college, in Missoula. I thought that if she and I were close by, my parents might want us all to be a family again."

Whoa. That topped all the reasons I'd had for coming home a year and a half ago.

"She's at UM?" I said. "That's great—only a hundred miles away. She live on campus?"

Merrily nodded, her expression livelier than it had been all morning. "In Jesse Hall. She's driving up for Christmas with a friend."

"That was my dorm," I said, memories flooding in. Mostly good, but I'd been haunted back then by my father's death during my senior year of high school, and I'd spent too many hours alone in my room or walking the riverfront trails. I'd been so self-absorbed I'd barely noticed the tall, good-looking guy from Minnesota who'd crushed on me. Fortunately, Adam hadn't forgotten me, and when our paths crossed again, we clicked.

"Ashley loves it," Merrily said. "She's always wanted to know about my parents. I haven't told her what happened back then—my prison stint, or their reaction."

"Oh. She's never met them?" Not every family is as close as mine, but I tried to hide my surprise as I did the math in my head. Ashley had to be eighteen, and Merrily thirty-seven or eight. She must have gotten to the business of marriage and motherhood right after leaving prison.

Merrily shook her head. "My parents had cut off all contact, so I stayed in Billings after my release. I made some bad choices young, but at least that was a good one." Her soft lips curved upward, and she transformed from plain to pretty. She couldn't be thinking of her marriage, if she'd gotten a divorce, and while I'd only been to Billings a few times, it didn't seem a likely source of her misty memories. She'd left, after all.

No, I decided, that smile was meant for Ashley. I smiled back.

"Your sister seems to get along with your parents," I said. Holly Thornton Muir was my cats' vet, and I'd run into her in the village several times, coming out of the antique shop with her mother or her children. Too late, I remembered Taya's terrible insult, comparing Merrily to her sister.

A complicated expression crossed the other woman's face. "Holly accepted Ashley without hesitation, and she's done her best to persuade our folks, but no luck. Still, I couldn't give up. I moved back, and I keep trying to talk to them. Maybe this town hasn't changed much after all."

That made me squirm.

"I'm being unfair," Merrily continued, her tone apologetic. "My family's dysfunction isn't Jewel Bay's fault. Though I do wonder if anyone ever called my mother on her behavior."

Good question. My mom might know. But I could understand how family and village might be intertwined in Merrily's memory.

"So you're working at the Building Supply. I hope that's going well."

"Yeah. I've always been good with numbers and organizing."

I grinned. "I knew I liked you."

"Erin?" Lou Mary called. "Ready to open?"

I glanced at the clock. Exactly ten a.m. Lou Mary's inner time clock never fails. "Flip the sign," I said, clapping my hands together. "Let's get this shopping season rolling."

Merrily slipped off her stool and stood in front of the jam display.

"Bet you missed huckleberry jam," I said lightly, and she picked up a jar. I gave her a quick tour of the shop, chatting about our locally made cheese, the fresh meat and poultry, and other staples.

"Don't forget," I told her a few minutes later as she zipped up her puffy red coat. "Tomorrow at one. I'll serve lunch. Bring enough cookies for everyone to take home half a dozen."

Though my mother had moved out when she remarried last summer and I'd moved in a few weeks ago, we'd agreed that the annual holiday cookie exchange should remain at the Orchard, the Murphy family homestead. Some traditions, my mother said, belong to the place where they began.

"I know just what cookies to make. It will be fun, meeting new people." Merrily set a box of truffles on the counter, next to the jams and soaps she'd chosen, gloves in one hand as she fished in her pocket for cash with the other. "I'll take these, too, to slip into a package."

"Love the gloves." Red-and-black Buffalo plaid, accented with small black buttons.

"A gift," she said, and a glow spread across her face. She gave me a quick hug. "Thank you, Erin. You've been so sweet."

Outside, she strolled down the street, shopping bag in one gloved hand, her red Santa hat dangling from the other.

"So what in blue blazes got into Taya Thornton?" Lou Mary said. This was her first Christmas at the Merc, though she'd worked retail more than forty years.

"I've never seen her so upset," I said. "It goes back ages."

"That business with Sally's ex embezzling from one of her companies?" Lou Mary asked.

Tracy's eyes widened. "I don't know that story."

"Sad, what I know of it," I said. "Merrily was fresh out of high school. She pled guilty to embezzling from the timber and property management company Sally Grimes inherited. Sally's husband ran it, but it turned out he was robbing her blind."

"What was Merrily's role?" Tracy paused while sorting food-themed ornaments for the tree in the window, the final touch. I'd have offered to help, but I'd learned that when it comes to decorating the shop, Tracy is happier and the results are better if the rest of us stay out of her way.

"That, I never knew. She helped Cliff Grimes in the office. She pled guilty to some kind of theft—I don't know the right term. He insisted on a trial where he blamed her for everything, but the jury didn't agree. They convicted him. He died in prison." I shuddered. "Anyway, her parents disowned her. After all this time, they still want nothing to do with Merrily or her daughter."

"Such a shame." Lou Mary rested one arthritis-swollen finger against her perfect coral lip. The bright reds and greens of the season didn't suit her coloring—a natural redhead, hair slightly enhanced to counteract the effects of age—so she ignored them. Today, she was dressed from tip to toe in soft camel, a double strand of rough carnelian beads wrapped around the base of her turtleneck. "And I thought my ex took the cake."

"Merrily served less than a year. Whether because she was so young, or because Cliff Grimes was a scumbag, I don't know. Anyway, this fall, she showed up here." I sipped my cocoa. "Literally here, looking for a job, but I'd already hired you." Whether we could afford two employees through the winter remained to be seen, but Lou Mary had become such an asset so quickly that I was determined to make it work.

"Points for chutzpah," Lou Mary said, her tone both admiring and incredulous, though she and Sally were friends, so I expected she'd heard part of the story. "Returning to the scene of the crime."

"And to such a warm, welcoming mother," Tracy said, sarcasm dripping.

"Which is so weird. Taya Thornton was my kindergarten teacher. I loved her—especially at Christmas. She brought cookies every Friday, and we made the best Christmas crafts." I'd found a dusty box of them when Adam and I cleaned out my mother's attic. The box sat in my old bedroom, waiting for me to sort through it.

"I can imagine the shame," Lou Mary said slowly, thoughtfully, "but not holding on to it for so long. Hard feelings chip away at a person."

"Anyway, Greg Taylor hired her at the Building Supply, in the office. People raised their eyebrows—"

"Sally wanted to organize a boycott, get people to stop shopping there," Lou Mary said, shaking her head. "I told her she could have five minutes to indulge her wounded pride, but then she had to get over it. No reason to give other people power they don't deserve."

Not for the first time, I wondered what pain had made retail-savvy, smart-mouthed Lou Mary so wise.

"Greg said everyone deserves a second chance." I stood. "And that's all I know, except that I like her. She's what, five years older than me, so I never really knew her, but I'm looking forward to becoming friends."

"Would you have hired her, with her parents down the block and Sally across the street?" Tracy asked. She tucked a strand of her long chestnut hair behind her ear, exposing a miniature red ornament. The other earring was green. "If you'd had an opening?"

As if "opening" had been the magic word, our front door opened, the chime ringing. I greeted the customer, a loyal shopper, cheeks pink from decorating. She picked up half a dozen jars of the Merc's huckleberry jam and another six of cherry preserves—her annual treat for her children and grandchildren.

I rang up her purchase, giving her an extra jar as part of our rewards program, and pondered Tracy's question. Sally hadn't been the only person who thought Merrily should have stayed away, for her parents' sake. But this was Merrily's community, too. How much more should she be punished? Home can be a powerful draw—a year and a half ago, I'd left a great job in Seattle as a grocery buyer for SavClub, the international warehouse chain, to come home and go into business with my mother. Then last summer, I'd been forced to consider whether the life I wanted with Adam would mean leaving Montana, but I'd been spared that decision.

"Three weeks to the big day," the customer said, bringing me back to the present. "Are you nervous, or excited?"

"Yes," I said, feeling the heat rise in my cheeks even though I didn't know whether she was referring to Christmas or the wedding.

She touched my hand. "You'll be a beautiful bride."

I nodded, my lips trembling, my reply stuck in my throat.

Fresca returned as the customer departed, the hug she gave me longer and tighter than usual, the warm, tangy scent of her perfume comforting.

"How are the Thorntons?" I asked.

She frowned, fine lines visible around her dark, moist eyes. "Sometimes, I don't understand people."

"Amen to that."

"We'll have to be extra kind to that family this year. Including the girls. Bill and I are going shopping. Call someone about that soffit before the ice works its way in and causes more damage. See you this evening." She gave me another hug, then left by the back door.

And then it was down to business. As if by that magic of the season Lou Mary had invoked, the Elves gave way to shoppers, and we hustled to pack up bags of jam, pickles, and preserves. My mother's Italian sauces, pastas, and spreads sold briskly. Luci the Splash Artist had created a new pine-scented soap in the shape of a Christmas tree, and by noon, I had to fetch another case from the basement.

A customer commented on the sagging garland and the gaping roof line, and I laughed it off, but the problem was no joke. I called my brother, Nick, and left him a message. He'd been a big help since his return to Jewel Bay last winter, but building repairs took a back seat to his real work. He's a wildlife biologist studying wolves and wolverines, and tracking his comings and goings would require a high-powered GPS. Adam had learned a lot about home repair since we'd bought the house, but I didn't want to ask him to take this on—he had enough to do, finishing up the painting and other details in our own remodel. And it was my family's building, not his. Not yet.

Tracy finished the windows and dragged me out to the street to take a look.

"They're terrific," I said, and meant it, though I knew she'd fuss over them all season long. One window showcased our products around a small artificial tree decorated with toy kitchen wares and strung with popcorn garland, burlap bags of kernels from a central Montana farm at its base. My favorite ornament was the miniature red frying pan.

In the other window, a vintage toy train circled a tiny version of Jewel Bay, featuring the Playhouse, the chalet-style Inn at the north end of the Village, Red's Bar, and Murphy's Mercantile.

"Simply perfect," I said and gave her a one-armed hug. "Now go home and feed that puppy."

A warm glow spread through me. Much as I love happy customers, they don't happen without happy employees.

Back inside, the scent of lavender mingled with cocoa and coffee. Lou Mary handled the customers while I checked stock and got ready for the Art Walk. If Decorating Day is the village at work, the Art Walk is the village at play. The dozen-plus galleries stay open late, and the merchants join the fun, welcoming shoppers and browsers alike. As I swept up bits of caramel corn, I wondered whether Walt and Taya would participate.

I was glad I'd invited Merrily to the cookie exchange. Sugar and spice are remarkably good for the spirit, especially among friends.

Two

*D*ark falls early this far north, this late in the year. At five o'clock, I stepped outside to survey the village. It had truly become a winter wonderland, with enough snow to evoke the season but not enough to keep the shoppers and revelers home.

This wasn't a big sales night. This was a night for villagers and visitors to celebrate, to greet old friends and meet new ones, and to see what temptations the artists and shopkeepers had created. The streets and restaurants were full. Every roof line sparkled, and the bright faces reflected the glow.

But it was chilly and I hadn't tossed a coat over my red turtleneck, so I hustled back inside.

We were at full strength tonight, with Tracy handing out samples of her chocolates and Lou Mary chatting up every would-be customer. Fresca had returned to serve as semi-official greeter.

"Erin, congratulations!" Carole Hoover, a trim, dark-haired woman, took both my hands in hers and leaned forward, our cheeks brushing. Behind her, Ike, her husband and the long-time undersheriff, beamed.

"Adam is a lucky man," Ike said. Even in jeans and a parka, he had a commanding presence. "Now that you're about to be married, maybe you'll stay out of trouble." He winked.

"Plenty of trouble to keep me busy here." I spread my hands. "And congratulations to you, on your appointment as sheriff. January first is the day, right?"

"Yep. Thanks." A shadow swept across his narrow face. The current sheriff had announced plans to retire when his term ended in a year, but cancer had forced him to quit early. The county commissioners had appointed Ike to fill the seat, and though he and I had disagreed a time or two, I had no doubt that he was the right man for the job.

And while he'd been in the Merc plenty of times on official business, this was a night for fun. "Help yourself to cocoa or hot spiced wine. Snacks on the back counter. 'Tis the season."

The Hoovers drifted off, pausing at the handmade pottery and wineglasses, talking and gesturing in that abbreviated way couples develop. Discussing gifts for the family, I hoped.

A customer standing next to Luci's soap display asked if we had any hand sanitizer. "No," my mother replied, "but check Jewel Bay Antiques down the street. I saw some there in Santa dispensers."

"Oh, how darling," the woman said, and I mentally rolled my eyes. Even in Santa dispensers, I thought the stuff reeked.

"Oh, gosh. Look how busy you are! This is going to be a fabulous holiday season." Heidi Hunter, owner of Kitchenalia across the street, took my arm and drew me behind the front counter—the cash-wrap, in retail parlance—and lowered her voice. "Now, what happened this morning with Taya Thornton and her daughter?"

"Heidi, I hate spreading gossip," I said.

"It's not gossip if it's true. Besides, you were there."

I made a *yeah-maybe* noise. Better, I rationalized, to report what I'd seen so unspoken questions wouldn't cloud the party tomorrow. And so the truth wouldn't get embellished beyond recognition. I gave Heidi the nickel version.

"That's horrible." Heidi's eyes widened, as blue and sparkling as the sapphires and diamonds in her tennis bracelet, a gift from an old boyfriend. "Can you imagine screaming at your own daughter in public? Or shunning her for years?"

No, I could not.

Heidi let out a slow breath, her elegant blond hair brushing her shoulders. "I know you kids all adored her in the classroom, but ever since they opened that shop downtown, I've thought Taya had a screw loose. I mean, nobody needs that many antique mercury glass ornaments."

"She just loves Christmas."

"There's passion, and there's obsession. I've got to get back to the store, but I wanted you to know—someone from Minnesota called and ordered every piece of Le Creuset cookware on your registry."

My turn for the wide eyes. "Every pot and pan? That's hundreds of dollars. Who—?"

Her eyes twinkled. "I can't tell you. Just make sure you leave room in your new kitchen cabinets."

She blew me a kiss and swept out the door. Though a registry at a sporting goods store would have been more his style, Adam had gone along with the housewares theme, as he had with most of the wedding folderol. Even a small, close-friends-and-family wedding was turning out to be a bigger deal than I had planned on.

Of course, when it comes to my family, every event is a big deal. And Adam's family … Well, the Zimmerman clan remained a mystery to me. After weeks of *will they or won't they* drama, the older twin brothers Adam called Cain and Abel had cancelled, claiming they needed to finish a project at their construction company by year-end. He'd almost seemed relieved. His mother worried about flying alone, so Adam had booked her on the same flight as Tanner Lundquist, his best buddy since the first day of first grade. Tanner would stay with us at the Orchard. Mrs. Zimmerman and the Contis, my mother's family, were booked at the Lodge. The Murphy clan all lived in Jewel Bay, thank goodness.

"Hey there." A pair of strong arms wrapped around me from behind, along with the familiar, not-unpleasant scent of woodland sweat and damp wool.

I wriggled around for Adam's kiss. "I was just thinking of you. I didn't hear you come in."

"With this crowd? You couldn't hear Santa's sleigh bells. Time to kick 'em out and go light that tree."

We grabbed our coats and ushered the stragglers out, then I locked the door and slipped my gloved hand into Adam's. He's tall, with an outdoorsy lope to his stride, dark unruly curls, and a smile that lights a flame inside me. It might have taken me nearly fifteen years to notice him, but I was all in now—hook, line, and sinker.

Villagers streamed toward the north end of Front Street, and we merged into the flow. A few feet ahead, Candy Divine wore a Santa hat adorned with a pink polka dot bow and Minnie Mouse ears.

A young boy's sing-song voice broke through the chatter. *"Jingle bells, Batman smells, Robin laid an egg."*

Landon, my favorite nephew—okay, my only nephew—bounced into view, sporting reindeer antlers on his Santa hat. Chiara and my brother-in-law, Jason, trailed behind him. "Merry Christmas, Auntie Erin!"

"Merry Christmas, little guy," I said. "Where'd you learn that song?"

"He knows all the words," Chiara said, sounding as if she'd heard them one time too many. She and I are often mistaken for each other, though she's got a couple of years on me and I've got her beat by a couple of inches and a few pounds. We've got the same heart-shaped faces and coloring, and both of us wear our straight, dark hair in collar-length bobs. Now, though, her belly distinguished us.

"There are more words?"

"Sure," Adam said, and he and Landon sang—though it was more shout than tune—as we made our way up the street.

"Jingle bells, Batman smells. Robin laid an egg. The Batmobile lost a wheel, and the Joker got away. Hey!"

Chiara shook her head, but she was smiling.

We slowed in front of the antique shop to admire Father Christmas and the forest creatures. I crouched to peer at the artificial snow, letting the others drift ahead. Their snow looked so much more realistic than what we'd used.

Sally's words broke my concentration. "I can't believe that Thornton girl came downtown today. After all she put her parents through. Some nerve she's got."

She wasn't talking to me. I kept my head down, not wanting to be seen. A poker face is not one of my talents. *So much for the new and reformed Sally*, I thought as I waited for her and her companion to pass. As Lou Mary had said, letting go of old hurts is tough, but necessary. Last winter, my family had finally learned who was responsible for my father's death, and I had to admit, the thought of how long the killer had gone free still frosted me now and then.

I waited until Sally Sourpuss and her companion had gotten lost in the crowd, then I caught up with my family and we stood together as the villagers sang Christmas songs. Old Ned Redaway threw the switch and lit up the sixty-foot blue spruce that towered over the small square wedged between the Jewel Inn and Dragonfly Dry Goods. Kathy Jensen, the Dragonfly's proprietor and a family friend, invited us in for a toddy, and we sipped and chatted happily.

Then Adam and I headed out. Had the night grown colder, or had the warmth dissipated with the crowds?

"Give me five minutes to make sure the shop's tucked in," I said as we neared the Merc. Inside, I locked away the change drawer and iPad we use as a cash register, and made sure everything was unplugged and secure. I handed Adam a basket filled with cocoa, chai mix, and Christmas napkins for the cookie exchange, and led the way down the hall.

"Pooh." I pointed at the tiny snowdrift that had blown in the back door.

Adam wriggled the door open an inch or two, shut it, then opened it again. "You need new weather stripping."

"What's this?" I bent and picked up a brown paper sack, sand shifting inside. "Did someone leave us a luminaria that blew out?"

Along with an unlit candle, the bag held a bar of Luci's lavender soap, a bottle of lotion, eight dollars in ones, and a note scribbled on the back of a grocery store receipt.

"'I stole these during the Art Walk,'" I read out loud, "'but I felt guilty, so I'm returning everything except the huckleberry jam for my mom. She deserves a Christmas treat.'"

I stared at the note, then looked up at Adam.

"Little miracles everywhere," he said and kissed my forehead.

Three

Making a house your own is always a challenge—especially when it's the house your grandparents built, the house where your parents made their life together, and the house where you lost your first tooth, whiled away long summer afternoons beneath the cherry trees, and mourned your father.

But I love a challenge.

And as I tied a red ribbon around the last bag of almond bianchi, my favorite Christmas cookies, and placed them in a basket on the oak library table Adam and I had scavenged from the barn at my sister's place, I breathed a sigh of relief. I ran my hand over the timeworn wood. We'd refinished the table and chairs ourselves. Set with red and white flowers and my grandmother's pressed glass bowls and candleholders, it was perfect.

Everything was perfect.

"YOO-hoo!"

Including my timing. I rushed to the front door, where my guests stomped snow off their boots and called out greetings. Behind Heidi came my childhood BFF, Kim Caldwell, a deputy sheriff newly promoted to chief detective. A gang of Murphys plowed through the snow, including my cousin Molly and her mother, my mother, and Chiara. And April Ng, the newest member of Chiara's gallery. Everyone carried a basket, bag, or box of holiday goodies.

I stood on the stone walkway and welcomed them, grateful to Adam for shoveling this morning's snow. After the last woman crossed the threshold, I stretched up on tip-toes, peering down the hill and the long, curving road to the highway. No sign of Merrily Thornton.

Maybe she was feeling bashful, the newcomer in her hometown, already the subject of uncomfortable talk and now the star of yesterday's Front Street shout fest.

Inside, my friends and relatives had shed their coats and begun poking around.

"Hey, sis, looking good." Chiara nodded her approval of the reconfigured living and dining rooms and our Christmas decorations. "Is that Cowboy Roast I smell?"

"The heck with coffee," Heidi said. "Where's the champagne?"

We sipped and chatted, and shared remodel stories. I'd made quiche and a fruit salad, and bought mini *pain au chocolate* from Wendy at Le Panier. On a trip to the kitchen for another bottle of champagne, I checked my phone, but Merrily hadn't called.

"Where's Adam this afternoon?" someone asked.

"At the Athletic Club. They're putting on a kids' swim-and-sweat day, then opening the North Pole Shop, where the kids can buy presents. Everything is under three dollars."

"Wish they'd had that when mine were small," my aunt said.

"Landon could hardly wait," Chiara said. "He loves having secrets from us."

"And those are the kinds of secrets you don't mind him keeping," my aunt added.

Pumpkin the cat wandered in and put a paw on the coffee table, pulling herself up to sniff the treats. "Not for cats," I said and tapped her sweet white foot. She lowered it and turned her sights on Heidi, who lifted her plate out of the way.

"Plumpkin, behave," Heidi said.

"Have you had her checked for diabetes?" my aunt asked. "That old cat of ours got real sick, and Dr. Muir—Holly—put her on insulin."

"Dr. Muir, the vet. That always cracks me up," my cousin Molly said.

"Actually, Pumpkin's lost quite a bit of weight since I got her," I said. "The dust-ups with Sandburg are good exercise."

Pumpkin had come to live with me last February after a tragedy left her ownerless and homeless. Even without the extra weight, the orange tabby was quite a bit bigger than Sandburg, the sable Burmese I'd brought home from Seattle. They'd started out wary and gradually became good friends, but friends with claws.

I picked up plates and suggested we refill our coffee and libations before divvying up the treats everyone had brought. My mother followed me to the kitchen with a stack of dishes and set them in the sink. The new sink, next to the new dishwasher, across from the new fridge, surrounded by the new cabinets.

"I should have redone this kitchen years ago," she said.

"And spare me the fun?" The project had gone smoothly, all things considered, but I was glad we'd been able to remodel before the big move.

"Well, it turned out beautifully. And you've done a lovely job decorating. But don't you think the tree should go in the living room corner?"

Where it had always been. I tamped down the teensy bit of irritation welling in my throat. After nearly forty years in this house, my mother was bound to have mixed feelings at seeing the changes, despite her delight that Adam and I had bought it. She'd been happier moving into Bill's place on the river knowing the homestead would stay in the family.

"With the smaller table, we thought we'd try it in the dining room." I picked up the coffeepot. "I love it in front of the new windows."

"It's perfect. Don't mind me."

The slight tremble in her voice caught me by surprise, as did the tear she quickly wiped away. I kissed her cheek. She slid her arm around my waist, and we ambled into the living room.

Where the talk had turned to Merrily Thornton.

"You saw it all, didn't you, Erin?" Molly held out her cup. "We'd already finished decorating the real estate office, so I went up the street to help decorate the Inn. But Sally Grimes said it was awful, Merrily and Taya screaming at each other."

"Poor Walt," my aunt said.

I filled Molly's cup. "Sally's exaggerating. Merrily barely let out a peep. I'd hoped she'd join us this afternoon. She could use a few friends in town."

"Probably too embarrassed," Chiara said. "Even though she wasn't the one behaving badly."

Logical explanation, I knew, but I couldn't shake my worry. Merrily had been too excited by the invitation to blow it off. Besides, this was my first party in the new-old-new-again house. I'd felt a strong connection to her, and I wanted her to see the place.

"How's the new job?" someone asked Kim.

"Great," she said. "The detective roster is filled now, and we've got two new patrol officers starting the first of the year. Being fully staffed will make a big difference."

Amen to that. No matter what the job, hiring is a perennial pain in the patootie.

In the dining room, we oohed and ahhed over the offerings. Date pinwheels, spritz cookies, bourbon balls. Candy cane cookies studded with crushed peppermint. Big, soft coconut macaroons dipped in chocolate. Jam thumbprints. Fudge ecstasies—crackle-topped cookies that make me ecstatic.

"No biscotti?" Heidi said. "Isn't it a law that every Italian must make biscotti?"

"Everyone makes biscotti," I said, "Italian or not. So what's the point?"

"You brought peanut butter cookies?" Chiara asked Molly, who is not half Italian.

"They're my favorite," Molly answered. "Everyone loves peanut butter cookies. These are simple—six ingredients."

"But they're not *Christmas* cookies."

When it comes to cookies, my sister and I were on the same page. Certain traditions must be followed.

"Lou Mary made the bourbon balls, and Tracy sent double-chocolate truffles. They're sorry to miss the fun, but someone had to run the shop today." Each woman had packed her contributions differently—gaily decorated bags, goldfish boxes, holiday-themed paper plates—and I packed up one of each for my staff.

Later, as my friends and relatives tugged on their boots and buttoned their coats, I glanced out the window. Giant flakes had begun falling, the kind that look so pretty and add up so fast.

I pulled Kim aside and held her cookie basket while she zipped her jacket.

"I wonder what happened to Merrily," I said.

Physical opposites though we are—Kim tall and slender, with piercing blue eyes, her blond hair in a no-nonsense cut; me shorter, curvier, with olive skin and dark eyes—we rarely had trouble following each other's train of thought. She was about to tell me not to worry, not to see bugaboos around every corner.

"Erin, don't worry. I'm sure she decided she'd rather stay home than chit-chat with people who know the worst about her."

"Does anyone ever know the worst about us?" I handed her the basket. "It felt like we clicked. Like she wanted to be friends."

"Coming home is complicated," Kim replied. "We both know that."

After what I'd witnessed the day before, I could only agree.

When it comes to home maintenance, Greg Taylor is no fool.

He and his staff had stocked the front of the Building Supply with bags of sand and ice melt, snow shovels, and roof rakes. A nearby display held packs of wire hooks for ornaments, spare light bulbs, packing tape, and other holiday miscellany.

But where was the weather stripping I needed for the Merc's back door?

I'd started my Monday morning at the Merc, shoveling the sidewalk, then setting up the till and getting our weekly deposit together. Lou Mary arrived at nine thirty on the dot, and we polished the place to a shine. Once the door opened at ten, I'd dashed out on an errand run.

Judging from the parking lot, I'd missed the Monday-morning contractor rush. And judging from the lack of a sales clerk at the front counter, they weren't expecting much business this time of day.

I poked my head around the end of an aisle leading to the back offices.

The older redhead who works up front stood in Greg's doorway, one hand cradling her other elbow, one knuckle in her mouth. I'd been in and out of here oodles of times since we started the remodel, when every project took twice as long as planned and required multiple trips to the hardware store. But despite my great memory for names, I could never remember hers. I needed a rhyme—Jeannie-beanie? Joni-joni pony tail?

"Thanks," I heard Greg say. "I'm sure there's a simple explanation. I'll look into it and get back to you." Then he hung up and charged into view.

"I called her house and cell, but no answer," the redhead said. "Car trouble, maybe?"

"Let's hope so." In his late thirties, Greg stood a shade under six feet, his thick, nearly black hair shot with streaks of gray. "Oh, Erin. Hi."

"Hi. Is something wrong? Family okay?" In the interests of fitting into my wedding dress in three weeks, I'd skipped my usual morning stop at Le Panier. Greg's sister, Wendy Taylor Fontaine, had been a childhood chum and occasional nemesis of my sister. Since I've been working next door to her, she's transformed from an irritatingly quiet but sharp-eyed observer to a good friend. Brother and sister were normally unflappable.

But something had shaken Greg.

"What? No, they're fine." He rubbed a hand over his forehead. I'd thought him super-cute when I was a kid, and time had been good to him. The cashier slipped past me, heading to her post. "It's Merrily Thornton. She didn't show up for work this morning. And now, I've gotten a call from the bank manager."

Oh, no. Merrily hadn't done something stupid, had she, proving her mother right?

"Greg. You need to see this." I recognized the balding, fifty-ish man sticking his head out of the adjacent office as Cary Lenhardt, the long-time bookkeeper. I hesitated, then followed Greg, stopping on the threshold. Inside, a pair of desks stood back to back, one littered with sticky notes, pens, and paper clips. Clustered on a small shelf above it were pictures of kids on sports teams, a family photo with an RV, and a white football emblazoned with the Seahawks logo, next to a Seahawks coffee cup crammed with pens and pencils. Cary's, I presumed. A computer screen glowed, and a paper coffee cup appeared to be in use.

The other desk was its exact opposite, as neat and orderly as a furniture store display.

Except for every open drawer.

"There, in her bottom drawer," Cary said, gesturing to the tidy desk. Merrily's desk, I presumed. "In the cigar box."

Greg leaned down and pulled out the box. Set it on the spotless surface and shot Cary a nervous glance before lifting the lid.

The box was stuffed with cash.

Greg sank into the nearest chair and buried his head in his hands. I could only imagine the pain and betrayal. I felt it, too, and I wasn't the one who'd hired her.

"Is that why the bank manager called?" I asked from the doorway.

Greg raised his head, eyes not quite focusing, as if just remembering who I was. "She and Cary finished up the deposit Saturday morning, and she took it to the night drop. The deposit slip listed several hundred in cash, not counting the checks, but there was no cash in the bag. The manager assumed it was an oversight. But Merrily is always here by eight a.m."

Except today. And with her history, it was too much of a coincidence.

I wasn't surprised by the amount of cash in the deposit, given the nature of their business. At the Merc, eighty percent of our sales are by credit or debit card, and the balance skews higher in summer. The one item that regularly sells for cash is our truffles, at seventy-five cents apiece. Although I supposed that a careful thief could squirrel away a little at a time, and before long, fill a box.

"How much is in there?" Cary said at the same time as Greg said, "We need to call the sheriff."

"I'll do it," Cary said. As he reached for the phone, his hand brushed his coffee cup and it wobbled, then righted itself without spilling.

Greg lifted the cash out of the box, his hands trembling, and began counting. Stopped, started over. Turned to me. "Would you check my count?"

"Sure," I said, stepping into the room. I sorted the cash by denomination and counted twice, the bills rough between my fingers. Tore a sticky off a pad on Cary's desk and wrote the total. Seven hundred fifty-two dollars.

Greg rested his elbows on his knees, hands clasped beneath his chin, the knuckles white. A distant look clouded his dark eyes.

The cash had lain on top of a small framed photo of a striking teenage brunette sitting on a sandstone rock. Gold letters and a year slashed across one corner marked it a senior portrait.

"Mind if I look?" I said, and at Greg's grunt of approval, I reached for the photo. Beneath it lay a few small trinkets and a plain white envelope, the kind birthday cards come in. The envelope was blank. I slid out the contents. Three shots of the same girl—one in a strapless gown, one in her soccer uniform, and the third cradling a Corgi, the happiest-looking of dogs. I flipped them over. *Ashley*, the back said, with a date, each in the same handwriting. A mother's handwriting.

The final picture was of Merrily with her parents and sister. No date, but I guessed she'd been about to finish high school, twenty years ago. I'd been in junior high, and remembered coveting a pair of my sister's sandals similar to the ones Merrily wore. Taya, her pixie-cut hair still blond, sat between the two blond girls on an antique oak bench, Walt behind them, beaming. Everyone was beaming.

A "before" picture.

Cary finished his report and hung up the phone.

"You checked the deposit, right?" Greg flung the words at the bookkeeper. "It's your job to verify the deposit."

"Hey." Cary took a step back, hands in the air. "I did my job. What she did afterwards isn't my fault."

"Isn't it unusual to make a deposit on Saturday?" I said. "Especially in winter, when the bank isn't open? We make ours on Monday." The bank was my next stop.

Greg looked at Cary, who shrugged one shoulder. "It was easier to do it that way when I started—I don't remember why—and we just kept doing it like that."

I understood. In my years at SavClub, I'd learned the value of regularly reviewing every system, especially the routines we follow without knowing why. But small businesses typically don't make that kind of review a priority. They think they don't have time. I aimed to not fall into that trap at the Merc.

At a knock on the doorframe, we turned our heads. The redheaded cashier—*what was her name?*—announced that the sheriff was here.

It wasn't actually the sheriff. Today's representatives were Chief Detective Kim Caldwell and the new guy, Detective Oliver Bello.

"Missing employee, missing money," Bello said after introductions were complete and Greg had summarized the problem. "Seems clear enough."

"But why leave the money behind?" I said.

"Why are you here, Erin?" Kim asked.

"Weather stripping," I said, as if that explained everything. When her expression made clear that it explained nothing, I turned to Greg. "Not sure if I need a whole new thingy, or some of that stuff you press into place." I tried not to be too obvious about wanting a moment alone with him, but he got the message.

"Easier to show you than call an employee. Cary, can you show the detective what we found?"

A minute later, Greg and I stood in an aisle with all the emergency insulation a girl could want. Overhead, the sound system played Christmas carols.

"Try these and bring back what you don't need." He put a black rubber door sweep and a bag of sticky-backed foam rubber strips into my hands, then his face crumpled. "Erin, this can't be happening. She can't…"

"I know. I don't want to believe it, either. But it sure looks like you have a thief, and it sure looks like it's Merrily." Saying so hurt my gut, despite the evidence.

Then I remembered how Merrily's face had lit up when she talked about Ashley, and I frowned. Odd enough to leave cash behind, but pictures…

Greg let out a long sigh, fraught with fear and shame. Humans. Some of us are quick to blame others for anything that goes wrong, and some of us are slow. Others would rather blame themselves.

"I never should have hired her," he said. "Profits have been down lately. Now I know why."

"You wanted to give her a hand."

"I keep thinking she'll come walking in the door," he said, "and we'll realize this was all just a mistake."

But meanwhile, he had two detectives waiting. That made my leaky door and sagging soffit seem like a piece of cake.

Four

Most Mondays I use the drive-through bank window, but curiosity got the better of me, so I parked the Subaru at the Jewel Bay Bank and Trust and went inside. Though space needs had forced headquarters to move to Pondera years ago, the local branch was thriving, in a 1910 sandstone structure much like Murphy's Mercantile. A tasteful addition had created the drive-through and offices with a view of the bay.

I handed my bank bag to the teller and glanced around while she added up my deposit. The sharp chemical-lemon scent of furniture polish stung my nostrils. Wide bands of gauzy silver and gold ribbon had been draped above the tellers' stations, catching glints from the big milk glass lights that hung from the tin-paneled ceiling. Greenery accented with more ribbon and clusters of pine cones hung below the counters and in the etched glass windows of the doors. In Seattle, where I used to live, holiday decor would have included an oversized menorah or a string of dreidel lights, but Hanukkah touches are rare here. I made a mental note to add one or two to the Merc's windows.

"Here you go, Erin." The teller handed me my cash bag, the deposit slips inside. "All present and accounted for."

On my way out, I dragged my feet past the manager's windowed office. A man I didn't know sat in the chair, eyes on the screen, fingers racing over an adding machine.

Thwack! Someone smacked into me, and I staggered sideways. My accidental assailant and I grabbed each other, steadying ourselves.

"Pamela!" I said. Pamela Barber and I had met a few months earlier, at the bank's Pondera branch. A shapely woman of about fifty, she wore a pencil skirt and a jacket with a stylish peplum.

"Erin. I am so sorry," she said. "Totally my fault—not watching where I was going."

"It's okay." I followed her gaze to her office. The only holiday decor was a bowl of peppermints and a fading photo of three young children with Santa. "I heard you moved down here. I guess this isn't the best day to congratulate you on the promotion. Is something wrong?"

"Not two weeks on the job, and I have to call in an auditor."

"Let me guess. I just came from the Building Supply. Their deposit came up short, and you have to make sure the problem isn't on your end."

Her mouth tightened, confirming my suspicion. "We're called the Bank and Trust, but trust is tricky sometimes."

"Truth to that," I said.

A few minutes later, I parked behind the Merc and carried my building supplies inside. The door sweep I could probably handle, but not the roof. I could call the contractor who did our kitchen remodel, but we'd have to wait weeks when all we needed was a piece of plywood cut and screwed into place.

Thinking about the door sweep reminded me of the regretful thief. What had made her change her mind? Jewel Bay looks prosperous, but there are pockets of poverty and need that surprise even the natives, like me.

I dumped my load and headed next door to brief Wendy. And to re-caffeinate—she and her baristas buzz the best espresso in town.

"Erin, it's terrible!" Wendy said the moment I opened the pine green door. "Merrily's missing and so is part of the bank deposit." Wendy shares her brother Greg's dark hair and eyes and intense features, though on her the effect was leavened by her uniform of brightly colored cotton pants and cherry-red rubber clogs. Today, a streak of raspberry jam marred her white chef's jacket.

She isn't chatty, but I've acquired a reputation for sleuthing since returning home. Talk spreads through a small town like flames through a forest in August. And half the town stops by the bakery every day. So she shares what she hears with me.

If it weren't for Merrily's history, people would assume she was sick or had car trouble. They'd think she got stuck in a snow bank—not that she took off for Vegas.

It didn't make sense. Why steal the cash, then leave it behind?

And the photos she'd tucked away so carefully.

Forget it, Erin. None of your business. My tummy growled. Surely I could eat one almond croissant without wrecking the fit of my wedding dress.

"I know—I saw Greg," I said. "He's still in shock. But I'm sure she'll turn up, and that there's a simple explanation."

Wendy looked doubtful. "I hope so. For his sake, and her parents.'"

Like salons and museums, the Thorntons never open their shop on Mondays, even in the season, sparing me the dilemma of whether to stop in and warn them of the coming gossip storm, or pretend I didn't know a thing. Which I didn't, not really, thank goodness.

I blew Wendy a thank-you kiss.

Back in the Merc, I huddled in my tiny office under the eaves, like a hobbit anticipating second breakfast. I took the first delicious, hot sip, and the first crunchy-sweet bite.

Heaven.

And then I dove into paperwork, posting sales and cutting vendor checks. Our business model is a hybrid of standard retail and consignment—we buy some products outright, like Rainbow Lake Garden's fresh produce, sell others on a percentage, like Luci's soaps and Monte Verde wine, and produce a few ourselves, like Fresca's pastas and sauces and our coffee, tea, and chai. All our food is grown or prepared in Montana, and we insist on high-quality, natural ingredients. Organic when possible. Real food, sustainably grown.

After all, if it's made in Montana, it must be good.

Nick had sent a text. WHAT'S UP? I SHOULD BE BACK IN TOWN IN A DAY OR TWO.

BLDG NEEDS U! I texted back. Technically, Mom owns the building and the business, but she says she holds it in trust for the three of us and expects Nick to do his part with the upkeep when he can.

I raced through the rest of the paperwork before going downstairs to spell Lou Mary. Unlike Tracy, who runs home midday to check on her dog, Lou Mary often eats lunch at the counter, especially if my mother or one of the other vendors is working in our commercial kitchen, so she can visit and observe. Today, though, she stepped out to meet a friend.

Fresca had come in while I was out, and was finishing up a batch of our newest line—salad dressings in both ready-to-pour reusable bottles and make-your-own packets. I filled her in on the news from the Building Supply.

"Let's hope it's all a simple mistake, or a misunderstanding," she said, then got back to work.

I unpacked a box of soup mixes from a new vendor, breathing in a hint of thyme, and found a place for them on the dry goods shelf. We'd already tried each variety—product testing is part of the job—and I expected them to be a popular winter item.

As I worked, I thought about the investigation, and the changes in the sheriff's office. Kim had brought Detective Bello around a few months ago after he'd been hired, introducing him to prominent players in town. I hadn't seen him since, until this morning. Jewel Bay isn't incorporated, so as head of the Village Merchants' Association, some folks refer to me as the mayor. I defer that honor to Ned Redaway, proprietor and namesake of Red's Bar, an institution nearly as old as the Merc. Bello seemed nice enough, but I'd learned to be wary of newcomers. Too often they blast in, charmed and charming, then convince themselves they understand the town because folks are open and friendly. Or they try to change it to make it like the place they left.

Bello had irked me this morning, with his *know it all, seen it all* expression. I couldn't blame him for assuming Merrily had disappeared with the money—I feared as much, and Kim must have told him about Merrily's conviction. But I felt sure there was more going on, starting with Merrily missing the cookie exchange yesterday.

I'd just finished with the soup when Lou Mary burst in the front door, shucking her camel hair coat as she surged past me. "So sorry I'm late."

Outside, the village clock struck twelve thirty. Lou Mary was many things, but late wasn't one of them.

She hung up her coat. "Erin, have you heard what they're saying about Merrily Thornton? That sweet girl."

Typical of Lou Mary to call a woman a hair shy of forty a girl, but from her, it sounded like a compliment.

"Rumor is she absconded with the Building Supply's bank deposit," she continued. "Picking up where she left off."

"That sounds like Sally talking," Fresca said. "But until we know what's actually happened, don't you think we owe Merrily and her family the benefit of the doubt?"

A deep flush bloomed on Lou Mary's cheeks. It wasn't like my mother to chide a woman her own age—she saves that for me.

"Francesca"—Lou Mary always calls my mother by her full name—"I've cautioned Sally against bitterness, as I know you have. And against idle talk. But Merrily's reappearance has reopened an old wound. Let her lick it a bit among friends, as long as she doesn't make a public fuss."

I watched, fascinated, as these two wise women, so very different but filled with mutual respect, negotiated their approach to the difficult woman across the street.

"Just a bit," my mother conceded. "Easier to nurse a grudge against Merrily, I suppose, than to believe her own husband would steal from her, especially when they had a child together. But I never thought an eighteen- or nineteen-year-old girl could have planned all that." She untied her holly print apron and hung it on a hook.

"Sally won't be the only one who thinks Greg Taylor is getting what he deserved, trusting Merrily the way he did," I said.

"Better to be too trusting than too suspicious," my mother replied.

"And better yet to be busy," I said as the front door opened and a gaggle of women chattered in, fresh from lunch and ready to shop.

I love gaggles of women at Christmas. Helping them kept my mind off Merrily Thornton and my to-do list. What was I thinking, planning a Christmas wedding? And meeting Adam's family for the first time to boot?

"Your window displays are so cute," one of the shoppers told me. "The train chugging through the snow to reach the village."

"They haven't found that woman yet," another said, a jar of jam in each hand. "Huckleberry or cherry?"

"Try one of each," I said, then, fearing I knew the answer, "What woman?"

"The one at the hardware store who they think took off with the deposit."

I worked the back of my neck with my fingers. Word was spreading fast. The shop line rang, and a moment later, Lou Mary handed me the phone.

"Erin," said a tense, male voice. "It's Greg Taylor. I need your help."

"Why? What? What's happened?"

"I—I went searching. I couldn't believe—I had to find her."

Something in his tone raised an alarm in my brain.

"Where are you?"

"Rolling River Farm." The Thorntons' place. "In the schoolhouse. Erin, she's here. And I think she's dead."

Five

You've got to come," Greg pleaded. "The sheriff is on the way, but I don't want to deal with this alone."

I grabbed my coat and keys, made sure Lou Mary didn't mind handling the shop floor alone, and dashed out. A few minutes later, I turned the Subaru off the highway onto the frontage road leading to Rolling River Farm.

The main house on the Thorntons' place, a large white pseudo-Colonial, dates back to another of Jewel Bay's founding families, though the last survivor had sold to Walt and Taya thirty years ago. It came with a majestic barn, still in use, a bunkhouse, and other out-buildings. The Thorntons moved an abandoned one-room country schoolhouse onto the property and reclaimed it, complete with old-fashioned desks, a shelf of early readers, and a vintage wood stove. Before Walt retired from the timber business and they opened the shop downtown, they ran a holiday antiques and crafts fair in the schoolhouse.

A classic design, red with white trim, it sits south of the barn, several hundred feet from the house. Giant twin spruces flank it, and the woods lap at the back door.

Out front sat Greg's pickup and an older tan Taurus I presumed was Merrily's. I parked beside the truck.

As I got out, the sight of flashing lights at the corner up by the highway caught my eye, and I sprinted to the schoolhouse porch where Greg waited. His flannel-lined navy jacket hung open, his head bare. His gloveless hands kept going to his face. He breathed out heavily through his open mouth, shaking his head.

"I can't believe it. Who would do this?"

I moved past him to the threshold but didn't go in. Didn't need to. Through the open door I could see Merrily Thornton on her back on the pine plank floor, one bare hand outstretched, the other flung across her body. Around her neck wound a string of Christmas lights. Her wide, blank eyes stared at nothing. The bluish tint to her skin contrasted with her puffy red coat. A couple of feet away lay one red-and-black plaid glove.

My own gloved hands flew to my chest, crossing as if in prayer. After all she'd been through, to come home and die.

Questions flooded my brain. How long had she been dead? Why had she come here, to her parents' place?

Who had killed her?

Tires crunched on the snow. An ambulance, followed by two marked sheriff's vehicles, Kim in one, Bello in the other. On TV, emergency services and patrol deputies usually show up first, detectives later. But around here there are too few officers covering too much territory, so whoever's closest responds.

Beside me, Greg's face went ashen, his eyes unfocused. "No one will ever trust me again."

I was puzzled. Wasn't the problem not his trustworthiness, but his trust in Merrily?

Bello headed straight for us while Kim circled the building. Though detectives don't wear uniforms, they both wore black suits and long wool coats.

"Who found her? You, Taylor?" Bello said.

Greg nodded. "After you left the Building Supply, I decided to search for her myself. I just—I couldn't believe she'd rob me and take off, no matter how it looked."

Kim returned from her perimeter circuit and stood behind Bello, a foot or two from the bottom step. Even in flat shoes, she had a couple of inches on him.

"First, I went to her house," Greg said. "Then I came here, and I found—I found her."

"Why come to her parents' farm?" Bello asked. "And Miss Murphy, why are you here?"

"I called her," Greg said.

Kim pointed to the open door. "Quiz session later, Bello. Body first."

We watched from the porch as Kim gestured to Bello to check the space. He peered behind the big teacher's desk and into the two small back rooms while she knelt beside the body. Then she called to the ambulance crew hurrying forward.

"Transport only, I'm afraid."

I slid an arm around Greg and led him down the steps, tiny snow-flakes melting on our cheeks.

"Why here, Greg? Why the schoolhouse?" I made no effort to keep my voice down. Greg's behavior was curious, and I wasn't going to let suspicion of him spread to me. But I did have questions.

His Adam's apple bobbed. "It was her special place. Like mine is the hayloft in Uncle Frank's barn."

And mine is the tree house my grandfather Murphy built in the cherry orchard.

But I sensed more, and waited.

"We were friends in high school, though Merrily was a year ahead. Our crowd hung out here."

"Nick, too? You guys palled around a bit." My brother and Greg, my sister and Wendy, pairing up by age. At four years younger than the boys and two years younger than the girls, I'd always felt left out. But I'd had Kim.

"Sometimes. By junior year, he was already into tracking and stuff. Dancing with wolves, we called it. Merrily's parents didn't mind us using the schoolhouse, but after they finished the restoration, they kicked us out." He paused, remembering. "Actually, things had already started to change. Merrily graduated, and then..."

And then her friends started college or found jobs, and she went to prison.

"Her happy place, huh?" Bello said. How much he'd heard, I didn't know. As he sauntered closer, he pulled a small peppermint candy cane out of his coat pocket, unwrapped it, and stuck it in his mouth. "Miss Murphy," Bello said, and pointed toward my car with his candy cane. "Why don't you wait over there? We'll talk to you in a minute."

"It's okay, Oliver," Kim said. "We'll interview them both formally later. But right now, I want to hear what happened."

He raised the candy cane to his mouth. "You're the boss." Then he turned to Greg. "So you were saying why you came out here. Some kinda hunch?"

"What, you don't believe in those in Florida?" I couldn't help myself.

He ignored me. Kim shot me a *careful* look.

"It made no sense," Greg said, "your theory that she took the cash from the deposit and split. First, it was only a few hundred dollars."

Criminy. She'd paid cash in my shop, hadn't she? Had I inadvertently taken in stolen bills?

"And as Erin said this morning, why take off without the money? If she'd been stealing from me, which I don't believe."

"You're a trusting guy," Bello said. "That why you called Miss Murphy?"

"I called her because—" Greg broke off and ran his hand over his hatless head. "I've known Merrily since we were kids, and finding her—it sucked. Erin's been through this before."

Finding a friend dead. That I had. And he was right—it did suck. But was I meant to be a friend or a smokescreen?

"Greg," Kim said, her tone frank but not harsh. "You know what Merrily did twenty years ago."

Greg sank back against the porch rail. "Does it matter why I thought she'd come here? I was right."

"Now, we may not have a lot of snow in Florida," Bello said, "but I do know it's like sand. Anybody walks through it, they leave their footprints. All I see is yours."

Beside me, Greg stiffened.

"Which means," I said, "that she's been here since before the snow started last night. She was supposed to be at my place at one—right, Kim? You were there. She didn't come, and she didn't call."

"Medical examiner will give us an idea how long she's been dead," Kim said. "Overnight in an unheated building complicates things, though."

"Well, who else saw her? Did her parents know she was here? They can't see the schoolhouse from the main house, but they can see it from the driveway. Even if they didn't recognize her car, wouldn't they have wondered who was out here? When—"

"Erin," Kim said quietly. "Trust us. We'll ask those questions."

Sooner rather than later, from the looks of it. A silver SUV pulling a white cargo trailer crept down the driveway and parked alongside my Subaru. The car had barely stopped when Taya Thornton flung open the passenger door and jumped out, pushing back her fur-trimmed hood.

"What's going on?" she demanded.

"May I ask where you've been?" Kim said.

"Not until you tell me why you're here," Taya replied.

Walt came up behind her. "Down at the Lodge, delivering a vintage sleigh for some Christmas parties. Your father can vouch for us. What's going on?"

"I have some sad news. It's Merrily."

"What has she done now?" Taya's harsh tone gouged my heart.

Kim took a deep breath before responding. "I'm afraid she's dead."

Nothing about Taya and Walt Thornton's relationship with their elder daughter was anything like what I expected. Neither was their reaction to her death. Taya stared at the detectives, then let out a shriek, a high, whistling sound like an osprey closing in on its prey. She flung herself against her husband's chest. He pulled her close, wrapping her grief in his.

A gust of wind tore at my hat and hair. The light snow that had been falling since I arrived turned hard and pellet-like, stinging my cheeks. I wanted nothing more than home and cocoa and Adam. Or the Merc and my mother.

Kim spoke to the Thorntons. "Where can we talk?"

Taya jerked out of her husband's embrace and charged toward the schoolhouse. "I want to see her."

Now that she's dead?

Beside me, Greg shuddered.

Oliver Bello blocked her way. "I'm afraid that's not possible, Mrs. Thornton."

The sound of an approaching caravan caught all our attention, lights flashing, sirens off. Two more sheriff's vehicles. In that split second of distraction, Taya scooted around Bello, up the steps, and inside. Bello tore after her, Walt on his heels. Though I couldn't see into the building, I could hear Taya's wail.

Half the county could have heard her.

Ike Hoover, still coroner and soon to be sheriff, jumped out of his rig. He reached the foot of the steps as Bello hauled Taya down them, Kim behind him with a firm grip on Walt.

"Under control, boss," she told Ike. He sized up the situation with a slow, sweeping glance that paused on me, then kept on moving. Behind him, uniformed deputies unpacked their cameras and forensic gear.

The wind whipped up and Kim told me to leave, promising that I'd be interviewed later. Deputies would stay on scene for hours, photographing, measuring, checking every inch. Darkness would fall, but they'd keep working under big lights. They'd tow Merrily's car to the county garage and send her body to the state crime lab in Missoula for an autopsy.

But the terrible afternoon held one more terrible surprise. Taya Thornton twisted out of Detective Bello's grip and marched up to Greg Taylor.

"This is all your fault." And she slapped him in the face.

Six

The pink neon cat in the window of Muir Veterinary beckoned, and I turned into the small parking lot fronting the highway as if drawn by a magnet.

As Greg had said, I'd been through this before, but that didn't stop me from feeling the loss. From feeling like the world had turned topsy-turvy. My eyes were hot and scratchy, my throat raw. Merrily had worked so hard to stay on the right path and rebuild the family she feared she'd destroyed, and now she was dead.

And I didn't trust her parents to mourn her properly. So though I knew I shouldn't, though the detectives would give me heck for it, I decided to call on Merrily's sister.

The only sign of the season was a cardboard box labeled X-MAS on the grubby vinyl floor in the entry. Apparently, Holly Thornton Muir hadn't inherited her parents' love of all things Christmas.

When I said the matter was personal and urgent, the receptionist led me past the treatment rooms to the office the doctors Muir shared. Animal and antiseptic smells mingled. No sign of Jack Muir, but Holly sat behind the big desk littered with stacks of patient charts, catalogs and dogalogs, and who knew what else. Merrily's desk at the Building Supply had been spotless. Clearly, Holly did not share her sister's passion for order and talent for organizing.

"Erin, hello." Holly stood, eyes bright, smoothing her light blue cotton tunic, plain but for a dark blue embroidered logo—a dog and cat nuzzling each other, above the name *Muir Veterinary*. She was shorter than Merrily, and slimmer, but with the same straight, pale hair, drawn back in a ponytail. "What brings you here?"

I opened my mouth to speak, then closed it, forcing myself to breath slowly, calmly. "Holly, this really isn't my place, but I thought you should know. Something's happened." *What are you doing, Erin?* But there was no backing out now.

"My dad?" she said, her voice rising with worry.

"No. No, it's Merrily. She's—she's been killed."

One small hand flew to her mouth, the patches of color on her cheeks deepening. She sank back into her chair, and her hand slid down to her throat, fingering the bronze chain that slipped out of the vee of her tunic, her only jewelry besides a plain gold wedding band.

"How—what—do my parents know?"

"They do." I told her what I knew, wishing I could comfort her, but the big desk stood like a bulwark between us. Although the cats were our main connection now, I'd always liked Holly. She'd been a senior when I'd been a freshman. A science geek, like Nick had been, and nice to the younger kids.

I looked around for water and spotted a small, glass front refrigerator. Tried the handle, but it was locked. For drugs, no doubt. I stepped out to the front desk and asked the receptionist for water. Told her Holly had had some bad news, and asked if her husband—known as He Dr. Muir, as opposed to She Dr. Muir—was around. In with a punk pug and his person, she said, but assured me she'd send him in the moment he was free.

I returned to the office. Back turned, Holly gazed out the window to the mountains beyond. Even from the doorway, I could hear her heavy breath. Several framed photos sat on the credenza below the window—Holly with her husband, Jack, and their son and daughter. Pictures of the kids, including one of the boy, about nine, in a basketball uniform, a ball cradled in his arms. A shot of Walt and Taya on the schoolhouse steps.

But no pictures of Merrily or her daughter. As if they didn't exist.

A moment later, Jack walked in, thanked me with not a little confusion, and took his shaking wife in his arms.

"If there's anything I can do, give me a call," I said. No one ever calls, but you say it anyway.

And with sadness in my heart, I slipped away.

∞

I turned off Hill and drove down Front, the only street running through the village. My eyes were drawn to the Thorntons' shop window. The woodland scene no longer seemed so tranquil.

Part of me thought I should stop in the bakery to let Wendy know that Merrily had been found, but I didn't have the heart. Besides, she'd ask about Greg, who could be under arrest by now, for all I knew. Anyway, since the baby came along, she tried to get away after the lunch rush, so she'd probably left already.

But there was no escaping Lou Mary. She'd heard my side of the conversation with Greg—she deserved an explanation for my sudden departure. Fortunately, the Merc was quiet for the moment, so I filled her and Fresca in.

"Merrily is—dead?" Lou Mary covered her mouth with one hand, reaching behind her with the other for a stool. "So young. And she had a daughter."

"Oh, darling." Fresca put an arm around me. "How dreadful. Do Walt and Taya know? They must be devastated. What about Holly?"

"Umm, yeah. The Thorntons drove up right after the sheriff. And I stopped to tell Holly." Who hadn't said anything about calling Ashley, and in my own muddled state, I hadn't thought to ask.

"I'll take a dish up to the house. Salad and a ready-to-bake rigatoni. Although I can't imagine they'll want to eat. Their child. Oh, Erin." Mom hugged me again, then leaned back, gripping my shoulders. "You are not going to get involved."

"No, of course not. It's Christmas. We're busy. The village—"

"You're getting married in two and a half weeks."

My throat got tight. She didn't need to remind me. Adam Zimmerman was Mr. Right, no question. At thirty-three, I was ready. We had a sweet house getting sweeter every day. And yet...

My mother has an uncanny knack for reading my mind. "Pre-wedding jitters are natural, Erin. But if there's something more worrying you..."

"No. Not a thing." Not about Adam or our future. Though it might be weird to marry a man without meeting his family. Not that I'd had a chance—between my job in retail and his in recreation, travel opportunities were almost nil. Adam had spent a few weeks in Minnesota lending Tanner a hand last summer, and I'd hoped to visit and meet the family then, but the shop had been too busy. Which was a good thing, but it did feel odd.

"No," I repeated. "I just can't imagine what I was thinking, planning a wedding for Christmas Eve."

She smiled. "Everything will be perfect. You'll see."

"From your mouth to the wedding fairy's ears." I tried to smile but wasn't sure it worked. I'd seen dead bodies before, far too often, but Merrily's death, coinciding with the theft of cash from the deposit bag, troubled me. Light snow had fallen off and on for days, filling in the killer's footprints. She could have laid there, dead or dying, for hours before being found. Maybe even before the bank manager's call and the discovery of the cash in her desk drawer.

Kim had said the temperatures would complicate the ME's time of death calculation. We needed an eyewitness.

What's this "we" stuff, Erin? Got a mouse in your pocket?

Mom released her grip on my shoulders. "If you're all right, darling, I'll head out for the day," my mother said. "The salad dressings are done, and we should be good on chai mix through the end of the season. That was a great idea."

"Thanks, Mom."

I kissed her goodbye, then watched Lou Mary work with a customer trying out lotions.

"See my knuckles?" Lou Mary extended one hand, a jar of green salve in the other. "They were so swollen, so cracked and dry, I'd have been mortified to show them to you. They're still not going to win any beauty contests, but when I heard that young Luci and Bill the herbalist were cooking up a salve, all natural, especially for arthritis, I volunteered to be the guinea pig. And you see the result."

The customer saw. She reached for the jar and studied the label.

I love retail.

I do not, however, love all Christmas songs. Somewhere—at the Building Supply, I suspected—I had picked up a nasty earworm. I shuffled through my mental playlist for an antidote song to banish all hints of Grandma getting run over by a reindeer. *No*, I screamed silently as the second most irritating tune popped into play. Go a-*way*, Jose Feliciano. I do not *want* a *Feliz Navidad*.

Upstairs, I waited for my computer to boot up. Why would Merrily steal again? Why had she stolen in the first place? No one seemed to know.

My phone buzzed. I hoped it was Nick, saying he'd pick up a sheet of plywood and fix the rotting roof line this afternoon.

But the message was from Adam. CHANGE IN PLANS. PROMISE NOT TO FREAK OUT. I'LL TELL YOU TONIGHT.

Oh, great. That just about guaranteed that I'd freak out. What else could a person do?

A person could get to work.

∞

Ten minutes to closing, I was on the shop floor, helping a woman interested in our beef and pork, when the front door chime rang ominously. Or maybe it was the sound of the heavy heels rapping on the plank floor, heading my way.

"This sausage is seasoned with fennel and red pepper," I told the customer, ignoring Oliver Bello in his black suit and his black boots with the Cuban heels. He was working on another of those baby candy canes. A smoker trying to quit? "More flavor than heat. Just the right amount of fat—it bakes or fries nicely."

"Same farm as that thick-cut bacon? We love that on Sunday mornings."

She took a pound of each, along with enough goat cheese and Fresca's sundried tomato and artichoke pesto to take a tray of bruschetta to her bridge club holiday party. I carried her selections to Lou Mary at the front counter, then acknowledged Bello.

He stood in the middle of the shop, arms crossed, frowning. "Where can we talk? In private."

"Welcome to the Merc, Detective," I replied. "Lou Mary, go ahead and lock up when you head out. I'll take care of the till later." I led Bello upstairs. The sloped ceiling wasn't an issue for him—even with his heeled boots, he wasn't much taller than my five-five. Who says men aren't as vain as women?

I took the desk chair, a black Aeron that Tracy had found used for a song, and gestured toward the only spare seat, the rolling piano stool in the corner. "Sorry. Space is tight. How can I help you?"

He gathered the tails of his black wool coat and sat, a small notebook in hand. The coat gave off a whiff of cigarette smoke, and I thought I'd guessed right about the candy canes. No wonder he was so grumpy.

"I understand you witnessed an altercation between the victim, Ms. Merrily Thornton, and her parents."

Anyone could have told him that—it had happened in public. But I doubted the too-proud Thorntons had confessed to a street fight with their daughter. "Just her mother. And I don't know that I'd call it an *altercation*. That's two-way. This was all Taya. Merrily stood there and took it." As though she'd heard it before. And maybe she had, in the two months that she'd been back in Jewel Bay. Saturday's incident might not have been the first shaming.

I told him what I'd seen and heard.

"What did Mrs. Thornton tell your mother when they went inside the antique shop?"

"You'll have to ask her."

"Oh, believe me, I will." He made a quick note. "No one else was present?"

54

"Elves were everywhere," I said, then saw his puzzled expression. "Decorating Day in the village is a big deal. Most crews were finished, but people were chatting, admiring the decorations, cleaning up. The way Taya shouted—they couldn't help notice. Sally..."

"Sally?" he prompted. He shifted wrong, and the wheeled stool nearly scooted out from under him.

"Sally Grimes," I said. "She owns the kids' shop across the street. She heard it all. You know Merrily pled guilty to theft ages ago. The business she stole from belonged to Sally. Her husband ran it, and Merrily worked for him. Merrily got caught up in his grand schemes to get rich off his wife, then dump her."

Even the basic facts were ugly. I had a hard time believing the Merrily I'd met had done such a thing. But she'd been a kid, and kids do dumb things. If they're lucky, they learn from it.

"Pretty gutsy, coming back here," he said.

"She did her time. She wanted to come home." My throat tightened and my vision blurred. "She shouldn't have had to pay for a twenty-year-old mistake with her life."

"You are surprisingly naive, given your reputation for interfering in criminal investigations. Such as stopping at the veterinary clinic to inform Dr. Holly Muir of her sister's death."

"Sorry." I deserved his criticism, and I knew it.

"Hmmph. But then, I see that you're the trusting type," he said. I cocked my head in a question, and he continued. "Downstairs just now. You let your sales clerk close up. Do you know she didn't help herself to cash?"

"I leave her and my other employee alone with cash all day. We've never had a problem."

Bello gave me a long, studied look. "Then you've been lucky. So far. But I understand. You and the victim were friends. You're defending her."

"I liked her. I thought she needed a friend. And I can't fathom parents disowning their child."

"Looks like they were right, though," he said.

I pursed my lips. "I don't believe she was stealing from the Building Supply. Greg gave her a second chance. Why throw that over for a few hundred dollars?"

"She fits the profile to a T. Middle-aged woman in a trusted position with no history of violent crime. She knew how to steal money while hiding her tracks. Embezzlement is a habitual crime."

Was thirty-eight middle-aged? I shuddered. Five years to go, then. Bello couldn't be much more than forty himself.

Despite my decade in the grocery business, I'd never been directly involved with an embezzlement case. But as I mentally ran through the stories I'd heard, I realized he might be right. They did all seem to follow a pattern. Except... I frowned.

"Merrily was only eighteen or nineteen back then. And she was after-school office help. That doesn't fit the pattern." Nor did Cliff Grimes.

"Proves she had a larcenous nature," Bello said.

Was that a variation on *the exception that proves the rule*? I never had understood that idea.

"Tell me about your conversation with Mr. Taylor," he said.

"Mr.—oh, Greg. He called, told me he'd found her, and asked me to come to the schoolhouse." The chair squeaked as I leaned back. Bello's cheek twitched, and I sat up. "Wait. You don't think he killed her. That's impossible. Greg would never—"

He tilted his head and I stopped. He *did* suspect Greg.

"Maybe he met her at the schoolhouse, last night, before the snow fell," he said. "Lured her. Confronted her about the theft. He admitted he felt betrayed and angry. How better to cover his tracks than to call a friend who would never doubt him?"

"You think he called me to provide cover." A sour taste dripped down the back of my throat, and I didn't admit I'd had the same thought. "But if she stole from him, why would she meet him at such a private place? Especially on her parents' property, after the way they treated her?"

"Maybe he followed her there. We have only his word that he hadn't seen her since Friday afternoon when he left work. Or it might have been the other way around. Maybe she lured him. Maybe he was the intended victim."

"Now you're guessing." As was I. "Is Greg under arrest?"

"Not yet," Detective Bello said, and his words sounded like a warning. To watch my step, or to keep my distance from his chief suspect?

Seven

After Bello left, I locked the front door and grabbed a bottle of Pellegrino. The tiny white Christmas lights in the windows gave the shop a ghostly twinkle. Outside, the streets were nearly empty, the skies dark. Only two weeks to Solstice and the return of the light.

The cool fizzy water eased the ache in my throat. Oliver Bello mixed a sort of Cuban machismo with cop swagger and short man syndrome. And he was a know-it-all. I'd been accused of that myself a time or two. Nothing pee-ohs a know-it-all like seeing ourselves in someone else. But he must be a good cop and a decent guy, if Ike Hoover had hired him and Kim approved.

Northwest Montana did seem like a curious place for a Miami cop to land, though. Especially one without snow boots.

I took another swig. Much as I didn't want to believe Merrily was a two-time thief, the evidence did point that way. But Greg Taylor a killer? I didn't know what had happened with the deposit or in the schoolhouse, but I couldn't believe Greg had misjudged Merrily so badly or been driven to violence. Despite Bello's taunt, I was not naive.

Greg's explanation that he thought Merrily was in trouble and didn't think she'd run off with a few hundred dollars made sense.

Especially with more cash, and those precious mementos, left behind.

The old brass cash register on our front counter is mainly for show, though I adored playing with it as a kid. These days we use an iPad to track sales and process credit cards, and keep our cash and checks in a vintage metal sewing kit. As I lifted the metal lid, I couldn't help but think of the cigar box in Merrily's desk drawer.

Bello's gratuitous comments about my trusting nature and being lucky "so far" had stung, but he had a point. Even when cash on hand is limited, every business needs systems to protect itself. Internal losses—shrinkage, in retail terms—are a huge problem, and they can cripple or kill a small operation. My mother had limped along without much in the way of systems, and when I took over, I changed some of that. But not when it came to cash handling.

I counted out the cash on the front counter, each denomination a small pile, then pulled out what we needed to stock the till in the morning.

A pounding on the glass startled me. I bustled around the counter and opened the door.

"Wendy, what are you doing out there? It's freezing."

She shivered in her thin white chef's coat. "I was hoping you'd be here. That new detective just questioned me."

I led her to the kitchen counter and poured her a steaming mug of spicy chai. "Slow down and tell me about it."

"I came in to help Max prep for a catering job tonight. Christmas party. My mother has the baby." Shoulders hunched, she cradled the mug close to her chest, then raised her eyes to mine. "Detective Bello thinks my brother is a killer. They held him all afternoon, though he's home now."

"At this point, the detective has to suspect everyone. And frankly, Greg is behaving oddly. Why did he go out to the schoolhouse?"

"To look for Merrily. Oh." Wendy was distraught, and a tad sleep-deprived, but now she understood. "No, Erin. I don't believe it. You know what happens when someone is suspected unfairly. First the theft, then talk about murder? Even when the real killer is found, people will be convinced he was hiding something. And the Building Supply will be hit hard."

I did know. Barely eighteen months ago, the Merc's former manager turned up dead in Back Street, not far from our gate. Fingers pointed at my mother, and our business suffered. My whole family suffered.

We'd seen the effects of change in Jewel Bay before and fought back. Decades ago, when a bigger, shinier grocery store went in up on the highway, Murphy's Mercantile became a relic. When the hardware store moved out to join it, expanding into a full-scale building supply, the original townsite by the bay nearly became obsolete. The locals were stubborn and creative, though, and over time, with persistence and new blood, they reinvented downtown into "Jewel Bay, the Food Lovers' Village." Restaurants, retail shops, and galleries had made the village a destination with its own identity.

And the Merc was its heart and stomach.

But major losses aren't easy to recover from. And a town without a hardware store quickly falls apart.

"You've got to do something," Wendy said, setting her mug down with a thunk. "Talk to Kim. Get her to see Bello's wrong and call him off."

"Listen, Wendy, I can't do that. She needs to let him do his job. And so do we." Kim knows I've got good instincts and that I've learned a few things about bad guys—and gals. But she never hesitates to remind me I'm not a cop.

"Then *you* have to investigate." Wendy reached across the counter, grabbing my hands in hers. "This is my brother. You *know* him. You know he couldn't kill anyone."

I did know him. And I knew that we can't always be as certain as we'd like about what other people would and wouldn't do. I had a hunch Greg hadn't told me everything. I squeezed Wendy's hands and released them.

"Greg said he and Merrily were friends in high school, that they hung out together. That's why he knew where to find her. But there's more to it, isn't there?"

Wendy looked away and rose. "Oh, Erin," she said, ready to cry. "Why is helping people so complicated?" She tried the door, but the lock sticks sometimes. I reached past her to fiddle with it, and as it snicked open, I saw a battle in my friend's eyes.

Fear, or worry? A desire to protect—but whom?

Criminy. What was she afraid to tell me? Afraid it would hurt Greg, not help him?

Wendy stopped in the doorway and turned, her brown eyes boring into mine. "Please, Erin. You helped Nick when they suspected him. I don't know how to help Greg. But you do."

I swallowed hard. It was one thing to believe I could be useful, another to make a promise. "Let me think about it."

She gave a quick nod and was gone. Back behind the counter, I slid the day's cash and checks into the bank bag, grabbed the cash box and iPad, and headed upstairs. Greg had no reason to kill Merrily before he discovered the theft this morning, and it seemed likely that she'd been in the schoolhouse for hours—long enough for the snow to have covered any other tracks.

But Bello had suggested otherwise. Why? What did he know about Greg Taylor and his weekend whereabouts that I didn't? What did Wendy know? Did it add up to an alibi—or the lack of one?

In the office, I unlocked the wall safe my grandfather had installed and tucked the goods inside. Glanced at the time. I had an appointment of my own before heading home. Home, to whatever news Adam hadn't wanted to share on the phone. I grabbed my coat and my red boots, then reached for my tote, a soft, handmade leather model I'd bought last summer to mark a new phase in my life. A second chance, of sorts.

Which reminded me of what Greg had said about second chances. I had to admit, I felt a twinge of guilt mixed with relief. Had Lou Mary not come along when she had and proven to be exactly what the Merc needed, I could have hired Merrily and found myself in a similar position.

But for the grace of God, and all that.

A few minutes later, I tugged the Merc's front door shut behind me and spotted a familiar figure heading for Red's Bar.

"Hey, Kim." I caught up with her just before she shut Red's door. Still in her work clothes.

"Erin—hi. I didn't expect to see you." Her voice hit a higher pitch than usual, and she glanced around the bar quickly. I was making all my old friends nervous today.

"My home away from home," I said. Good food, good beer, right next door. Plus my mother owns the building. We'd stopped in the middle of the room, enveloped in a beery warmth. "Do you have a sec?"

She opened her mouth, then closed it, and I took that as a yes.

"I know you've assigned Merrily's death to Bello, but can you keep a close eye on him? Please? It's like he thinks the victim's scum and the killer's obvious, so that's the end of it."

"I assure you, Detective Bello will investigate thoroughly. There will be no rush to judgment."

Maybe not, but I wasn't convinced.

She tilted her head, studying me. "Why do you care so much, Erin? You barely knew Merrily."

I blew out my cheeks. "I'm not sure. It's almost as if there's no one to mourn for her. Her parents are so wrapped up in their brand of guilt and shame, and her sister wants to protect her relationship with them. That leaves Merrily's daughter, who's just a kid—"

"A daughter? Walt and Taya didn't mention her." Her brow furrowed. "Dang, that's messed up."

"All I know is she lives in Jesse Hall at UM. I don't even know her last name. Ashley something."

"We'll find her," Kim said. "And don't worry. Bello's only been here four months, but he knows the job. He helped me investigate a bar shooting in the West Valley, and the negligent homicide case from that boat crash last summer. I have my own cases, but he'll keep me in the loop."

"Oh, I heard about that. The ring of Santa Claus suit thieves. Has everybody lost their Christmas spirit?"

She smiled without humor.

I turned serious. "Bello seems to think Greg Taylor called me because he wanted to divert suspicion from himself. And I don't want to be played. But he did seem honestly shocked and upset. Not like a killer."

Anyone else might have asked how I knew so much about the reactions of a killer. Kim didn't need to.

"But if he is—if he did kill her," I continued, "then we have a double tragedy that's going to hurt a lot of people."

"I understand," she said. "I can't promise there won't be collateral damage, but remember, I love this town, too."

And that was as much as I could ask of her. "Thanks. Hey, I gotta run, but one more question. About Bello. How'd he get here?"

"Came up on vacation and loved it. When he got divorced, he wanted a change, and we had an opening."

Leaving the past behind, lighting out for the territories. A story as old as Jewel Bay itself.

Eight

"$\mathcal{N}$ow I remember why I swore I'd never make another wedding gown," Kathy Jensen said, though with her lips clamped over straight pins, decoding her muttering took some work.

"This isn't exactly a gown," I said. Dragonfly Dry Goods, her quilt and fabric shop at the north end of the village, had closed for the day, but we were in the workroom for my final fitting.

She grunted. "Close enough. Turn."

I obeyed, a tad disconcerted by standing on a low table facing a mirror. The resulting image reminded me of the popular book covers showing headless women in tight-fitting dresses, from the cleavage down. My silky white-on-white brocade brushed the top of my red cowboy boots, and swirled when I twirled.

"Two weddings in one family in one year. What did I do wrong?" she said, her ash-blond hair so heavy it barely moved as she inspected me.

For my mother's wedding in the orchard last summer, Kathy had designed a stunning-but-understated sage green lace number in what she and Fresca called tea-length. I'd had to make a few concessions to the weather, choosing a wide sweetheart neckline and ballet sleeves, just below the elbow. A local woman was knitting a red angora wrap, with yarn from sheep I knew personally, to ward off the chill. The wrap and my boots would add a festive touch.

At the moment, the slippery fabric was giving Kathy fits.

"Well, I think you're safe for a while. Nick isn't even dating." My brother's fiancée had been killed last February. Good-looking and self-supporting, with no disgusting habits or dangerous addictions—except tracking wolves—he was highly eligible, and several women had made their interest clear. He'd had a brief, disastrous fling last summer, then declared he wasn't ready for another serious relationship and disappeared into his work. "Actually, I've been trying to reach him. I saw him drive into town on my way here—home from Glacier, or Alberta, or wherever the wolves took him—but I don't think he saw me."

Kathy stuck the last pin in her cushion and made a circle with her finger. When I finished my slow pirouette, she reached up to tug at the bodice, then poked a finger around the neckline and pulled on one shoulder. Dress fittings are a bit like certain medical exams.

"The biggest challenge is your sister," she said, her words finally clear. "Am I going to need to take in a maternity dress at the last minute?"

"It's okay. Even if the baby arrives early, she says nobody will be looking at her anyway. Just me and the baby."

Kathy made another undecipherable sound, then told me to take off the dress, carefully. As if I needed reminding of all those pins.

Preparations were nearly done. I'd always wanted to get married at the Lodge, though I'd envisioned it in summer. But at Christmas, the place would be picture-perfect. Choosing a band had been a challenge after the bass player in my favorite jazz ensemble went to prison, but they'd regrouped, and a rock guitarist was going to join them for the reception, so we could kick up our heels.

"Shame about Merrily Thornton," Kathy said when I came out to the front room, back in my winter uniform of stretchy black pants, long-sleeved T, and a fleece jacket, my red boots in hand. "Her parents must be devastated."

"Hard to tell," I said. "The way Taya blew up at her Saturday, then carried on this afternoon. Has she always been so … dramatic? In kindergarten, I thought she was fun, but I was six."

"Yes, always," Kathy said. "Good thing Walt is so steady."

"It's funny how different they are. But they're both so passionate about Christmas, and the antiques." I slipped into my coat.

"They are a team against the world."

That's what marriage is supposed to be—the *team* part, anyway. Not the *against the world* part. And for sure not the *against our kids* part.

"So, how did the community respond when the scandal broke all those years ago? I was too young to notice."

"People were shocked, but no one blamed the Thorntons for what Merrily did. Except Sally, but that's understandable. People felt sorry for her. She hated that. Then she opened her shop downtown, and later the Thorntons did the same, but by then, the tensions had blown over."

I thanked Kathy and left. Outside I paused for another look at her windows. Crocheted doilies in shades of white and ivory had been hung to form delicate Christmas trees. With the shop dark behind them and only the glow from the lighted tree outside hitting the windows, the lacy forms looked like fairies' skirts.

I walked down Front Street, then around the corner to Back Street. Nick's Jeep was parked nearby, and I needed to talk to him about the roof, but it could wait.

After this crazy day, all I wanted was to go home.

∞

For weeks, when I opened the door to my childhood home, I'd been greeted by the smells of sawdust, Sheetrock mud, paint, and varnish. This time, it was ground beef, mixed with the piquant aroma of tomato sauce rich with oregano. Before meeting—or re-meeting—me and joining in my family's weekly food-fests, Adam had been indifferent to meals. Except coffee, which doesn't count. He'd quickly become a convert, and my mother had taught him to make her classic lasagna and her special basil vinaigrette. He'd learned well.

One more reason I call him Mr. Right.

"Hey, babe."

I tugged my arm out of my purple and gray jacket and let it drop to the floor, then slipped in to a sweet embrace. "Hmm. That tomato sauce tastes great," I said as we pulled apart a few moments later.

He gave me the grin I still can't believe didn't turn my head in college. Other things on my mind back then.

Silly me.

"Wine?" he called over his shoulder on his way back to the kitchen. "I opened that bottle Donna gave us for helping recruit new Elves."

I hung up my coat, shut the closet, and scooped up Pumpkin, who'd appeared as if by magic. "The red from Sardinia that guarantees a long and happy life? You bet."

He handed me a glass and I took a sip. *Mmm.* It would make a long life worth living.

"You heard about Merrily Thornton, right?" I moved to the newly redecorated living room, the full-figured orange tabby trailing me. No sign of Mr. Sandburg. He'd taken to hiding lately, and I wasn't sure if he was pouting over the move or exploring new secret places. "But first, tell me about this big change in plans."

"I can't believe Greg called you and you went out there." Adam sat on the couch and I took the other end, the cat on the cushion between us.

"The change in plans," I prompted.

"Ughh." He sighed heavily and set his wineglass on the coffee table, a pine trunk with rope handles we'd found in the Thorntons' back room. A dark curl fell over his forehead. "They're coming after all."

"Who? To the wedding?"

"The whole crew. Except my dad."

For reasons I didn't fully understand, apparently a mix of shame and agoraphobia, his dad rarely left town. His mother seemed sweet, though. When Adam told her we were engaged, she'd called, then sent me an album filled with photos, artwork, and school stuff from his childhood. He had never known she'd kept one. But the boys, Calvin and Alan, whom he called Cain and Abel, made me nervous. Identical twins married to cousins, they'd spent much of their adolescence torturing Adam, three years younger, and playing pranks on any adult unfortunate enough to cross their path.

"They're grown up now, Adam. They behaved themselves last summer when you visited, right?" He'd stayed with Tanner, helping his childhood buddy through chemo, but I knew he'd seen his family several times. "They run a successful business. They've got wives."

"Those women are saints. If they have kids someday, I can only imagine—"

The oven timer sounded and Adam bounced up and out of the room, leaving me to imagine what wild and crazy fathers he thought his older brothers might be.

"What do you think, Pumpkin?" I said in a low voice. "Are Calvin and Alan Zimmerman really the devil's spawn? Or is Adam still mad about the time in the seventh grade when they snuck his jock strap and cup out of his wrestling bag and replaced them with a pink lace thong?" Tanner had told the story last summer, and by the scowl it had put on my easy-going guy's face, I suspected it was the tip of the prank iceberg.

Where would they stay? So much for progress on my to-do list.

Careful of the cat glued to my thigh, I stretched, hooked a finger on the strap of my gorgeous handmade leather bag, and tugged it toward me. Got out my iPad and added *Call Lodge—twins?* to my list.

Adam had warned me from the start that his dad would not come—he'd only made the twins' double wedding because the church was two blocks from the house. So neither of us would have a father present. The idea of being "given away" didn't appeal to me, but I did want to walk down an aisle, and my mother and brother would do the honors.

I was getting married. I could hardly believe it.

Over dinner, I told Adam about the tragedy of Merrily Thornton and the strange behavior of Greg Taylor. And Wendy. "She wants me to investigate, but when I asked her about Greg's old friendship with Merrily, she changed the subject. Like she was afraid she might incriminate him."

"Families," he said. "Can't live with 'em, can't live without 'em."

The lasagna was herby and gooey, the way I like it. "Who'd have thought Mr. Mac 'N Cheese From a Box would become such a great cook? What's for dessert?"

The face I love took on a wicked slant as Adam leaned across the corner of the dining room table toward me.

A little while later, I wrapped myself in a fluffy fleece robe and scrounged under my side of the bed for my slippers. My fingers found something else soft and furry, and I pulled Mr. Sandburg out of his hiding place.

"You little stinker. Were you there the whole time?"

Back in his jeans and Henley, barefooted, Adam trekked downstairs to work on "the media room." Two weeks ago, he'd hung a blanket across the entry and pinned up a No Girls Allowed sign. I still hadn't seen the space. That was fine. The remodel had taught us both that even small projects can trigger major "discussions" if you're not on the same page. So when your partner says they've got a project to tackle, pour another glass of wine or beer and curl up on the couch with the cats.

Adam knew my penchant for investigating, and swore that my passion for justice and for this community were part of what he loved about me. He'd never tried to stop me from getting involved, and I knew he wouldn't try now.

But he had reminded me gently, when I told him how upset Wendy was, that I had a lot on my plate. The weeks between Thanksgiving and Christmas are pivotal for village merchants, including the Merc. Most of us make the bulk of our income in the ninety days of summer and depend on the holidays to give us a cushion against the winter doldrums. I'd added Lou Mary to the payroll this year, increasing our expenses. The Merc needed all my attention.

Not to mention the wedding. And we were taking two weeks off in mid-January for a honeymoon.

But I felt a draw to this case. The friendship with Merrily nipped in the bud. The parents who acted like her reappearance, and then her murder, were a personal affront. And the new detective who didn't grasp that I could see and hear things law enforcement might miss, or misunderstand.

As for actually getting Bello to listen, I'd cross that bridge later. *If* I came up with any useful facts or insights.

I didn't know a lot about Merrily. She'd grown up in Jewel Bay, on the picturesque Rolling River Farm. It was a working farm, though the Thorntons leased out the pasture and hayfields. Before retiring to retail—not the piece of cake newbies often expect—Walt managed timberlands for one of the big conglomerates. Not the company Sally had inherited. Hers was small potatoes, to mix my agricultural metaphors. But that timber connection might have been how Merrily got the job working with Sally's husband, the late, unlamented Cliff Grimes.

How much money had Merrily taken back then? Had it all been recovered? More questions.

I grabbed my iPad and started making notes, using my favorite mind map software.

Had Merrily stayed in Billings all these years? Another note.

The photos of Ashley in the cigar box haunted me. I'm thirty-three and Chiara and Wendy thirty-five, so that made Nick and Greg thirty-seven and Merrily thirty-seven or thirty-eight. She'd gone to prison at eighteen or nineteen, about the age Ashley was now.

By extending their spite to the next generation, Walt and Taya had deprived themselves of a beautiful granddaughter.

I shuddered. No family was perfect—certainly not mine, despite our reasonably peaceable weekly gatherings. But the Thorntons made no sense to me, devoted to one daughter and disowning the other.

That took me back to where the evening started, to Adam's family. Meeting them was the only thing about this wedding that had me worried. Thank goodness Adam is a rock. And Tanner would be there to help us both.

At the sound of footsteps on the stairs, I closed the iPad and picked up my wine.

I'm not one of those women who oohs and ahhs over every house, mentally redecorating it, or who curls up in the evening to watch

House Hunters or *Property Brothers*, cute as they are. Took me weeks, after Adam accepted my proposal and we decided to buy the place, to sift through all the ideas my mother and sister offered and figure out what I wanted. Our family friend Liz had insisted on a feng shui consult, too, to maximize the healthful flow of energy in the space.

We'd redone the kitchen and bathrooms, and created a master suite from two small bedrooms. Adam and I had done all the painting ourselves, and spent hours hunting for the right mix of affordable furniture, new and antique. Neither of us had much after years of cozy rentals. It was time for us to settle down and for the house to get an update. Still warm and inviting, still home to the traditions my parents and grandparents had begun. But *ours*.

And Adam had ideas of his own. The biggest was converting part of the basement into a cozy den. Now he stood in the doorway, grinning that loveable grin.

"Ms. Murphy, your presence is requested in the lower level." He held out a hand and we started down the stairs. At the landing where the stairs jogged, he told me to close my eyes, and led me the rest of the way. The sounds of Cold Play's latest surrounded us, and my bare feet touched a soft, looped carpet. Behind me, Adam put his hands over my eyes.

"Ta da!" He slid his hands away and rested them on my shoulders.

My mouth fell open. The giant flat screen on the wall, I'd known about. Tanner's wedding gift, it had arrived at the store a few days ago. On either side, built-in cabinets held stereo equipment, speakers, and other electronic doodads. Pieces from my glass and pottery collection sat on other shelves, and a panoramic photograph of Lake McDonald in Glacier National Park filled one wall.

"Chiara hung the art. The guys and I put the cabinets in Saturday when you were working. Bill laid the carpet last week."

The day I'd noticed a funny smell.

"We've got digital surround sound, though I haven't got the TV hooked up yet. The controls are hidden." He wiggled a switch on the wall, and the lights lowered, then rose. "Dimmers."

"You did all this yourself?" Two long couches could hold a crowd for a big game, or let us stretch out to watch a movie. An oversized chair was made for cuddling. Trays on the ottomans would hold food and drink, a book, or the remote.

"Don't sound so surprised."

I put a hand on his chest. "I'm sorry. It's just that you're the guy who thinks a calendar showing a different ski run every month is art, and who never bought a piece of indoor furniture in his life except a bed. Your friends never needed to take a table or chair to Goodwill— they just gave it to you."

"You like it? I even sent pictures to Liz to check out the feng shui."

"I love it. Oh, a wet bar. This is what you were doing when you said the plumber had to redo the pipes for the laundry and I didn't think they needed redoing!"

"Yep. I was hoping to update the bathroom, too, but that will have to wait."

"For our first anniversary," I said and reached up for a hug.

Because I knew that whatever else happened, whether a blizzard hit our wedding or his brothers hauled out their teenage pranks, whether my sister had her baby that day, or any of a million other things went wrong, the wine had already done its magic.

We would have a long and happy life here.

Nine

Two days in a row, I started the morning at the Building Supply. I got there earlier on Tuesday than the day before, and the place was buzzing with contractors picking up Sheetrock and screws and all kinds of whatnot for the day's jobs.

I found Greg in the electric aisle, talking with an employee about putting the LED bulbs on sale before a new supplier's first shipment arrived. "Don't know why the old vendor dropped us, but let's make some room."

"I'll make a sign," the other man said. "Merrily made a template I can use."

Greg flinched. "Do that," he said. The other man left and I called Greg's name.

"Surprised to see you again so soon," he said, rearranging his face from grouchy boss to affable retailer. Everybody in the Taylor family looks alike. Wendy and Greg hadn't followed their parents and older brother into the theater biz, but they had natural acting talent. "Did those items you picked up yesterday do the job?"

"Truthfully, I've been too busy to find out. Can we talk?"

For a moment, the facade slipped, his lips going straight, his shoulders sagging. Then he gathered an invisible strength and became the pleasant store manager.

"Erin, I know my sister thinks highly of you. And you certainly were a big help to Fresca and Nick when they were under suspicion." He tucked his chin, balancing on that edge between understanding and patronizing. "But I don't need you digging around."

Though his tone wasn't rude, his words surprised me. He'd been panicked when he called me yesterday, and he'd confided in me at the schoolhouse. What had changed?

"Did they identify another suspect? Make an arrest?" Because a killer was on the loose and we were all at risk until they did.

His mouth tightened, and a muscle in his jaw quivered.

"Boss." It was Cary Lenhardt, the bookkeeper. "I've got those deposit records you wanted."

That perked my ears. "Checking for more discrepancies?"

"Good to see you, Erin. Good luck with that drafty door." Greg gave me a firm, dismissive nod, and walked past me toward the offices, Cary in his wake.

The light bulbs might be going on sale shortly, but I needed an excuse now. I grabbed one. The other customers had cleared out, leaving the cashier alone at the front counter. It was the same redhead as yesterday. *Jeri? Jackie? No.* Her puffy, red-rimmed eyes told me that unlike her boss, she wasn't covering up her emotions.

I put the bulb on the counter and left my hand there, a universal sign of empathy. "I'm so sorry about Merrily."

"I know what they're saying—that money is missing, and because she stole from somebody once years ago, it must have been her." Not-Jeri's voice wavered, but with grief rather than uncertainty. "She was like a shelter dog, you know?"

I cocked my head, not following.

"They've been treated bad," she continued, "and you think they'd be mean. But instead, they're the sweetest dogs you ever had."

If that wasn't a testimonial to a life transformed, I didn't know what was.

"She brought in cupcakes and cookies. She lent me money when my tire blew between paydays. That doesn't sound like a thief to me."

Detective Bello would say it's easy to be generous with other people's money. And he might be right.

"Me, neither," I said. "I'm worried about her daughter."

"Oh, that poor girl. Ashley. Lives in the same dorm as my Jasmine. The sheriff's office said they'd send someone to tell her."

Older than I'd been when my father died, but not by much.

She reached under the counter for her phone, thumbs flying. "Let me text Jas. See if word's gotten out."

I waited, feeling a bit awkward.

"No reply. She must be in class." The cashier tucked her phone away and reached for my light bulb. "I'll let you know what I hear."

"Thanks. Merrily worked early Saturday, right? Were you on shift?"

She ran the scanner over the box and asked if this was going on the Merc's account, which made me feel worse about not knowing her name. I vowed to get us all name tags, so no one would have the same problem at the Merc. "Yeah, I was here Saturday. We counted the till together, like every morning. Then she and Cary finished up the deposit. She dropped it off on her way to help her folks decorate." She choked back a sob, and I was glad the place was nearly empty.

But her words changed the picture a bit. Could anybody be quite so conscience-free as to steal from her employer, then immediately go see the parents who'd shunned her for that very activity?

Everybody's got motives the rest of us can't see. But that sounded pure crazy.

"I saw her in the village. We talked. We had cocoa together." I scribbled my name on the credit card screen. "I liked her."

And I could see on the nameless cashier's face the impact of her death. Whatever Greg Taylor's reasons for trying to throw me off the scent, I was no sweet, clingy shelter dog. I intended to be a pit bull who held on and didn't let go.

∞

On the sidewalk in front of the Merc stood a very pregnant woman, one hand on her low back as she squinted at the roof line. My sister.

I made a half U-turn to slip the car into a diagonal spot and climbed out.

"You gotta get this fixed," Chiara said.

"The soffit's all rotted. Nick did some repairs last winter, so I was hoping he could fix it."

"He's busy, Erin. What about Adam?"

Winter isn't usually a wildlife biologist's busy time, but even after traipsing around the woods with Nick last winter, there was a lot I didn't understand about his work. "He's worked so hard on the house, I didn't want to ask. He finally let me see the basement, by the way. I love it."

Her smile mirrored my own, her cheeks pink from the fresh air. "It was great fun, especially knowing you didn't have a clue."

"I didn't. Adam is full of surprises." I told her about his brothers' change in plans and his nervousness.

"Twins are like that sometimes," she said. "Bonded in the womb and all that. Sounds like Adam always felt left out, until he found Tanner."

"Tanner says they saved each other."

"It's only for a few days," she said. "They can't get too wild. Besides, they are going to love you."

We hugged and I watched her waddle across the street, feeling like the luckiest little sister on the planet.

Monday's sales had been surprisingly good, so when Tracy and Lou Mary arrived, we restocked and crossed our fingers. Heidi says in the kitchen shop at Christmas, people take more time early in the month. Later, they spend less time and more money, especially the men.

"Hey, you two. Help me puzzle this out." I showed my staff the bag Adam and I had found outside the back door, with the soap and lotion, cash, and note.

Tracy read it twice. "Now that's a first."

Lou Mary pondered. "Someone who walks around with a pocketful of one-dollar bills. A waitress, maybe?"

"Yeah. Or a busser—she's young. Lives at home," Tracy said.

"Ask at the restaurants," Lou Mary suggested.

"Good idea," I said. "Thanks."

"You're welcome, By the way, the cookies from your party are divine, but I'm surprised you didn't make biscotti."

I rolled my eyes. "Just because I'm half Italian, everyone thinks I have to make biscotti."

I spent the rest of the morning in the basement, packing orders for shipping. My brother-in-law, Jason, had set up our online store last winter, with help from Luci the Splash Artist, a talented graphic designer as well as a soap maker. Since the online store had gone live, orders had steadily grown. To my surprise, in-store orders increased, too. Customers were willing to pay for the convenience of a wrap-and-ship purchase, and let me stand in line at the post office instead of them.

But my after-school shipping clerk had graduated, and I hadn't found a new one.

Back on the main floor, Tracy was taking advantage of a brief lull to make up more gift baskets. My idea, and a brilliant one, I don't mind saying.

I headed up to the office. Catalogs from our suppliers were flooding in—online and in the mail—and half a dozen sales reps had called to talk up their products and special offers. It made sense to order now, when stocks were high and prices low. Estimating how many tea tins or labels we'd need in the next six months wasn't rocket science. How many compostable plastic forks and how many picnic baskets. You figure out what you've sold, estimate sales growth, and bite the bullet.

But that takes time. Not to mention I had a Christmas season to get through, a family of future in-laws to prepare for, and a wedding to put on.

That called for truffles. Fortunately, we keep a box of rejects in the office and I plucked out one with an illegible swirl. Raspberry or cherry?

"Mmm. Green tea."

That reminded me that Merrily had bought a box of truffles on Saturday, and my throat tightened.

Dang, dang, dang. I really thought we could become friends. You can never have too many. Even in your hometown.

I wiped away the tear forming in my left eye, and focused on my supply inventory. And because my mind jumps around, I thought about the Building Supply and the light bulb sale, then my conversation with the cashier. She'd said she and Merrily counted the till together every morning. Putting two employees on the job is an excellent safeguard. Whether Greg had started the practice when he hired Merrily or before didn't matter, but I wondered what other protections he might have put in place.

Like having two employees prepare the deposit. The cashier said Merrily and Cary had finished it up before Merrily took it to the bank, and Cary had said something similar yesterday.

Maybe the bank did have an internal problem. I'd heard about a credit union manager in another town who'd thrown her bosses off for years, whiting out the actual cash-on-hand figure and writing in a higher amount so the totals would balance.

Too bad the crooks among us can't put their ingenuity to use making the world a better place.

But what I couldn't see was how the coverup of embezzlement inside the bank could be connected to Merrily's murder. Or how it might explain the cash in the cigar box.

Humans. When they baffle you, reach for chocolate.

Jen

'Tis the season," Rosemary said. I stacked my last load of packages on the post office counter.

"I keep telling customers: Get your orders in by the fifteenth if you want delivery by Christmas. But you know there will be stragglers."

"Yeah." She laughed. "And I'll be one of them."

I didn't even want to think about Christmas presents. And so far, I hadn't. Would anybody mind if a Christmas bride skipped that part?

And wedding favors. Boxes of truffles would be perfect. *Bingo!* If I ever had time to put them together.

"Shame about Merrily Thornton." Rosemary rested her hands on the plastic tub of Merc packages. "She came in every morning to pick up the Building Supply's mail and every afternoon to make the drop off. That girl worked hard."

Mail. Truffles. "Did you see her Saturday? She bought a box of truffles to slip into a package, and I'd assumed she meant a Christmas gift, but if she was mailing a box ..."

"Saturday? I was off." Another clerk in a blue postal blouse, a navy turtleneck underneath, came into view, and Rosemary relayed my question.

"Yes," the other woman said. "She was sending a care package to her daughter—goodies before finals. She sent that girl a box or a card every week. Texts and emails are great, but there's nothing like good, old-fashioned mail."

"Nothing like," we all agreed.

"Do you remember Ashley's last name? I'd like to send her a note. Merrily must have come straight here from my shop."

The clerk opened her window and gestured to the man behind me in line. "Hansen, Johnson ... Ten thirty, quarter to eleven? We open at ten and the early customers had come and gone, but the noon rush hadn't started yet. Larson, that's it."

Every business has its rhythms. "Thanks, both of you. See you soon."

Ashley Larson, Jesse Hall, UM. Who needs fancy databases or the victim's personnel records? Small-town talk gave me all the info I needed to find Merrily's daughter. Now what? I would send a condolence note. What else did knowing the girl's name and whereabouts tell me?

Nothing. But learning that her mother sent her a card or a package every week—that was not a woman who would risk a return ticket to prison for a few hundred dollars squirreled away in a cigar box.

I turned the key in the Subaru and cranked up the heater. Grabbed my iPad from my bag. Not many people know you can create a timeline with a simple Excel template. I'd discovered the tool while planning product launches at SavClub, a hair-pulling task.

Merrily had left the Building Supply around nine, dropped off the bank deposit, then driven down to the village. Where had she parked?

Across the bridge at the south end, I guessed—the direction she'd gone when she left the Merc. Her purchase had been the first sale of the day, and the iPad would tell me the precise time, but it didn't matter. I just needed a general idea of where she'd been over the weekend.

I knew where she *hadn't* been Sunday afternoon—my house. Had the killer struck then? Too soon to say. Too many variables. Maybe a simple change of heart about attending the cookie exchange, as my sister had surmised. But I didn't think so.

I tucked the tablet away and put the car in gear.

At the cookie exchange, Molly had said Merrily lived up the street from her. As the newest member of the Jewel Bay Realty team ("Call us for a real gem!"), Molly came in early and worked late. Typical Murphy workaholic ways, though I had to admit, much as I love selling things, a career in real estate sounded like a bad dream to me.

But my cousin loves it. And she loves double mochas. On my way to her office, I detoured toward Le Panier. As my hand hit the doorknob, I recognized the woman on the other side, struggling with a tray full of coffee cups, a bag of pastries sitting precariously on top. I held the door for Pamela Barber then grabbed the bag of pastries and followed her to her car. Opened the passenger door and waited while she settled the coffee safely on the floor and took the bag.

"Thanks, Erin. We've got more visitors from headquarters this morning, so I'm buttering them up with lattes and croissants."

"A yummy plan," I said. "Still tracing that short deposit? The one that may or may not be from the Building Supply?"

"You know I can't talk details, but nothing slips past you. Let's say there are a number of possibilities." Her expression turned somber. "I don't blame you for thinking what you're thinking, Erin. But I made the best of my second chance. Please believe that."

I did. What I knew about Pamela Barber's past wasn't common knowledge, but I had no reason to doubt she'd trod an honest path every day since. I wished her good luck.

No sign of Wendy in the bakery. Michelle took my order for a double mocha and a double skinny latte. A single mother of two who makes the Energizer Bunny look like he's sleepwalking, she'd started working full-time at Monte Verde Winery since last summer's events. But she worked here every morning pulling espresso shots *and* helped Max on catering jobs. She said she'd miss the activity in the village too much if she quit, but I suspected she appreciated the chance to earn extra dough at Christmas, for her kids.

"Michelle, an odd thing happened the other day." I told her about the bag and the note. As she listened, she lifted her brows in an *I can relate* gesture. "The dollar bills made us think of tips, and the note sounds like she's a kid. You know all the restaurants and caterers. Any idea who it might be?"

"No-o-o, but I'll ask Max if it might be one of the bistro bussers. A kid who's working but can't buy presents may be paying for everything herself."

"And going without some of the basics. Like socks and decent underwear." And nice soap.

"Exactly. It's a bigger problem in this town than people think. Let me ask around."

"Thanks."

Moments later, hot fragrant cups in hand, I paused in front of the Thorntons' shop. Dark. Not even the tiny white lights around the display window glowed, and the twinkle in Father Christmas's eyes seemed dulled.

A few doors down, Molly accepted my offering gratefully. "What do you need this time, cuz?" She knew me well.

"Nothing from your files." I sat and took the first sip, more of a hint-of-foam-and-flavor-on-tongue than an actual taste, since the coffee was so hot. "Merrily lived near you. Do you know which house? And whether she was buying or renting?" Molly kept her finger on the pulse of real estate the way I focus on retail.

"Oh, sure. She lives—lived—in Granny G's old house. Renting, I'm sure. If that house ever comes on the market, I'll snatch it up myself."

Gwendolyn Gottfried Taylor, who'd died last spring, had been known throughout Jewel Bay as Granny G. She'd been a powerhouse, a true family matriarch.

Not to mention Greg and Wendy's grandmother.

Now I was more certain than ever of a hidden connection between Greg and Merrily. And more uncertain of Greg.

"Any chance you saw Merrily between, say, eleven o'clock Saturday morning and noon Monday?"

I could almost see the gears clicking and whirring in my young cousin's brain. She'd been a big help last summer, untangling the ties between suspects and witnesses, and she wanted to be helpful again.

Don't we all?

One freckled cheek scrunched up, one blue eye half closed. "Sorry. I didn't see her. I didn't see anybody hanging around the house. No strange cars on the road."

"No worries," I said, though I had plenty.

Molly held her mocha close to her face. "Erin, do you think her parents killed her? She's been back here for months. Blowing up at her in public—that's like, so not good ju-ju on Decorating Day."

On Decorating Day, we are all Elves in service of the Christmas spirit. Friends and strangers helped out together, and the work got done. But Taya, who adored Christmas and looked like an elf herself, had been spitting mad.

Walt? He'd been sad. Protective—not of his daughter, but of his wife. What had he said? *It's best that you stay away.*

Best for whom? And why?

I let out a long slow breath. "I have no idea."

$$\infty$$

Back in the shop, I refilled the sample bowl of Jewel Bay Critter Crunch and made a fresh pot of Cowboy Roast. We were set for the afternoon customers.

The sound of boots stomping off snow in the hall told me Tracy was back from her lunch break and vet visit.

"Polka aced his checkup," she announced, her round, pretty face aglow. "Dr. Muir couldn't believe how big he is for six months."

"Holly's back at work so soon?"

"No. He Dr. Muir." Miniature Dalmatians hung from Tracy's ears, the closest thing to Harlequin Great Dane earrings she'd been able to find. "John—Jack."

"That's so funny," Lou Mary said. "When a person has exactly the right name for their job."

"An aptonym," I said. "Like Candy Divine. Or Dave Barber." Pamela's ex, who is a barber. Or a pair of Pike Place Market merchants I'd shopped with in my Seattle days—Vinny the wine seller and Pepper who owns the Spice Shop.

"He said Holly's taking a couple of days off, to help her parents. I guess they're pretty freaked out, despite disowning her." Tracy snapped open a Diet Coke. "Merrily, I mean."

"That probably makes it worse," Lou Mary said. "Now that she's dead, there's no chance of reconciliation."

"I got no sense they wanted that," I said, picturing the elder Thorntons on Decorating Day and outside the schoolhouse, when they heard about their daughter's death.

"You never know what's in someone's heart," Lou Mary said.

Tracy took a long swig. "The clinic staff were pretty upset. Merrily worked there part-time for a few weeks before she got the full-time job at the Building Supply a couple of months ago. And she still did the clinic's books. The receptionist was going nuts, trying to find someone new this time of year."

That took me by surprise. If Merrily did the books for her sister and brother-in-law's veterinary clinic, then they must have been on good terms. And they trusted her.

What did Walt and Taya think of that? Had they even known?

"I guess her ex is on his way. From Billings," Tracy continued. "Long drive."

Eight hours in winter, halfway across the state.

"By the way," Lou Mary said to me, "your favorite detective would like you to stop by the sheriff's office."

I suspected she did not mean Kim Caldwell. I gave her a tired nod.

Over lunch upstairs, I returned a few emails and updated our Facebook and Instagram pages, highlighting our newest and grooviest food and gifts. Always a balance, keeping the focus on food, and keeping it real. Selling truffles and caramel corn wasn't enough. We had to be seen as a viable supplier of eggs and bacon and pasta, too. Fresh, local, and competitively priced. A challenge in this crazy climate, especially in winter, when I didn't mind if more of our income came from pottery than pork. 'Twas the season for gifts—and the profit margin is higher.

Thirty minutes later, I headed out.

Granny G's old house, where Merrily had lived, was a tidy bungalow on the Stage Road, the original road north out of Jewel Bay. In these days of space stations and hybrid cars, stagecoaches seem like figments of Western movie makers' imaginations, but the valley is criss-crossed with roads named for long-ago stages. They remind me to slow down, and take the long view.

The driveway hadn't been plowed or the sidewalk shoveled. A set of footsteps, made by a large man in large boots, led to the side door and around to the front porch. A second set trailed them—also male, but in regular shoes, judging by the slip marks.

A sheriff's deputy and Detective Bello, no doubt, though they'd left no barricades or yellow tape to signal a crime scene.

I guessed that the ex—Larson, I presumed—would stay here, with Ashley. Holly and her husband lived a few miles north, in an area where even locals need a map. Walt and Taya's spacious home sat close to town, but I suspected they would not welcome their granddaughter or her father.

A shovel leaned against the wall by the side door, and I got to work clearing a path to the small covered front porch.

The ex did have me curious, though, and I hoped Merrily's parents would show him some courtesy. Unless he was a creep. But she hadn't made it sound that way.

I stopped to catch my breath, glad for my knee-high snow boots. It must have been about thirty degrees, and I'd worked up a light sweat. The rest break only fueled more questions. Who would handle funeral arrangements? Her parents? Her ex, on their daughter's behalf? Poor girl.

Reverend Anne would know. She might even tell me. We aren't Methodists, but Anne is an old friend—she hung out with Chiara and Wendy growing up, and I remembered her in the kitchen and garden of this very house. Adam and I had asked her to officiate at our wedding, giving me a good excuse to swing by her church for a chat.

The snow was light and I finished quickly, then fetched the basket I'd brought. A bag of Cowboy Roast, a jar of plum preserves, cheese, and crackers—a few things that might soothe a grief-stricken visitor. I set it on the porch and peeked in the kitchen window.

A cherry red KitchenAid mixer stood on the counter, bits of dried dough clinging to the beaters. Cookies covered two cooling racks. A bag of powdered sugar lay nearby, and I pegged the cookies as Russian tea cakes.

The realization punched me in the gut. Merrily hadn't changed her mind. She had meant to come to my place Sunday. She'd have needed to leave here by twelve thirty. Red-striped cellophane bags and a spool of red ribbon sat on the kitchen table, but she hadn't started packing. Sugaring the cookies, then counting them into bags, tying them up, and tucking them into a box or tote would have taken a good half hour. That meant she'd left the house before noon on Sunday.

Why? Not of her own accord. Not with all those cookies as witnesses. Bello's theory about the call that lured her made some sense. I knew from Kim that law enforcement could request phone records, but getting them sometimes took days.

As far as I knew, Greg had no motive to kill her until Monday morning, when he discovered that the deposit had gone missing and found the cash in her desk.

Who had wanted Merrily Thornton dead before that?

And where was the killer now?

So many questions, so few answers.

But I'd learned, in business and in crime, answers don't come knocking on your door. Like Jack London said about inspiration, you have to go after answers with a club.

Eleven

I was about to drive away when a sheriff's rig pulled up behind me. And who should approach but Detective Oliver Bello himself, slipping and sliding on the slick surface of the freshly plowed road.

"Since you can't be making a social call on a dead woman," he said, "you must be investigating. I wish you wouldn't."

"I heard that Merrily's ex was on his way, and I thought it might be nice—neighborly—to shovel the snow and leave him a few things he might need."

His brow furrowed. "How did you hear that?"

"It's a small town, Detective. We talk to each other. And I hear you wanted to talk to me."

"You need to come in and make a formal statement, ASAP."

"Sure. But while you're here, let me show you something." I climbed out and led the way to the front porch, the detective struggling behind me in the snowy driveway. "Better get yourself some good winter boots."

He grunted. I waited for him to join me on the porch, then pointed in the kitchen window and explained my theory.

"Let me get this straight." He rubbed his hands together in their thin black leather driving gloves. "You think she was—what? Kidnapped? Because she left a plate of cookies behind?"

"You're the one who said she was lured away," I said. "You've got to get those cookies in the sugar while they're cool enough that the sugar won't melt but warm enough that it sticks."

"We made a thorough inspection. No signs of anything amiss."

Meaning no spilled flour or scattered pecans. No spoons on the floor. "The cookies are amiss. She was obviously planning to come to the cookie exchange at my house. What made her change her mind?"

"Someone lured her to the schoolhouse and killed her. Your friend Mr. Taylor, perhaps. Her boss. Why else would a woman rush out of her house without her coat or purse?"

I craned my neck to see what he was pointing at. Merrily's black leather cross-body bag lay on the seat of an oak Windsor chair next to the back door. She'd grabbed her keys and nothing else.

Now *that* was amiss.

"You've got a point," I said, though he was missing the point about the cookies. "But if someone lured her away, it was before Sunday afternoon, before she could pack up those cookies and bring them to my house."

He fixed me with a steady glare. "Miss Murphy, I understand that both my predecessor and Undersheriff Hoover tolerated your attempts to interject yourself into official investigations out of friendship, and perhaps a touch of pity. Let me be perfectly clear: I have no intention of letting you do the same on my watch."

And with that he turned and slip-slided away.

∞

The detective had made my Jell-O rise, but I am not anti-law enforcement. Some of them are my best friends. And my mother always says to do the things we don't want to do first, so we don't have to keep thinking about them.

So I drove past the church to the sheriff's satellite office, tucked in a pair of extra rooms in the back of the firehall, a stone's throw from downtown.

I parked beside Bello's rig and went inside. The office had never been high on atmosphere or aesthetics, but now it felt positively grim. The weather, maybe. Or the new guy.

Deputy Oakland sat at the battered gray metal desk in the outer office. Before I could say a word, he handed me a clipboard with a few sheets of paper attached. "Hey, Erin. Good to see you. We've typed up what you told us yesterday. Read it over, add anything we've missed. Sign and date. You know the drill."

See, I told myself. It's not that hard to be friendly, to let the citizens feel like they have a stake in the investigation, even a role to play. The new guy could learn a few things from the deputy about attitude.

"Thanks." I took the clipboard and sat in a chair near the door to the inner office, open a few inches. Though I couldn't see Bello inside, or see him stand and walk to the door, someone got up and shut it firmly.

I glanced at Oakland, a heavy-set man who'd been on the job for years. The mustache he'd shaved last summer had grown back.

"He takes some getting used to," the deputy said. "But he's not a bad guy."

Coming from him, that meant a lot. I focused on the statement. Debated how to phrase my observation. Finally, I wrote *I believe, based on the baked but unfinished, unwrapped cookies in the victim's kitchen, that she intended to come to my house Sunday afternoon, but was prevented from doing so by ... By what?* All I could think of was TV cop lingo ... *a person or persons unknown.*

I read it over, signed it, and handed it back to Oakland.

"Deputy, any preliminary word on the time of death? Or the cause?"

His eyes flicked toward the closed door.

"She wasn't strangled with the lights, was she?" I made a clawing motion near my neck. "It's instinct. Someone tries to strangle you, you fight. You kick. You struggle to get free. If it's even possible to strangle someone with an electric cord."

"Oh, you'd be surprised what people can do with an electric cord," the deputy said, and a shock rippled through me. "But no, she wasn't strangled. More than that it's too soon to say. When we get the preliminary report ..." He flicked his eyes toward the inner door.

"Tell your boss he needs new boots," I said and left to the sound of laughter.

$$\infty$$

Half Irish, half Italian, I'd been raised Catholic, but when my father was killed in a hit-and-run and God defied all my prayers by holding no one responsible, I'd left the church. In my years away, in Seattle, I'd found spiritual solace in long walks along Puget Sound and on drives through the Olympic Rain Forest and hikes through the Cascades. In truth, any place with trees, as befits a girl raised in an orchard.

With the mystery of my father's death solved last winter, I now understood that the guilty party had not gone unpunished but been tortured in mind and heart by what had happened. But I had lived too long without the institution to forgive it for failing me back then.

Still, a wedding needs a celebrant. The Reverend Anne Christopherson, once a wild child and now a Methodist minister, had been the obvious choice. Besides, she didn't care if Adam and I rarely darkened her doors. She only wanted—and she actually said this—a chance to shine God's light on us.

I parked outside the Methodist church, a block away from the high school. The pastor's study lay off the vestibule, and her door was open. I didn't have much time, but it wouldn't take long to find out if Anne would talk to me about Merrily and her parents.

One foot over the threshold of the book-lined room, I realized she was not alone.

"Erin," the pleasantly plump blond minister said in her reassuring, caramel-smooth voice. "I'd like you to meet Brad Larson."

The man stood and I stuck out my hand. "Erin Murphy."

"Brad is Merrily Thornton's husband," Anne continued as if I hadn't spoken, and realization struck. So caught up in my own doings, I'd barely noticed the road-worn dark blue truck out front, the one with Yellowstone County plates. Billings plates. "He's here to make arrangements."

She made the euphemism sound as if it were the most natural thing in the world.

"Erin Murphy," Brad said, the lines across his high, pale forehead creasing. He wore jeans and a light blue denim shirt. Work clothes. I doubted he knew the fashion gurus were dictating that denim-with-denim was trendy. A "statement." "You helped Merrily when her mother got so upset."

"How did you—did she tell you?" Had she called him before she was killed? Did he know what had led her to change her plans so abruptly that she left dozens of cookies on the kitchen counter? Did he know who might have killed her? "And I'm sorry, I had the impression Merrily was divorced."

"Holly told me." He ran a hand through what was left of his fine blond hair. "We filed, but the divorce wasn't final yet. I was hoping..."

"I—I'm so sorry for your loss. For you, and your daughter."

His exhale was ragged, his eyes downcast.

"Erin, was there something you needed?" Anne prompted. Her royal purple tunic, caftan-esque, was ministerial, but the bold shade overwhelmed her fair coloring.

"Uh, no—not really. I just—the wedding." My hands rose and fell in the air like birds drunk on the fermented cherries left behind on the trees. I turned to Brad. "Two and a half weeks. Lots of last-minute details."

He curved his mouth in acknowledgment, though it was not a smile.

"Brad, if you don't mind me saying this," I said, "Merrily said Ashley didn't know about her past. Her time in prison." I raised a hand to stave off interruption. "And it isn't any of my business. But half the town knows. If Merrily were still alive and Ashley visited for Christmas, no one would say a word. But with her... gone, and questions about money missing at the Building Supply... Well, she'll hear the talk. Might be better if you tell her everything first."

The room was silent, as if the walls needed time to absorb my words. My stomach turned sour and jittery. *You should have kept your mouth shut.*

"Why don't we all sit down?" Anne said.

"Ashley is the light of my life," Brad said simply. "Top of her class. All-state soccer, recruited for the college team. Heart as big as the sky. She's wanted to be a vet since she was five. If she keeps getting scholarships, she'll make it."

96

"You probably haven't been to the Building Supply yet," I said, sinking into the soft leather chair in front of Anne's desk. Brad resumed his seat, his heavy work boots flat on the floor. He must have been exhausted by the long drive.

"The police think the owner killed her," he said.

I glanced at Anne. She'd known the Taylors and Thorntons as long as I had. Nothing but sympathy showed on her round face.

"They do," I said to Brad, "though it's hard to believe. Everyone she worked with liked her. She kept your daughter's picture on her desk." In her desk, in the bottom drawer, but he didn't need to know that. Though it was odd. "We all know why she left Jewel Bay years ago, but I'm curious why she came back."

"Merrily felt she had unfinished business here. With Ashley in college—" He raised one shoulder, the gesture of a man who didn't quite understand what had become of the life he thought he had. "I couldn't leave Billings. I run the family business. She worked there, too. She'd never lived entirely on her own, and I guess she thought it was time."

"What kind of business?" I said.

"Plumbing," he replied, gripping the arm of the chair with a reddened hand, the nails scrubbed clean. "My grandfather started it, then my dad took over. He still works full-time, though he lets me run the show. Merrily ran the office and did the bookkeeping."

I stared at him. Out of the corner of one eye, I noticed Anne's mouth gape open then close as she composed her features.

"It was never a problem," Brad said. "She came to us fresh out of prison. She desperately needed money and bookkeeping was all she knew how to do. It was my mother who wanted to give her a chance. Part of her religious mission, community service."

"A good woman," Anne said.

"The best," he replied. "My dad watched Merrily like a hawk. He even hired a CPA to review the books every quarter. Merrily handled the cash for the Girl Scout troop and the PTA—she had a gift for numbers and keeping things organized. No trouble, ever."

Until she came back here. Curiouser and curiouser. "Did she talk to you much about her parents?"

He shook his head. "Didn't take me long to fall for her, and then we got married. For seventeen years," he continued, "my family was her family. Her parents returned every letter she sent, unopened. They never showed any interest in Ashley, their own granddaughter. And yes, they knew about her. Holly tried to get them to see reason, but no."

"Merrily knew it would take time to heal that breach," Anne said. "She was willing to wait."

"She took responsibility. She reformed." His tone fired up. "They refused to give their own daughter a second chance. And she may be dead because of it."

We sat there, the three of us, Brad breathing heavily, Anne holding the space in her quiet way, me wondering. Wondering why he and Merrily had separated. Wondering if he really did know everything about the embezzlement twenty years ago.

Wondering where he'd been Sunday.

And why he thought her death had something to do with her parents' behavior.

Then, without hearing my questions, he answered them. Or at least, made my questions about him irrelevant.

"They rejected my daughter without ever knowing her," he said, his voice at the soft crack stage. A man who felt that wound so deeply might have lashed out at his still-sort-of in-laws. But he would not have harmed the mother of his child.

I touched his sleeve. "Tell your daughter everything. It will be painful, I know, but better for her to hear the details from you now than to be angry with you later over the secrecy."

He yanked a blue bandana out of his pocket and blew his nose. "Why would this Taylor fellow kill Merrily? I don't believe she stole from him. The woman I knew would never do that."

Was he saying he wasn't sure she'd stolen the money the first time?

Now that was an intriguing thought.

Twelve

I hate running late. Especially when there's no one to blame but myself. I always think I can squeeze in one more thing. But no matter how many productivity tools and apps you download, the day only has twenty-four hours and you can only move as fast as you move.

On the other hand, what I'd learned from Brad Larson was better than any tidbits I could have squeezed out of the good reverend. Merrily's not-quite-ex had confirmed my instinct that she had genuinely longed to reconnect with her parents. To forgive their trespasses and ask their forgiveness in return.

Walt and Taya's overblown sense of shame stemmed, I thought, from fear that others would see Merrily's misdeeds as proof that they were lousy parents, despite all outward appearances. And despite Holly's upstanding life. Or maybe Holly's normalness made Merrily's criminal record seem all the worse.

Lordy. Adam and I wanted to be parents. But thinking about the Thorntons made me worry what we might be getting ourselves into.

I swallowed the last bite of my black bean burrito from the taqueria and pulled into the Lodge's nearly empty front lot. The burrito had been a risk—car food usually is—but skipping lunch was riskier. I wiped my hands, grabbed my bag, and trotted into the main building, a historic log treasure. The Lodge and guest ranch is Jewel Bay's secret weapon—classic log buildings that evoke another era, with just the right amount of farm implements and taxidermy on the walls. And after nearly a century in business, the Caldwells have a pretty good idea how to please their guests.

"Sorry I'm late," I told Trinka, the events coordinator, one of the few Lodge managers not part of the Caldwell family. A log popped in the big stone fireplace.

"No worries. Thanks for the heads-up," she said, perpetually chirpy. "Your call gave me a few minutes to book those additional rooms you asked for, and make a new seating chart for the dinner. We usually split up out-of-town families if they aren't in the wedding party, so they can get to know the other guests."

Criminy. The seating chart. She showed me a screen on her iPad with the plan we'd worked out, then switched to a new layout. She'd put Mrs. Zimmerman—Diane—with my mother and Bill. One twin-plus-wife had bumped cousins from the Murphy uncles' table, while the other had been foisted on the Contis, my mother's brothers and their wives.

"That should work," I said. My aunts and uncles could handle a jokester or two.

Sisters-in-law. I'd never had any and was about to get a pair.

We walked down to the Carriage House, where the ceremony would be held. The sky was crystal-clear and the snow sparkled in the sun—a true bluebird day.

A horse-drawn sleigh would deliver my mother, sister, and me to the Carriage House, then after the ceremony, take Adam and me up to the main lodge for dinner. Guests would be shuttled in the red Jammer, a retired Glacier Park bus that one of the elder Caldwells had managed to snare ages ago. Then Santa would come with gifts for the little ones, and the grownups would return to the Carriage House for drinks and dancing. Adam and I would spend the night here, and we'd all gather at the River House—Mom and Bill's place—for Christmas morning.

All the years I'd been hanging out with Kim, I'd never actually slept in one of the cabins, with their peeled pine beds and comfy quilts, Pendleton wool blankets slung over the log-and-leather chairs.

Trinka pointed as we walked. "I've put Adam's mother in the cabin closest to the main lodge, and given his brothers and their wives a two-bedroom close to the lake."

She had it all worked out. I rubbed a thumb across my lucky stars.

In the Carriage House, Trinka showed me what would go where, from the table with the guest book to our chairs and Anne's podium, and later, the bar and band.

"You're a pretty low-key bride," she said. "At this point, most women are on the verge of panic."

Was I as calm as I looked? Either I hadn't gotten to the freak-out stage, or I was in denial.

Or, everything was so right that panic wasn't necessary. I was marrying the love of my life in a place I adored, with everyone I cherished around me.

Okay, so meeting Adam's family had me anxious. But what could go wrong?

"You're making it all easy," I said, and meant it.

"Thanks. The florist will deliver the poinsettias and floral arrangements in time for the rehearsal—you've chosen a festive but tasteful scheme. Now let's get you back to the Lodge to go over the menu with Chef Kyle. Wendy Fontaine is making your cake—that will be scrumptious."

We picked our way back to the main lodge over the curving, snow-packed road, not saying anything. I'd forgotten how quiet the ranch is during the winter, with a skeleton staff and few guests. Not like summer, when families from all around the world congregate for an active vacation—hiking, sailing, riding, singing around the campfire.

In the lodge, Trinka ushered me to the small private dining area off the kitchen, then excused herself.

With my holiday hours, and the extra time we'd spent on remodeling, moving, and planning a wedding, Adam and I had been skipping the Friday night pool games at Red's that were a staple of fall and winter. The death of Nick's fiancée had wrought another change in the gathering. All that meant I hadn't seen much of Kyle lately.

People often assume he and Kim are brother and sister, not cousins. Tall, slender, and blond like all the Caldwells, Kyle had been a Navy chef, and came home to follow his dream of running the Lodge kitchen. Unlike most chefs, he wears black and a baseball cap, but the way he cooks, who cares?

Kyle entered carrying a big silver tray. "I'm thinking three appetizers for each evening," he said. The rehearsal dinner and the wedding dinner. "Your choice, but I wouldn't repeat more than one. This is butternut squash with mint on crostini."

I bit in. "Oh, my gosh. That is fabulous." I took another nibble. "And pistachios?"

He beamed. "You're the first person to identify the pistachios in one try."

I couldn't come up with a joke about nuts that he wouldn't twist, so I reached for the next offering, a mini lamb skewer.

"Made my own mint sauce," he said.

"Perfect. Not too sweet."

"You're really getting married. I can't talk you out of it."

"You are so full of it," I said. "At least I know you'll be in the kitchen during the ceremony, so I don't have to worry about you raising your hand and saying you object."

"I have a sous chef." He waggled his eyebrows. But it was all in fun.

Kyle's risotto cake with chives and Parmesan was as yummy as the others. I tried two mini tarts, one filled with my mother's sun-dried tomato and pine nut pesto, the other with a fresh snap pea pesto. Red and green, for the season, served with a cheese platter.

"One more," he said, and slid the final plate in front of me.

I sniffed. Fishy. Took a bite. Wrinkled my nose and put the rest back on my plate. "Trout?"

"A lake trout canapé with roasted red pepper and caper garnish." He made an X next to it on his list. "Only one reject. That's not bad."

He boxed up the leftovers for me and I thanked him for the taste test. I slowed as I drove by the horse barn and arena out of habit. My favorite mare, Ribbons, was away at the winter pasture with the rest of the Caldwell herd.

I squinted. Was that who I thought it was? It couldn't be.

It was. *Walt Thornton.* I parked and trudged to the barn, the snow crunching beneath my feet as I cut between the trees. He'd disappeared. I hoped Taya wasn't with him—I wanted to talk.

Though the horses had been moved months ago, the air inside carried the fragrant aroma of horse sweat mixed with fresh grass, baled hay, and sweet oats, and a hint of horse manure. I'd spent half my childhood at the Lodge, learning to ride and care for the horses.

The sneeze snuck up on me and I doubled over with the force of it. Chiara says my sneezes should be measured on the Richter scale. This one could have blown the roof off the old building.

"Who's there?" a male voice called.

I straightened and squinted into the dark. "It's me, Erin Murphy. Is that you, Walt?"

No reply.

"Walt?" I couldn't imagine what he was doing here, let alone hiding in the shadows. For a man whose daughter had just been killed, he was acting awfully wierd.

But then, no etiquette book covers a situation like that.

A bare bulb flicked on in one of the horse stalls and I squeezed my eyes shut, flashes of light stabbing the backs of my eyelids. I opened my eyes slowly and took one step forward.

There, in the stall, stood Walt Thornton next to the biggest, ugliest Nutcracker I had ever seen. Ten feet tall, maybe twelve. His mock bear-skin hat nearly scraped the rafters, and his huge clenched teeth would scare even the biggest bah-humbug. Next to the statue, Walt was a scrawny midget, though his grin was nearly as big as the Nutcracker's.

The ballet may be a classic, but I have never understood the appeal of fake wooden soldiers. Can you actually crack a nut with them?

"Wow. That's um…big," I said.

"Remember that show they filmed up north, by the ski hill? *Christmas in the Woods*. I bought all the props. We had a big auction a few weeks ago. These are the pieces that didn't sell."

I vaguely recalled hearing about the sale. A decorator from Alberta had come in the Merc and mentioned it. I had a much better memory of her purchases—I'd made three trips to her car, toting her bags and boxes. We heart Canadian tourists.

"We called it Santa's Workshop in the Barn." He led me from stall to stall, showing off the props. Santa's golden throne. A fake igloo big enough to sleep in. Snowflakes six feet across, trees already decorated, wrapped boxes large enough to hold a person with lids that lifted off. A five-car train for transporting children or elves.

"We'd probably have sold it all in July," Walt said, "when the shopping malls are planning their holiday displays. But I didn't want to store the stuff until then. Not sure what I'll do with these pieces. Donated tons of lights to the Elves."

Walt's daughter had been killed and a string of light bulbs wrapped around her neck.

I bit my tongue. Literally—the salty taste of blood stung.

Poor, clueless Walt. Or maybe his love of Christmas gave him comfort when he most needed it.

"I always thought Christmas was Taya's thing," I said. "In kindergarten, we started cutting out snowflakes and candy canes the day after Halloween."

A soft smile crept across his face. "Our first date was dinner and a movie in a big mall. On our way to the restaurant, we stopped to get our picture taken with Santa. How could we not fall in love with the holiday?"

Of such simple moments are traditions born.

"Is that how the girls got their names? I always assumed they were born near Christmas."

"Merrily was," he said. "December twenty-sixth."

Not quite three weeks. Dying so close to a birthday seemed doubly sad.

"Holly's birthday is in July," he continued, "but once we started the theme, we stuck with it."

Like they'd stuck with the shunning?

I shivered inside. Walt's Christmas cheer was gone, washed away by the silent tears streaming down his gray-stubbled cheeks. I touched him on the shoulder, and he crumpled against a wooden post.

"I never believed—" he said. "I never wanted—" He interrupted himself with huge gasps for air. "And now, she's—and we'll never—"

Never what? Forgive her? Get her forgiveness? No point asking. I stood beside him, my hand on his shoulder. Then he straightened and pulled out a handkerchief.

"Walt," I said gently. "Were you in touch with Merrily? Despite Taya's objections?"

He drew in a big, noisy sniff, the kind that gets stuck in your throat and chokes you if you aren't careful. He nodded.

"And you knew about her daughter? Your granddaughter?"

Another nod.

For seventeen years, Brad Larson had said. Merrily had been nearly nineteen when she went to prison, and Ashley was now a freshman in college. People often toss out inaccurate numbers, and kids sometimes start school early.

If I'd guessed wrong, I'd mortify him. If I were right…

"Merrily was pregnant when she went to prison, wasn't she? And you knew."

His head wiggled and waggled in all directions. "I was never sure if the judge knew, or just guessed. But Merrily made me swear not to tell Taya."

"And the father, Walt? Is that why you didn't want Taya to know?" It would be too cruel if your daughter not only stole from her boss but also got pregnant by him. At least, if you believed it was all the woman's—the girl's—fault.

"She never said, but we guessed." Another sniff as noisy as a horse's.

"Who told Taya about the baby? Holly?"

"Years later. She meant well, trying to get us back together. But Taya stuck to her guns."

Was that a note of admiration I heard? I couldn't fathom. In his view of the world, their daughter had betrayed them, and he could choose her or his wife.

107

They didn't seem to have wondered why she stole the money, if she had. Was it for the baby? Not according to Brad Larson, who'd said she'd been desperate for a job.

I sighed. Humans, and the tangled webs we weave. Had the judge imposed a light sentence so mother and child could start a new life together as soon as possible, in freedom? Or had the judge considered Merrily little more than an unwitting accomplice of Cliff Grimes? Or even his victim?

"Her father is here—Merrily's husband, I mean. The father who raised Ashley. He'd like to meet you, and introduce you to her."

The tall man in front of me, the man with the sad eyes who had always been so gentle and kind, spun away on the heel of one cowboy boot. I could not think him a killer, but the wife he was so determined to protect?

Maybe.

Without a word, Walt disappeared among his prizes. The show-pieces intended to evoke the Christmas spirit, to create an impression of joy and happiness.

It was nothing but a comfortless facade, and as I walked toward the big sliding barn doors, I thought the giant dolls and fake trees a touch shabby, their luster dulled. As I passed the first stall and glanced in, even the Nutcracker seemed to droop.

Thirteen

Grief slays each of us differently. And while I understood from Walt Thornton's reaction that his daughter's murder cut him deeply, I did not understand much else about him or his wife.

And I'd spent far too much time away from the Merc today. It's a close second to the Orchard for my happy place, and I could hardly wait to get back to work.

I turned off the highway, still thinking. The Thornton girls didn't look much alike, despite both being fair-skinned blondes. Though Chiara and I are unmistakably sisters, Nick is cut from entirely different cloth.

In the photo I'd seen, Ashley didn't resemble mother or aunt. The height could have come from Walt. And she was brunette. But teenagers color their hair these days.

Yeah, right. They color their hair purple or add lime green stripes. Do blondes of any age go dark, unless it's an actress for a role?

In the Merc's back hall, I shucked off my coat. My mother had been making marinara sauce this morning, and the scent of an Italian herb garden clung to the air.

"Erin, hi!" Candy Divine greeted me in full pinkness, from her fuchsia-streaked hair to her hot pink Uggs. If Minnie Mouse were a candy maker, she'd look like Candy, minus the tail.

The woman had grown on me since she first floated in to the Merc a year and a half ago on a cloud of pink sugar. Since then, her candy had gone from sticky lumps to the real thing, and she had cooked up a devoted following. Not devoted enough to support her, though, so I'd helped her get a job with Sally, using her design and sewing skills to fill the racks at Puddle Jumpers with princess dresses, dinosaur costumes, and other clothing sure to appeal to every five-year-old's grandmother.

That's what keeps this village thriving. Instead of seeing each other as competitors, we work together and boost the bottom line for us all.

"Hi back atchya," I said. "What's in your basket?"

"Sugarplums," she said in a voice so high and sweet it could shatter crystal. "Peppermint taffy, and nougat studded with candied cherries. And my very own handmade candy canes, in the colors of the rainbow!"

Candy canes made me think of Oliver Bello. Not so sweet a thought.

We oohed and ahhed over the selection, then Tracy and Lou Mary found space for the canes and created a display while I added them to our inventory. Love my automated inventory tracker. I took a moment to pop a few pics of the new goodies on Instagram with my phone.

"You been stitching up Christmas dresses?" I asked Candy.

"Yes. Now I'm designing for Valentine's Day. It's such fun." She popped a piece of taffy into her mouth, her next words a bit garbled. "Did you hear what happened to Ray?"

"What? No. What's going on?" The Bayside Grille is my favorite lunch spot, and the owner, Ray Ramirez, is a sweetheart, despite the scorpion tattoo that peeks over the crew neck of the snow-white T-shirts he always wears.

"Some customer trashed him online. Said she couldn't believe he put sauerkraut on his Reubens."

"That's what a Reuben is," I said. Ray cooks the beer-soaked sauerkraut in his kitchen and cans it in our basement. We sell cases of it, gallons of it. I aim to sell a liquid ton of it.

"I know, right? It's like complaining that your broccoli's green."

Tracy snorted. The doggies in her ears swung madly.

Candy swallowed the last of her taffy, her hands bouncing through the air. "Then, the little minx got all her friends to chime in, and his ratings went from, like almost five stars to barely two."

Minx? Lou Mary mouthed at me, her eyes approving. *That's good.*

"We can Yelp him," I said. "We've all eaten there. We can give him an honest rave, and boost his ratings."

"Oooh!" Candy clapped her hands. "Let's start a campaign!"

Gad, I love small towns.

I left them to work out their "Yelp for the Grille" plan and found my mother in the basement, sitting at the desk Nick had built himself last winter. Now that he had moved out of the barely habitable homesteader's shack at the Orchard and into the house Christine, his fiancée, had left him when she died, he no longer needed to hide away in a corner of the Merc's basement for warmth and WiFi. But that also meant he was harder to track down when I needed him. I knew he was around. So why was he too busy to help me with my building? With *our* building?

"Hello, darling," my mother said. "How did your fitting go last night?"

"Great," I said, holding up one of Candy's canes. "No calories in these, right?"

She smiled and the world righted itself. A stack of cookbooks on the small desktop caught my eye.

She followed my gaze. "I'm working on a few menus for the family visits. The big day will be here before you know it."

"Speaking of, I've got news." I hooked a stool with a foot, sat, and rolled closer. "Adam's brothers are coming after all." I didn't tell her how weirded out he was.

"Oh, good." Her eyes lit up, then she got serious. "You've hinted at some tensions, but it will be lovely to meet them. We'll give them a big Montana welcome."

She hadn't heard all the stories Adam had told me, stories his boyhood buddy Tanner swore were true. How the twins played every prank in the book, from taking each other's tests to going on each other's dates. They'd had a thing for jokes with snakes that didn't go over so well with the other kids in the neighborhood.

And I hadn't told my mom that after their father lost his job and hid out in the basement, and their mother's boss refused her a loan against her paycheck, they ate nothing but Cheerios and ramen noodles with frozen peas for a week. Chiara's response to the stories had been that we represented what he hadn't had, what he wanted, what he would work his adorable backside off to create with me.

My sister was right. I had no doubts about Adam's commitment to me and our future. He'd known what he wanted to make of his life, and that he needed to leave Minnesota to get it. He liked to remind me that when I came back to Jewel Bay and he recognized me as the girl he'd let get away in college, he'd seen a second chance and grabbed it.

My mother reached for a notepad with an *F* in classic script on the top and her favorite green pen to start a new list. My love for organization—and office supplies—is genetic.

Which reminded me of Merrily and her penchant for organization. That desk, that kitchen. We'd been kindred spirits.

"We'll need corsages for his mother and the girls. It's Diane, right? We'll put snack baskets in the cabins. I know the Lodge leaves coffee and cookies out, but we'll give them something with a bit more substance." My mother is never happier than when she's figuring out how to feed people. "Any food allergies that you know of? I'll call. Do you have Diane's number?"

I found it and read it to her. "Mom, there's something else I want to talk with you about."

"Overwhelmed with wedding details, darling? Just ask—you know I'll help any way I can."

"No, not that." I told her about seeing Walt Thornton at the Lodge, and how he refused to meet his granddaughter. My mother listened intently, palms open in her lap.

"It's as if Merrily was dead to them," she said. "Then she came back to life, and died again. I can't even imagine."

"How will Ashley deal with this? With grandparents who rejected her before they even met her?"

"She may know more about her mother's past than her father realizes," Mom said. "After Taya learned about the girl, she told me. She'd worked out that Merrily had gone to prison pregnant. Thank heavens her sentence was short, and with good behavior, she made it even shorter."

"Did you ever talk to Taya about the shunning?"

Mom sighed. "I tried. She cut me off instead. That taught me a lesson about interfering."

A lesson I suspected she hoped I would learn. "But how could they treat their daughter that way? And their granddaughter?"

"Families are complicated. And some people respond to emotional injury better than others." My mother leaned forward, hands on her knees. "Becoming a parent is to open yourself to the deepest love, and the deepest heartache imaginable. Nothing hurts like watching your child suffer. When Nick lost the love of his life, when Chiara had those miscarriages, when you..."

"When I what, Mom?" I said, not sure I wanted the answer.

She let out a long sigh. "When you went off to college after your father died, I knew one word from me and you'd zip home faster than boo. Selfishly, I wanted you here to comfort me, but I knew that would be a mistake. You were lost in your own grief, and I had to let you stumble your way into the world."

She reached out, the tips of her fingers stroking my cheek. "And darling, you have done so beautifully. My heart is about to break with love for the three of you, for Landon and the new baby, for Adam and Jason and Bill."

I scooted closer and for a long moment, we simply held each other. Then I rolled my stool back and met her gaze.

"Thank you, Mom. But I didn't sense that Walt felt any pain for Merrily's pain. I heard only anger and shame at what she did to them. That's how they look at it. As if everything she did wrong, she did to hurt them."

"Taya said much the same thing when we went into their shop. It was surreal—the place all glowing with holiday spirit, and so little of it in her."

Remembering Saturday morning brought back the image of Sally Grimes, on the sidewalk in front of her shop. She'd been mighty peeved at the sight of Merrily, and by her return to Jewel Bay in general. Me, I understood why she came back. The longing for home. How geography shapes your relationship to space, people, life. Growing up on picturesque family properties didn't guarantee family harmony, but it did create a bond to the place.

"Mom, who do you think fathered Merrily's baby? Was it Cliff Grimes, Sally's husband?"

"Oh, darling, I don't know. Leave Sally out of this. Delve into the murder if you have to, but let that go."

I wouldn't ask Sally. Bad enough that her husband stole from her and had been poised to abandon her and their daughter, Sage. Family money and property hadn't made for an easy life, though she and Sage had mended their relationship.

But let go?

That was a promise I couldn't make.

Fourteen

Some days, on my way home, I forget where I'm headed and start to turn at the road leading to my old cabin. Despite all the work we've put into the house, I find myself surprised at times to be living at the Orchard again. To see the stars shining through the cherry trees as I drive in. To see Adam's perpetually filthy Xterra in the carport.

To be greeted not by Pepé, my mother's Scottie, but by my—our—cats.

And by Adam, pulling on his coat. "Hey, cutie. How'd it go at the Lodge?"

"Great. Kyle sent home samples." I lifted the box. "Although I'm going to have to be careful with these, not to mention all those Christmas cookies."

"I'll take care of them for you." He grinned and gave me a kiss. "Gotta run. SAR training."

Once a month, on Tuesday nights, Adam changes hats from kids' camp and rec guy to wilderness medicine guru, and teaches the Search and Rescue squad the latest cool stuff.

"Back around ten," he said and reached for the door. Stopped, disappeared into the kitchen, and came back a minute later, a half-eaten peanut butter cookie in one hand and two more in the other. "I always tell people to take emergency rations. These are great, by the way."

Molly's unChristmas cookies. I rolled my eyes.

In the kitchen I checked the cats' food and water and stared into the fridge. It didn't offer a lot, a sign that I hadn't been home enough. I made a salad and a plate of Kyle's appetizers, careful to leave some of each for Adam. And all the trout canapés.

My uncle the vintner had shipped us several cases of wine for the wedding, but we hadn't tasted them yet. No time like the present. I popped the cork—such a satisfying sound—on a California red and poured a smidge into a glass. Sniffed, swished, sniffed—luscious.

Took the first sip. *Oh my.*

I filled the glass and carried it and my plate to the dining room, on the theory that eating greens now would make up for the cookies I knew I'd eat later, and that I'd eat less at the table than on the couch.

The herbed squash crostini was as good now as it had been this afternoon. "Bad for cats!" I called to any felines in earshot, then grabbed my iPad from my bag at the front door before the cats could try my dinner for themselves. Set the iPad on the table and opened the wedding project list. Back at SavClub, I'd been trained in maintaining project lists and identifying the next action, but sometimes there were too many "next actions" for any twenty-four hours.

Appetizers, I typed, and added the crostini and lamb skewers to the rehearsal dinner menu. The others would be perfect for the wedding dinner. The crostini was good enough to serve twice.

I sipped Uncle Joe's red blend and studied the list. We had the wine, and I'd met with the events coordinator—I checked those items off with glee. My dress and accessories—check. My mother was repurposing her wedding dress. Chiara and I had gone shopping and found a maternity dress that would do nicely for her, whether she was still pregnant or not. I was too excited to get a new niece or nephew—if they knew the sex, they weren't saying—to fuss about her dress. Or whether we might need a last-minute substitute.

Adam, Tanner, and Nick had chosen matching suits with coordinated shirts and ties, all tailored and ready to go. Chiara and my mother had outfitted Jason, Landon, and Bill.

No matter what else happened, we would look fabulous.

But I needed to check on the flowers. Test cakes with Wendy—Adam wanted to be part of that. Find thank-you gifts for Reverend Anne and our attendants, although neither Chiara nor Tanner would expect anything. Plan the wedding favors and table decorations, and rope a few friends into helping me set up. I'd booked the photographer months ago, and Adam had taken charge of the music. He said he didn't want a bachelor party. His brothers might have other ideas.

I scanned the guest list. The flood of early RSVPs had slowed to a trickle, but I had questions about a few couples and wasn't sure how to follow up. Trinka at the Lodge had told me to plan on a handful of last-minute changes, but also said that the no-shows and surprise guests would probably balance each other out.

We had an appointment to get the license tomorrow. Adam had told me to update my passport, and the new one hadn't arrived yet. But we had time for that.

My mother had scheduled hair appointments and a spa day—I should add Adam's mother and the twins' wives.

No wonder people eloped. Trinka had said some brides started feeling homicidal at this point, and I understood why.

But I had murder on the mind for another reason as well. Merrily Thornton was dead. Money was missing. Greg Taylor couldn't seem to decide whether he wanted my help or not.

I took my dishes to the kitchen and Pumpkin trotted after me. "You smell fish, don't you, Miss Kitty?" I cut a tiny bit of the trout off one toast and set it on the mat next to her dish. She scarfed it up like the finest caviar.

I refilled my wine and created a small dessert plate. Set the cat in her fleece-lined bed by the gas fireplace on the wall between the living and dining rooms, converted from wood in the remodel. Sandy's bed was empty.

On the wall next to the living room hung the one piece of art I'd left in place. A serigraph landscape, the lake and mountains stacked in receding layers of color. Kim and I had made the print together in art class, senior year. Before the accident that killed my father and nearly destroyed our friendship.

It wasn't my friendship with Greg Taylor, or even with his sister Wendy, that was driving me to investigate, though I wanted to help them. It was much more personal. I'd been appalled by how Merrily's parents had treated her. And though I couldn't explain it well, not even to myself, I felt guilty. So unfair, that a woman would be forced to work so hard to prove herself worthy of the love of friends and family that I took for granted.

The loyalty I felt to her did surprise me. But sometimes, we meet someone and feel an instant connection. Some people might say it's one soul recognizing another. Some would call it instinct, and others imagination gone wild. I'd felt it when she came in to the shop on her job hunt, but hadn't acted on it. We'd gotten a second chance at friendship, and lost it.

And I'd been a kid who'd lost a parent tragically. Though I hadn't met Merrily's daughter yet, and like me, Ashley did have one loving parent left, the unfairness of it all made me determined to do everything I could to help the police find the killer.

Besides, I had a tool that works wonders.

In the living room, I sank into the brown leather chair—a housewarming slash wedding gift from our family friend, Liz Pinsky, who knew how much I'd loved its twin when I lived in their caretaker's cabin. The moment I picked up my iPad, a small sable cat leaped on to the arm of my chair.

"Ah, so that's what it takes to get your attention," I told Sandy. "A warm lap and a plate of cookies."

Sandburg turned himself around, then settled down and wrapped himself in his tail, ignoring me. A few feet away, in her bed by the fire, Pumpkin raised her head, then went back to sleep.

My trusted assistants, doing what they do best.

Nobody knows about the Spreadsheet of Suspicion. Call it my secret weapon. The detectives have their murder books and white boards. I've seen them, and they work. Timelines are great when you need a linear approach, and mind maps are perfect for brainstorming. But for full-scale organizing, I love me a spreadsheet. Nothing works better to corral my questions and clues, the whats and whys and whos.

I created a column for Merrily and listed the key facts surrounding her murder and the theft at the Building Supply. Then I added what I knew from the twenty-year-old crime, which was not much, at this point.

The wine went down beautifully—a complex blend of fruit and spice. Sandy twitched his tail, and I gave my attention to the spreadsheet. Catalogued the photos and other items in the cigar box from her desk as best I could remember.

I slipped the cat off my lap and headed for my old bedroom, which we were treating as a temporary storeroom. Dug out a box I hadn't unpacked yet. Snicked open the latch of the wooden Swiss puzzle box, one of several my grandfather had brought home after the war. My version of Merrily's cigar box, minus the cash.

Slipped the old theater token into my pocket. Though I wasn't sure it had anything to do with anything, it made me feel a little closer to Merrily.

Back in the living room, the cats hadn't moved. I plucked a peanut butter cookie off the plate. Not bad. Not bad at all.

The next name I wrote was Greg Taylor. The first question? Motive. The second, whereabouts, which I shortened to *whabouts* to keep the columns uniform. Bello surmised that Greg might have had reason to kill Merrily even before discovering that she'd betrayed his trust and stolen the cash from the deposit—*if* she had stolen it. What if he were right? What if Greg had already harbored suspicions? Laid some kind of trap and caught her, then waited for the moment...

It wasn't impossible. Wendy had begged me to investigate, then backed off, fleeing the Merc when I asked one too many questions. Did she know something that might incriminate Greg? Was there some other connection—or tension—between him and Merrily?

"What else, Sandy?" I said. "Who else?"

Burmese cats are known talkers, but mine was keeping his own counsel tonight. I took a bite of one of Lou Mary's bourbon balls. Strong, with a kick and plenty of substance—just like her.

Had someone from Merrily's more recent past wanted her dead? No doubt prison bred deadly enemies, but that was too long ago.

Another embezzlement victim would fit Bello's theory that embezzlers follow predictable patterns. But her only other employer had been her husband's family business, and Brad swore she'd never stolen

121

a cent from the plumbing company, or the community organizations she'd worked with.

What about Brad himself? You could never rule out a spouse, even when they said all the right things, as Brad had. He'd given the impression, true or not, that the divorce was her idea. Had his resentment reached the danger point?

I added his name.

Truth was, I didn't have enough info yet to know what might really have happened. The Spreadsheet of Suspicion was raising more questions than it answered.

I lifted Sandy up gently and placed him in his bed. He let out a soft moan.

What if I was wrong? What if Bello had it right?

No. I didn't believe Greg Taylor was a killer, not for one minute. But there was more to the story than he'd told me, and Wendy knew it.

I frowned. Did that put her in danger? Murder is rarely random. Killers have a specific reason and a specific target.

The rest of us weren't at risk. Unless we stumbled too close to the truth.

I heard the front door open. Ten already? Time flies when you're probing crimes.

"Hey, babe." Adam enveloped me in a hug, his lips finding mine, and I forgot all about secrets and spreadsheets.

"Now that's what I call CPR," he said a few minutes later. "What have you guys been up to while I was demonstrating defibrillators?"

"They've been dreaming of mice," I said, waving at the cats. All of a sudden, my spreadsheet seemed silly. So I fibbed. "And I'm working on a checklist for the shop. Open and close procedures, who to call when stuff goes wrong—things the staff will need when we're away."

Our honeymoon in January would be my first vacation since taking over the Merc. Not that I had any idea where we were going. Adam said he'd tell me what to pack the day before we left.

"Doesn't your mom know all that stuff?" He plucked a piece of my aunt's fudge off the cookie plate and answered his own question. "No, I guess she doesn't. Leave any of those appetizers for me?"

"Of course," I said. While he was in the kitchen, I grabbed the iPad, saved the spreadsheet, and powered down, with one last thought.

I couldn't be sure until the time of death was established ... No one would tell me directly. I'd have to deduce it from the questions Bello asked, the avenues he followed. But if Merrily Thornton had died on Sunday, there was a good chance that while I'd been fretting over her skipping my first party in our new home, while I was worried about cookies and Christmas trees and what traditions to keep and change ...

While I'd been twittering over Christma-trivia, a woman who'd fought for everything she had was losing it all.

∞

A light snow fell overnight, so my first task at the Merc Wednesday morning was to shovel out front. Up and down the street, other merchants were doing the same, and we exchanged greetings and waves. The sidewalk in front of the Thorntons' shop had not been touched in a couple of days, so I toted my shovel up the block and cleared their walkway.

The elegant storefront looked so neglected and forlorn, the sight half broke my heart. Would the Thorntons reopen today, or skip the season entirely? Could they return to some semblance of normalcy? How would customers, and the other merchants, respond?

On my way back to the Merc, I spotted another hook about to pull out of our disintegrating soffit. Nick had texted late yesterday that he was busy investigating a possible new wolf den up north and wouldn't be able to work on the building until next weekend, at the earliest. So I'd called a construction guy my brother-in-law knew, but got no reply.

Inside, I called the builder again and left another message. "Who else can I call?" I asked the empty shop. Hearing no answer, I pondered a temporary fix.

I hauled out the ladder and set it on the slightly slippery sidewalk. Climbed up, wrapped a wire around the gutter, and reached for the sagging garland. Looped the wire around the garland and gave it a few twists. A stupendously bad idea, I knew—if the garland fell again, it would take the gutter with it, along with more of the soffit and a row or two of shingles.

I hate when the best I can do isn't enough.

I rested the shovel beside our front door and went into Le Panier for a warm-up. Sally Grimes, coatless, bent over the pastry case.

"Go ahead, Sally," I said. "You know there are no calories in December."

She stood abruptly, startled. "Oh, Erin. Don't be ridiculous." She snatched up her coffee and dashed out the door.

Wendy and I exchanged raised-eyebrow glances, stifling a shared laugh.

I'd promised my mother I wouldn't quiz Sally about Merrily Thornton. I never said I wouldn't tease her about croissants. But I did sympathize—it must be awful to have the wound left by her husband's betrayal ripped open after all this time.

"Bello's breathing down Greg's neck, watching every move," Wendy said over the burr and buzz of the espresso machine.

"I'm not sure your brother wants my help." I perused the pastry case, wishing my crack about calories in December were true. *Remember your dress ...*

Wendy's back was to me as she foamed the milk, but her white-coated shoulders stiffened ever-so-briefly. "Of course he does," she said, pouring my double shot and adding the milk, her tone less convincing than her words.

"Surprised me that Merrily was renting Granny G's house," I said.

The front door opened. Wendy's face froze, and her eyes told me not to say another word. "He-hello, Mrs. Thornton," she said. "Nice to see you back in the village."

"You." Taya pointed a finger at me, and I felt six years old again. I'd forgotten that sweet Mrs. Thornton had not suffered transgressors, whether the sin had been running with scissors or talking during naptime. "You think you're such a loyal friend, rushing to everyone's side. Has it occurred to you, when you stick your nose into other people's business, that there might be consequences?"

The heat in her words could have run Le Panier's ovens for a month.

I stiffened my spine. "I hope so," I said. "Otherwise, what would be the point?"

Taya's blue eyes flared. Then she made a half-pirouette and left as quickly as she'd come.

Leaving me feeling like a burnt-out Christmas bulb.

Thank God for double espresso.

Fifteen

Back in the Merc, my hands still shaking from Taya's outburst, I got ready to open. When Tracy and Lou Mary arrived, I retreated to the office to start the procedures manual I'd told Adam I was working on last night.

Why hadn't I thought of creating one before? Because we hadn't needed one, because I never took a break. I worked six days a week, seven in the height of summer. Wherever Adam was taking me for our honeymoon, I could hardly wait.

I finished the first draft and my latte at the same time, and printed out a copy.

"Tell me what you think," I told my staff a few minutes later, as I set the draft on the counter. "What else would you need to know when I'm not here?"

"I don't even want to think about that," Tracy said. Today the Queen of Cheap Chic wore all black, from knee-high boots to skirt to a cashmere turtleneck, a wide red leather belt wrapped around her waist. She noticed me notice and hooked a thumb in the belt. "Five dollars."

My eyes widened. "I should hire you to organize my closet. You've got three times the clothes I do in a house half the size."

"It's all in the accessories."

"Don't you worry one bit," Lou Mary broke in. "January is slow. We've already made a plan. In between customers, I'll wash every shelf and dust every jar in the place, while Tracy makes truffles for Valentine's Day."

"Truffles. I'm thinking three-packs for wedding favors. Gad, I am never going to get everything done."

I'd hired Lou Mary last summer to relieve the pressure on Fresca and me to work the shop floor. And I'd figured that hiring a second clerk would give Tracy more time for truffling, and keep her from opening her own chocolateria elsewhere in the village. The two hadn't become instant best buddies. But I'd given them time and space to work it out, and they had, thank goodness.

I left them poring over the list of procedures and returned to my office. Taya's comment rattled in my brain. What consequences did she fear? Or had she been threatening me? Greg had gone pretty far out on a limb in the name of old friendship. *Everyone deserves a second chance,* he'd said.

I opened the Spreadsheet, and zeroed in on TOD—the time of death. Sometime between noon Sunday, as the unfinished cookies showed, and noon Monday, when Greg found her.

That he'd found her was another reason I couldn't believe him to be the killer. But Bello had his reasons to suspect Greg. I outlined them: Someone—possibly Merrily, possibly a bank employee—had shorted the cash in the Building Supply's deposit after Merrily and Cary the bookkeeper had each counted it. A box full of cash was found in her desk drawer, although as far as I knew, she hadn't been back to work since she left with the deposit.

Which meant the missing cash wasn't in her stash—though there was no way to prove that.

All circumstantial.

But the kicker was the trust Greg had placed in her.

I leaned back in my chair. I was about to hand Tracy and Lou Mary the keys to the kingdom, the secret codes, all the details that make this place run. True, my mother would stop in regularly, and most customers pay by credit card, but I did not question their loyalty and honesty.

Famous last words?

Or was it better, as my mother said, to die trusting than to live by suspicion?

I stretched out my legs and crossed one foot over the other, fiddling with my fused glass heart pendant. It had been a gift from Adam last Valentine's Day, and I wore it often.

How would I feel if I were Greg Taylor, and an old friend betrayed my trust? A trust no one else thought she deserved?

I'd be furious. Devastated. Angry enough to kill?

Maybe, I had to admit, and that thought made me shudder.

I sat forward. But only if Greg had had reason to suspect her *before* Monday morning, when the deposit turned up short. And only if she'd still been alive that morning. If he tracked her down and killed her. But he had to have known at that point that he'd be the number-one suspect. He might have a temper, he might be too trusting, but he wasn't stupid.

Anyway, Greg hadn't left the Building Supply until late Monday morning, after the detectives finished their initial investigation. When he went searching and found her in the old schoolhouse. Bello believed he'd known where to find her because that's where he'd killed her.

Greg had called it her secret place, her refuge. That made sense.

What I knew about rigor mortis and lividity came from TV cop shows, and wouldn't fill the foil cup a truffle comes in. But I felt sure, from the way Merrily lay on the schoolhouse floor, that she'd been dead long before Greg found her.

I couldn't help Greg prove his whereabouts to Bello—he'd have to do that himself.

Was there a chance Walt or Taya had heard or seen something at the schoolhouse? Lights on the road, lights flickering through the trees, a shout. Or a shot—though I hadn't seen blood, I couldn't rule that out. Anything that alerted them to trouble?

But after Walt's reaction in the barn and Taya's angry shouts in the bakery, I wasn't sure they wanted justice for her.

Oh, no. No, Erin, don't even think that.

Too late. Walt certainly had the size and strength to kill his daughter. What about Taya? Merrily had been a few inches taller and quite a few pounds heavier than her mother. But maybe murder was like those stories of superhuman strength, where a tiny woman lifts up a car so her toddler can crawl out.

Where had *they* been during the murder window? I dashed downstairs.

"Lou Mary, do you know if the Thorntons were open on Sunday?" Most downtown merchants keep longer hours during the holidays. Though I'd been home baking cookies, the Merc had opened Sunday from noon to five.

She pursed her coral lips, remembering, then drew her leopard print glasses from her nest of pale red hair. She peered at me, one arthritic finger raised. "Now that you mention it, no, I don't think so. A woman asked about them—she'd seen some German glass ornaments there a few weeks ago and wanted to get a couple. A Christmas shop closing on Sundays in December seems odd, doesn't it?"

It did, indeed. But *odd* seemed to be the watchword of this case.

And I knew they hadn't opened Monday, though that was according to schedule. But they hadn't been home when Greg arrived, or when I got there. So where were they Sunday and Monday?

If my goal was to ask the questions Bello would overlook, then I'd leave it to him to track down their comings and goings. Besides, I didn't have the time. Murder is inconsiderate that way.

"Erin, Adam's on the line." Tracy handed me the shop phone. Adam knows I can't answer my cell when I'm on the shop floor, so if he wants to reach me, the shop line's the best option.

"Hey, good-lookin,'" I said. "What you got cookin'?"

"Sorry, little darlin.' Hope this isn't too unromantic, but I'm going to have to meet you in Pondera this afternoon. I forgot—county park and rec board meeting at three."

"That's okay." Our appointment was at two. "I'll figure out a way for you to make it up to me."

He laughed. "I'll plan on it."

∞

I called the Bayside Grille for takeout—Candy's story about the online trashing had gotten my mouth watering for a Reuben. When I dashed across the street a few minutes later to fetch it, the place was packed and I barely knew a soul. *Good.* Come January, there'd be no wait and I'd know someone at every table. Also good, but in a different way.

"If you liked your lunch," I said to the woman ahead of me at the register, "you might say so online."

"Oh, good idea," she replied.

"That was you," Ray said when it was my turn to pay. "Lunch is on the house. I've gotten seventeen four- and five-star reviews in less than twenty-four hours."

"Not me. Thank Candy Divine," I said, and Ray's eyebrows rose. "Miss Pink Sugar takes injustice to heart. Hey, a quick question." I told him about the remorseful thief, and our theory that she worked in a restaurant and lived with her mom.

He frowned, thinking. "Not unless it was a boy. We've got a weekend dishwasher, sixteen, messy home life. I make a point of sending extra food home with him."

A possibility, but the handwriting looked girlish. Was that a false assumption? I supposed the writer could have disguised their handwriting.

Back in the Merc, I ate at my desk while going over invoices and other bills. Not easy, with a hot, gooey sandwich, but I managed. We'd finish the year well in the black, thank goodness, and even start to build a cushion. It hadn't been smooth, and it hadn't always been fun, but running the Merc was in my blood.

As I clicked off the computer and got ready to meet my love, my cell phone rang—a call from the Building Supply.

"Erin, hi. Greg Taylor calling." He hesitated, and when he continued, he sounded less assured. "Need a favor. We've brought in a forensic accountant to re-create the last few months of records. But he's hitting a wall."

"A firewall?" I said. "You can't break through without a series of high-level passwords."

"Right. Isn't that part of Jason's background? Do you have his cell? I called his office, but the line goes to voice mail."

"Yeah. He worked in computer security in San Francisco." Before he and Chiara moved to Jewel Bay to raise Landon in her hometown.

He'd expanded into system setup and web design because in a small town, you can't afford to specialize. "I'll text you the number. So, are you saying you don't know how much money is missing?"

"It's more complicated than that. Looks like she falsified some records, created some phony accounts."

"Wow. Merrily did all that? And locked the files to hide her tracks?"

"That's Detective Bello's theory. One of them, anyway. He also seems convinced that I tumbled to it and snapped. He grilled every employee about my behavior and my temper. Had half the staff in tears. Even Lenhardt was miffed."

Lenhardt? Oh, right—Cary, the bookkeeper. "Does that mean the bank staff is in the clear?"

"Don't know," he said. "But I'm the one who hired her. There's been a hardware store in Jewel Bay since before there was a Jewel Bay, and I put it all at risk." His voice thinned and shook. "I can't believe this. How *could* she? How could she?"

My thoughts exactly.

Sixteen

Adam stood outside the courthouse sporting a big grin.

As we climbed the stairs to the clerk's office, all thoughts of firewalls and murder and motherless girls slipped away, replaced by anticipation. By joy. Happiness. Nervousness. From the way Adam squeezed my hand, I knew he felt it, too.

Gratitude. Love. So much emotion swirling inside me, my skin could hardly contain it.

We'd filled out the application online and now presented our IDs, paid the fee, and signed in all the right places. Got the paperwork our officiant and witnesses would need. Sealed the deal with a kiss, accepted the deputy clerk's best wishes, and headed out.

On the front steps, Adam kissed me again, a sweet, slow promise, before dashing off to his meeting.

As long as I was in Pondera, I decided to follow another line of thought. A wild hare, but those can be the most inspiring. I swung by the newspaper office and asked to see their archives. A twenty-something with a sapphire stud in one nostril set me up in front of a computer that provided access all the way back to 1980. That was decades more than the online archive, and plenty for my snoopful purposes.

The embezzlement from Beckman Timber and the charges against Merrily Thornton and Cliff Grimes had been big news for weeks. Some of the story I knew. Other details surprised me. Merrily had gotten the summer job as Cliff's office assistant not through her father's connections in the timber industry, as I'd assumed, but through Taya's friendship with Sally. Still, the aftermath must have left them both feeling betrayed.

Taya was a good ten years older than Sally, and they weren't neighbors. But unlikely friendships sometimes pop up in small towns.

Cliff Grimes had been away on a fishing trip when Sally opened the mail, found a tax lien, and called a CPA. Then she'd called the law. Cliff heard the news on the TV when he stopped at a favorite watering hole on his way home. He split for the border, but the bartender called the sheriff, and poor Cliff never saw Canada again.

Another article detailed the escape plan investigators pieced together. He'd been working on it for a while. It involved fast cars, fast boats, and secret accounts in banks on faraway islands.

It did not involve Merrily Thornton.

The whole business deflated my trial balloon theory that Walt and Taya thought she'd seduced Cliff and stolen from his wife. Discovering that their sweet-faced teenager was a manipulative gold-digger might have justified their anger and sense of betrayal.

What if he'd seduced her and planned to split? Talk about slimy.

It didn't help me understand her parents' reaction. But it might explain why Merrily had never spoken out against him.

I sipped the double latte I'd picked up on the way. It tasted thin, almost burned, unlike the espresso at Le Panier. At the time of Cliff's trial, about 75 percent of the missing money had been located. He claimed Merrily had taken the rest, but investigators could never find a trail between her and any of the stolen funds.

If she'd spent it on the usual teenage toys, they'd have been found and sold to pay restitution. Oh, now that was a thought. Had restitution been ordered? Had she paid it? Questions for Brad Larson.

Another thought made me frown. What if she'd spent the money on drugs? Surely not. Especially when she got pregnant.

I kept reading. Prosecutors had offered Merrily a reduced sentence in exchange for her cooperation. She declined, though the judge had handed down only the minimum sentence anyway.

My guess was she'd internalized her parents' lessons about shame too deeply. Testifying against Grimes would be ratting, blaming someone else for your own actions—even though he'd been a forty-year-old man stealing from his wife and she'd been an eighteen-year-old girl. And if she were pregnant, she might have taken the high road, choosing not to criticize her child's father.

Alongside the article on Merrily's guilty plea and sentence ran a sidebar on the phenomenon of female embezzlers. *Think you see a pattern?* the article asked. *You do. Ten of the twelve embezzlement cases we've reported on in the last three years involved middle-aged women with no criminal records, in positions of trust, working for small, family-owned businesses. Investigators say these employees work hard, rarely taking time off. They make themselves indispensable, which makes them less suspect—but many use the extra hours to rationalize dipping their hand in the till.*

I shivered. That echoed what Bello had said. Nearly every business in Jewel Bay could be described as small and family-owned. How many of us were vulnerable? A quick mental run down Front Street told me that the Thorntons' antique shop might be the one operation with no outside employees.

Although, as Cliff Grimes had proved, keeping it all in the family was no guarantee.

I kept reading. *"Success emboldens the larcenous employee," one expert said. "Not getting caught feels powerful, and the combination of power, having a secret, and getting something for nothing is addictive." Accidental discoveries are not uncommon.*

Like Sally Grimes picking up the mail for the property management company she owned but rarely touched, trusting her husband to manage it.

But what about the cash missing from the Building Supply's bank deposit? An example of that boldness?

Maybe Detective Bello wasn't so wrong after all—the profile of an embezzler did fit the modern Merrily. She handled money, although others did, too, and she had other duties. She hadn't been there long, but her friendship with Greg—and his trust—dated back decades. Though I couldn't figure out why she'd take the money now.

But the Merrily Thornton who'd gone to prison had been far different.

When men embezzle, the article continued, *they take larger amounts. Women buy extras for their families; men shop for show. In both sexes, financial straits often provide the initial push, triggered by gambling or other debts, but long-term embezzlement is driven by the desire for a more expensive lifestyle. Experts say it's nearly impossible to identify where all the stolen funds go, with much of it frittered away on pricey meals, spa days, and other indulgences.*

Not Merrily's style, by a long shot.

"Sorry to interrupt," the sapphire-studded receptionist said. "It's five thirty. We're closing."

"Oh, geez." I sat up with a start. Sure enough, it was dark outside the big windows. "That's okay—I found what I needed."

Maybe I had, I thought as I stepped around an icy puddle in the parking lot. But I didn't yet know how it all fit together.

∞

"Stupid halogens." Every glance in the rearview mirror was painful. The thin sheet of ice on the two-lane road amplified the brightness of the headlights behind me, and the sleety-snow angling down hard made visibility even worse.

The pattern embezzlers followed bugged me. If Merrily had stolen a pot of money twenty years ago and was stealing now, why hadn't she stolen anything in between? If leopards don't change their spots, as the saying goes, surely they don't change, then change back.

Had investigators not found Merrily's share of the money years ago because she'd hidden it so well? Or because she never had any?

Brad Larson said she'd been broke and desperate for a job when he met her, newly released from prison. If she'd had money tucked away—I pictured that cigar box—surely she'd have come back for it. But her life showed no signs that she'd dipped into a pot of gold, then or now. She rented a modest house, from a friend. She drove a dented ten-year-old Taurus. Her daughter went to a state school on a scholarship.

Had someone else found the hidden money and spent it? Her parents?

That dark idea gave me the chills.

I blinked at the brights bouncing off my mirrors. That truck was way too close. It fell back, and my grip on the wheel relaxed.

I'd only caught a glimpse of Merrily's kitchen and dining room. The table and chairs I recognized as Granny G's. The cookware was nice, but not pricy. Coffeemaker, decent. That KitchenAid would have been three hundred or more new, but she could have had it for years. Good coat, easy to find on sale. When she'd come to the Merc on her job hunt last fall, she'd clearly wanted a job, but she hadn't acted desperate.

So did all that signal that she had a small nest egg and was confident she'd find a job, or that she had a million bucks squirreled away? You can never tell, like the bag ladies or street men who live in one-room fifth-floor walk-ups and leave squillions to their grade school or an art museum where they sat in the café for hours nursing a single cup of coffee.

If she'd been stealing to support a more expensive lifestyle, she sure hadn't shown it.

The truck zoomed closer now, flirting with the centerline. "Go ahead," I urged the driver. "Pass, before we get to the curve."

What was I missing? What was staring me right in the mirror that I couldn't see?

I was determined to figure this out. Not just because people and their puzzles fascinate me. Solving cases, helping the community heal—it *matters*. My work matters—giving people good healthy food, helping folks make a decent living, being a cog that keeps the wheels turning.

But bringing about justice is bigger than me. And pursuing it, in my own way, meant even more than selling local cheese and hand-made truffles.

I eased up on the gas as I entered the big curve near the slough. Barely half past five and full dark. *Come on, solstice.* Wheat fields stretched along either side of the road, and in the distance, a light glowed on a shadowy farm building.

The word *community* stuck in my brain. It meant so much to us in Jewel Bay. Brad Larson said Merrily moved back home to reconnect with her parents. He'd implied that was behind their divorce—she'd been getting ready to move as soon as their daughter left home.

Why would she come back here and try to repair the relationship, only to wreck it?

The reports of those old crimes still baffled me. The articles described Merrily's work as an after-school and summer job. Merrily was a planner. Her mother was a teacher, her sister went on to be a veterinarian. Surely she'd planned on college.

That didn't sound like a young woman who would steal from her mother's best friend, have an affair with the woman's husband, expect to escape, and destroy all her dreams.

The bright lights flashed in my mirror. The truck I'd thought had dropped back safely now sped beside me. Without warning it slammed into my driver's door and pushed me toward the shoulder.

The wheel jerked loose in my hands. I tightened my grip and my instincts took over. Steer *into* a slide, I remembered my father saying. He'd never had the chance, sliding into a bridge at night, on a dark, icy road.

But this was no slide. The pickup—black? blue? I couldn't tell—held steady beside me and slammed into me again. In the dark, I couldn't have seen the driver even if I'd been able to take my eyes off the road.

He hit me once more, a metallic screech piercing the thick silence. A sharp flood of fear rose in my throat. Everything seemed so clear, yet I could see almost nothing. Nothing but the reflector on the post on the side of the road as the Subaru ran over it, down into the ditch.

Steer *through* the ditch, I told myself. Drive right on up the far side and into the pasture. The cows won't mind.

Partway up the slope, my trusty little car slugged to a halt, stuck in the mud and snow and ice. It rolled on to the driver's side, and I could hear the ice break. See the brackish water rise up the windshield. See it begin to leak in.

Adam. Mom. Chiara. Nick. The names tore through my brain. *Landon and the new baby.*

The babies I would never have.

I couldn't move my arms. Why was it so dark? Why was I so cold?

Seventeen

The voices moved in and out of the darkness. They asked me questions. Fingered my wrists and the side of my neck. Shone lights in my face.

I blinked. Tried to raise my hand to shield my eyes. It wouldn't move.

Darn light, too bright, too bright.

"Erin, can you hear me? It's Derek D'Orazi."

Who? Oh, right. EMT. Picture framer. Nice guy. Cute. Let me co-opt his phone last summer to take pictures of evidence before the sheriff tossed me off the scene.

"Talk to me, Erin."

I didn't want to talk. I wanted to sleep. If I kept my eyes closed, would they let me sleep?

"We're taking you to Emergency." He leaned in, and I smelled the tomato sauce and garlic on his breath. He obviously hadn't tried my mother's tomato sauce. She has a delicate touch with garlic.

"You're going to hear a loud thunk," he said, "and feel a bump. It's nothing to worry about—just us sliding the gurney into the ambulance, and the wheels folding up."

Somehow they'd gotten me out of the car, out of the water, and onto a gurney.

Wait. Out of the water? How had I gotten *into* the water? I tried to remember. A truck. A curve. I tried to sit up. Derek put a hand on my shoulder and pushed me back down. Lights flashed everywhere. Why wouldn't they shut off the lights? They were making my head hurt.

I tried to turn my head away, but all I got was another eyeful of lights, these from a sheriff's vehicle. A uniformed deputy stood on the side of the road, listening to a woman who was talking with her hands.

"Is she going to be okay?" I heard her call as the gurney rolled by. "I can't believe that pickup hit her and didn't even stop."

I opened my eyes and found Derek's face. "My phone. Call Adam. Call my mother."

"Already done," he said. "Detective Caldwell took care of it."

Detective Caldwell. Kim was on the case. I could relax.

∞

You wreck your car, you rip your skin open, you scare the bejeebers out of yourself, and they tell you to rest. But will they let you? *No.*

Hospitals are full of bright lights and sharp objects. And people who want answers.

Normally, I appreciate answers. My mother says my first words were a question—probably *Why?* Or *Why can't I have another cookie?*

But these were questions I couldn't answer.

"What happened?"

"Do you know who might have gone after you?"

"Does this hurt?"

Now there was a question I could answer. Pretty much everything hurt. And I still felt darn cold. After all the poking, prodding, X-raying, and who-knows-what-elsing, the ER doc told me I was a lucky girl.

I'd kinda guessed that.

"Nothing broken," she said, her voice almost as soothing as the Reverend Anne's. "Some scrapes and bruises, and that strained ankle will slow you down."

"Can I dance at my wedding?"

She smiled. "Unless you're getting married in the next couple of weeks, sure."

Uh-oh.

"No internal injuries that we can find," she continued, "but your blood pressure is a touch low, so we're going to let you rest another hour or two here in the ER. Keep you quiet."

"Good luck with that." The voice I'd been longing to hear spoke, and I turned toward it, despite the pain in my neck.

"Adam," I croaked. I raised my arms, though one was snared in the IV tubing. The doc stepped back and let him approach. He took my hand and fell to his knees.

"You think you can get out of marrying me by driving into a ditch full of icy water? No way."

"Darling." My mother flooded in, Bill and Nick behind her. She came to the other side of the bed and took my hand in both of hers. No matter how much pain I felt, it had to be half of what I saw on her face.

A minute later she broke the silence, glancing around the tiny room crowded with beeping machines. "What happened? Can someone please tell me what happened?"

"We're still piecing that together, Mrs. Schmidt," Detective Bello said. I hadn't noticed him come in. Over his shoulder, I spotted Kim, standing next to Nick. "Passerby called it in. She was coming from the other direction when she saw a large, dark pickup with standard Montana plates start to pass Miss Murphy's Subaru—"

"Very bright lights," I said. "Scary bright."

Bello focused on me. "Can you tell me anything about the truck? Chevy, Ford? Two-door or extended cab? Full bed or short?"

But all I could say—all I could see in my fractured memory was a dark truck, and my life ending at thirty-three.

Bello continued the story. "The witness pulled over to give him room—you know how narrow the shoulders are on that stretch. That close to the slough, the road was slick, and he was passing on a curve. She thought he was an idiot. But then he seemed to steer into your car deliberately." He peered at me from his post at the foot of the bed. "As if he wanted to hit you."

I nodded slowly, aware of a stabbing pain at the base of my neck. "Three times. I think he hit me three times."

"She says you fought hard to stay on the road, but the truck was too big."

"Who would do such a thing?" my mother asked.

Bello's eyes rested on me, the tug-of-war between us gone, the stakes too high. "Any idea?"

I told him the truth. "I don't know. But I think it has to be related to Merrily's murder, don't you?"

That, he wouldn't say. The detectives had more questions for me, though the doc kept a close eye on them. Kim leaned in close before they left. "Be careful. You've been my best friend since the fifth grade, and I'm not interested in opening up the job."

Despite the pain in my neck, I had to laugh.

Bello and Kim left, and Nick walked out with them, no doubt hoping to pry loose a few more facts. Bill gave me a hefty dose of homeopathic arnica and tucked the bottle in Adam's pocket. Homeopathic remedies don't interfere with prescription drugs, but not every medical doctor tolerates natural medicine, even when the practitioner is as well-regarded as Bill, and a relative of the patient.

Mom and Bill headed home, though not before extracting Adam's promise to call them immediately if anything changed. My Reuben had long worn off, and they don't serve dinner in the ER. I sent Adam to the hospital cafeteria with a promise to bring me back something.

I was alone when my ever-fatter, ever-slower sister and her family trundled in.

"What do you think you were doing?" Chiara said.

"Hello to you, too, big sister."

"I'm sorry." She lowered herself into the chair next to the bed and reached for my hand. It was a stretch, given her belly and the medical equipment, so we had to be content touching fingers. "I was so scared."

"Me, too."

"Auntie, your face is a mess," Landon said. He put a knee on the bed to climb up, but Jason grabbed him. "Hey, little man. Not a good idea."

"But I want to kiss Auntie Erin and make it better." He burst into tears.

"I'll take him." Jason started to pick up his son.

"Jason, would you stay?" I said.

Head cocked, eyes wide, he set the still-sobbing child down. Chiara pushed herself up. She glanced between us and led Landon into the hall.

"Let's sing," I heard her say, followed by his wobbly voice joining hers. *"We three kings of Orient are ..."*

"Great," I said. "I needed a new earworm."

"Sorry." Jason took the seat Chiara had vacated, bumping the IV stand with one khaki-clad knee. "Tough day in the first grade. When he heard about your accident, he completely fell apart."

145

"It's okay," I said, "though I'll be singing that song for days. Did Greg Taylor call you about breaking that firewall in the Building Supply's computers?"

"Yeah. Thanks. Interesting job. Took me most of the afternoon to make the first crack. She set up some pretty serious obstacles. But I'll get in and see what she was hiding."

"How did an assistant bookkeeper who did general office work have that kind of access? Not to mention that level of computer skill. And who knows you're on the case?"

"Good questions," he said. "I may be able to detect the digital fingerprints, see if I can identify who set up those blockades. The cops know I'm digging for evidence. They don't have the resources to do it themselves." He grew cautious. "The Building Supply staff know I'm there. I needed Cary's help on a couple of programs. Why?"

The thought had been torturing me ever since Bello reported the witness's account, confirming my own sense of what had happened. The thought that alternately made me want to back off and flee to Mexico, and fight harder than ever to find the killer.

"If I was hit on purpose, they might come after you next."

Jason sucked in his breath and leaned back. The sounds of his son's singing had faded away, but I knew he was thinking of his family. My brother-in-law, fiercely protective behind the sweet, nerdy façade.

"What about Lenhardt? Is he a target, too?"

"Could be," I said. "I don't know."

"He's got a kid on Landon's soccer team, and an older boy. Seems like a nice guy."

"I always thought Walt and Taya were nice, and they rejected their own kid. I thought Merrily was nice, and she may have betrayed a man who trusted her when no one else would. Heck, I'm starting to think Detective Bello is nice."

"You sounded pretty lucid until just now," Jason said and we both laughed.

The best medicine.

∞

The ER doc came in as I finished devouring the chicken Caesar wrap Adam had brought me, and said if I was that hungry, I was probably on the road to recovery. After one more good going-over, she set me free.

"Now I'm sorry I splurged on the basement," Adam said a few minutes later as he drove into Jewel Bay. "You're going to need a new car."

"And a new phone." I pushed a few buttons, but the thing just sat in my hand. "With a waterproof case. Not that I'm planning to plunge into the drink again anytime soon. Would you stop at the grocery store for some rice? I want to see if I can dry this thing out."

"The more you poke it while it's wet, the more likely you'll damage the battery."

"Probably right." I tossed the phone into my soggy leather bag and leaned my head back. It didn't hurt too much, though I expected to have a lovely black eye the next morning. "I still can't believe this happened."

Adam made a noise I couldn't decipher, as if he were trying to decide what to say. "Which brings us back to who did it. If you were hit on purpose, someone wanted to stop you from investigating. Who, and why?"

And what—if anything—linked the murder, the theft, and the hit-and-run?

The grocery store lot was nearly empty and he parked close to the front door. "Rice and what else? Tylenol?"

"No. I've got the arnica pills, and gel at home. How about ice cream? We've got chocolate-Cabernet sauce in the fridge." In summer,

147

the Merc sells pints of a local ice creamer's wares, but in winter, they take their truck and head south. Happily, I find Tillamook's Oregon Hazelnut and Salted Caramel an equally addictive substitute.

Adam dashed inside while I waited in the car. After a minute or two, I dug out my phone. Lights flashed, but nothing else happened. I dropped it back in the bag and stared out the window.

A movement caught my eye. The grocery store's electric doors swooshed open and a young boy emerged, followed by a man. Greg Taylor and his son, each carrying a bakery box. I opened the Xterra's passenger door and called out.

At the sound of his name, Greg stopped, then spotted me. "Hop in the truck," he told the boy, a miniature version of himself, minus the gray hair. "I'll be there in a minute."

"You're shopping late."

"His team won the sixth-grade basketball tournament over the weekend. He forgot to tell us the school is celebrating tomorrow and he's supposed to take cupcakes." Greg gestured with the bakery box. Then he saw my face and frowned. "What happened to you?"

"Got run off the road between here and Pondera. And I'm not sure it was an accident."

His eyes widened. "You're okay, though, right? Thank God."

"Yeah, thanks. Actually, I'm glad to see you. We've been friends a long time, Greg, and I know you're not so sure about me helping you prove you didn't kill Merrily." I watched as he lowered his eyes and shifted his feet. "But I don't think you were completely honest about your relationship with her. You hired her, sure. You also rented her your grandmother's house."

"She needed a place to live."

"She didn't come back here asking for your help, did she? She wanted to do this on her own, to prove to her parents and the town that she was a good person and wasn't here to take advantage of anyone."

"Nobody else would give her a job," he said. Not even me, though I hadn't actually had an opening. He tightened his grip on the cupcakes. "She was a good person. She didn't deserve to die."

"You said you two were friends, but it was more than that, wasn't it? And that's how you knew about the schoolhouse. What a special place it was to her."

In the bright circle cast by the parking lot lights, his skin looked sickly and the gray streaks in his hair more pronounced.

"In the cigar box in the bottom of her desk drawer," I continued, "along with the cash, were pictures and a few small objects. One was a token from the old Bijou theater."

Greg let out a ragged breath. His parents had met as theater students in college and spent a few years putting on musicals with traveling companies. They settled in Jewel Bay and took over the crumbling movie house, the Bijou. They started a community theater, and later, a summer company featuring aspiring young professionals. Eventually, the village foundation bought the building and remodeled it into the current Playhouse, managed by Greg's older brother.

The tokens dated back to the 1930s, and for decades everyone in town who'd grown up going to the Saturday movies had a stash of them, though the movies had stopped before I could collect any. They'd been used as tickets initially and, later, handed out in school and Scouting as prizes to be redeemed for popcorn or Junior Mints. For a few years after the movies ended, kids left the tokens on desks or passed them in the hall, to send messages—*meet me after class, meet me by the City Dock.*

Meet me at the schoolhouse?

"Did you give it to her, or did she give it to you and you slipped it back in her cigar box when we were in the office? So Bello wouldn't figure out that he was right, that you did lure her out to the schoolhouse?" Bello wasn't from around here. He wouldn't know about the tokens and their significance. But Kim would, and I knew that eventually she'd see the token and figure it out. If I didn't tell her first.

"What? No." Greg's head jerked back. "Erin, I swear—she was dead when I got there."

"What I don't know," I said, "is whether you figured out that she was pilfering cash, or whether she figured out that you were behind it. Weren't you a computer science major?"

"A hundred years ago. I haven't kept up with that stuff. Why would I steal from my own company?"

"You were angry because Merrily kept the truth from you. You thought you were better friends than that."

"I didn't kill her, Erin. I swear—"

The electric door opened and Adam walked out. At the sound of footsteps, Greg glanced over his shoulder, then back to me. "I swear to you, Erin. When I talked about second chances, I was talking as much about myself as about Merrily."

Eighteen

ou're supposed to rest," Adam said the next morning when I asked him to take me into the village and drop me off at the Merc.

"I can rest at work."

"Not what the doctor had in mind. She only let you go because your blood pressure came back up."

Sure. It rose every time I thought of dark pickups.

"I'm fine," I said. "No internal bleeding. No hypothermia. None of the things you're worried about happened."

The set of his jaw told me I was wrong about that.

"Sorry," I said. "Fresca will be in and out, and Chiara's across the street. Besides, Lou Mary will hover better than any nurse."

That brought a curve to his lips and a dimple to his cheek. Gad, I love that dimple.

Predictably, both Tracy and Lou Mary fussed, and I let them—not for my sake, but for theirs. I answered all their questions, except the one I wanted to answer most: *Who?*

But I was going to find out. Because you don't mess with a Murphy girl without paying the price.

I was sitting at the counter trying once more to resuscitate my phone when Wendy arrived.

"You tried rice on that?" she said.

"The phone or my face? Yeah, but I guess that trick only works if the battery just got damp. This got dunked." It spat to life like R2D2, with spurts and burps, red lights and green, though unlike the beloved droid, it did not spin its head in excitement.

"I brought medicine," she said and handed me a double nonfat latte and a paper bag.

I drank in the coffee scent, then took a bite of the *pain au chocolat.* "Thankth. Thizh wull fikth evryding."

She perched on a stool, her cherry-red rubber clogs the same shade as the upholstery. Today's cotton drawstring pants were a solid navy, a subdued choice for her.

Between bites, I answered her questions and asked about her baby, Stephanie. That brought a bit of color back to her cheeks.

"I almost forgot," she said after she slid off the stool to head back to the bakery. "Michelle wanted me to tell you she's got a lead, and a plan."

I frowned, puzzled. Oh, the bag with the note and cash. I'd asked the barista to help me identify the thief. But what did she mean by a plan? A project to rehabilitate teen thieves? "Oh. Great. Tell her thanks, and I'll pop in as soon as I can."

As she exited the front door, I smiled to myself, hoping Michelle knew that in Jewel Bay, if you suggest a project, you own it.

The phone had gone dark again. Silly thing was playing with me.

I limped upstairs and used the shop phone to call my cell carrier. They would be pleased to send me a replacement—for the small sum of three hundred and nineteen dollars.

I begged. I whined. "It wasn't my fault. I got run off the road by an unidentified driver. I tried rice. I took a hair dryer to the wires. Nothing." Which prompted them to remind me that attempting repairs myself would breach the warranty.

"On an electronic paperweight?" I said.

Then I rang my insurance agent. "If I hadn't heard from you by noon," she said, "I was going to call you myself. You okay?"

"Glad to hear the grapevine's working. Yeah, thanks. My car, not so much." We went over the details. An adjuster would inspect the damage later today. "Sounds like it's totaled, though," she said. "We'll need the crash report. Gotta get official confirmation before we can pay on an unknown driver claim."

Well, that stank. Creep runs me off the road and lands me in the hospital, and I'm the one who has to jump through the hoops.

I thanked her and hung up. My project list kept getting longer. I called the bank and made an appointment with Pamela Barber to see about a car loan.

Black eye or no, business details don't wait. I skimmed yesterday's sales info and scanned our inventory system for alerts. We were in good shape, except for our custom coffee blend. I called the roaster and placed a special order. Updated Facebook and Instagram, then added a social media section to the procedures manual.

Darn it, the carpenter still hadn't called back. Who else could I ask? I sent the Universe a message, asking for a referral. Sounds silly, but it works sometimes.

Then I opened my Spreadsheet of Suspicion and timeline. I had no new suspects, but I hadn't ruled anyone out, either.

Oh, wait. Hadn't the woman at the crash site referred to the truck driver as *he*? A generic *he*, or had she actually seen the driver's face?

I closed my eyes, trying to conjure up the image of a big, dark pickup. Where else had I seen one recently? Monday at the schoolhouse, Greg had been driving his own vehicle, not one of the small white company pickups he usually drove. A big pickup, dark gray. The same truck he'd been driving last night on the cupcake run with his son.

Brad Larson had parked his truck outside the Methodist Church. Also big and dark.

Who else? Last time I'd been at the Building Supply, I couldn't have thrown a stone without hitting one.

But if Merrily Thornton's death—like her life—taught me anything, it was that when it comes to other people, you never know what you think you know.

And a big vehicle can give a small person a sense of power.

I switched screens to the timeline.

"Erin?" Lou Mary called up. "The detectives are here to see you."

Detectives, plural. The office was too small to hold us all. I pushed myself up, wincing at the pain in my left ankle.

"Don't come down, Erin." Kim's voice. "I can't believe you're working. Actually, I guess I'd be shocked if you weren't," she said as she came up the stairs.

I sank back into my chair. "Any news?"

Kim, wearing dark green today, took the piano stool. Bello put one foot on the top step and leaned against the wall, arms crossed. "I've assigned the investigation of your accident to Detective Bello," she said, "because—well, because of our connection. I came along to see how you are."

154

"I'm okay, thanks. Don't you two think me getting run off the road is related to Merrily Thornton's murder? It has to be." My hands clenched and I felt the heat rise in the room.

Kim flushed and didn't reply.

"The whole situation could have been much worse if the witness hadn't been so quick on the scene," Bello said.

I shuddered at the memory, fresh and raw. "Any chance she could ID the driver? Or that she saw the plate number?"

"No to both," Bello replied. "She saw a face in profile. Male or female, she couldn't say. I'll admit, I've been surprised by how many women drive them up here."

That was true. Horsewomen. Boaters. Others who regularly haul trailers or large loads.

"You searched Merrily's house, didn't you, Detective? You saw she wasn't living large. How would she have known how to put up sophisticated firewalls and protected areas in the Building Supply's accounting software? And I'm guessing you didn't find a stash of money, either."

"No, we didn't," Kim said. "Although at this point, we don't know for sure how much disappeared, through the different schemes."

"But it's more than she left in that cigar box, and more than the few hundred from the deposit bag," I said. The spreadsheet was still open, and I prepared to share my suspicions. "Have you taken a close look at the bookkeeper? Cary Lenhardt?"

"Believe it or not, Miss Murphy, we have," Bello said. "I hate to sound harsh when you're not feeling well, but my job would be a lot easier if you stuck to selling soap and jam."

"So you do think my wreck is connected to the theft. And the murder. You're saying—"

"I'm saying, I am not fresh off the boat. I may not know what everyone in this town eats for breakfast or who went to grade school with whom, but you were very lucky last night. This is my case, and I am not interested in seeing one homicide become two." With that, Detective Bello stomped down the steps out of sight.

Stunned into silence, I stared after him, then looked at Kim. "Tell me more, Kim. I'm the victim here."

Hands on her knees, she pushed herself up. "You know I can't, Erin. Just...be careful."

∞

They'd searched for the missing money in Merrily's house. No doubt they'd scoured her car and rummaged her other desk drawers. I wondered if she'd hidden it at her parents' place—that could have been the reason she went to the schoolhouse.

And then I wondered about the package she'd mailed on Saturday. Maybe it had held more than truffles.

I needed to talk to Holly.

But to do that, I needed a car.

I limped downstairs. All was well in the shop. I headed out the front door and glanced at the hole in the soffit. At least it hadn't gotten worse. The garland swagged nicely—you'd have to look close to see my makeshift solution—and the gutter fix was holding.

"Thank you, building gods," I said out loud.

Across the street in Snowberry, April Ng sat behind the front counter with a pen and sketchbook. "Erin!" She dropped her things and rushed toward me, then stopped herself, hands flying up as if she were under arrest. "Is it okay to hug you? I don't want to hug you if it hurts."

"Hug away," I said. "I'm a firm believer in the healing power of touch."

She embraced me gently, then stepped back, surveying my face. "In a few days, you'll be able to cover that black eye with a little foundation."

"Thanks." I held up the once-stunning leather bag she'd made from recycled coats and manufacturers' scraps. Post-consumer and post-industrial waste, she called it. "Is there any hope?"

Snowberry is built on a shared passion for making art. April had joined after moving to Jewel Bay last spring with her husband and daughter. If anyone could salvage the bag, she could.

She took it in both hands. Surveyed the stains, studied the seams. Peered inside, her long black hair falling across her face. "Let me try."

"Thanks. Sis in?"

She nodded and pointed. I limped to the back room in my loose-fitting snow boots, hoping my bruised ankle would heal in time for me to wear my red cowboy boots and dance at my wedding. Someone had tried to stop me, and they were not going to succeed.

"No, you can't borrow my car," my big sister said two minutes later. "You just about got killed last night, and now you want to go driving around? Doing what, investigating? Besides, you're not even supposed to be on that ankle. How can you drive?"

"It's my left ankle, and it's fine." It was not fine, but I wasn't going to admit it.

"No," she repeated. "I can't believe Adam let you come to work. Although you probably didn't give him any choice."

I hadn't. "It's not that big a deal."

Clearly, she did not agree, and she was not handing over her keys.

A minute later, I was back on the sidewalk, pondering my options.

"I hear your luck nearly ran out last night," a woman said, and I turned to face Sally Grimes.

The way I saw it, my lucky stars had saved me. I knew that was Sally's way of saying she was sorry about the accident and glad I'd come through relatively unscathed.

"I'm fine, Sally. Thanks."

"Good. We wouldn't want two dead bodies in one week." She jerked her head toward the antique shop. "Now you see what comes of getting too close to Merrily Thornton."

"That's harsh. You don't think she learned her lesson? That she truly wanted her parents' forgiveness? And maybe even yours?"

Her chin quivered. From the cold, or emotion? Coatless, in suede loafers, she must have come outside when she saw me. "Funny, isn't it?" she said. "Funny-strange. I never blamed Taya for what Merrily did, but she was so mortified, she could barely stand to talk to me. Even after she and Walt opened their shop and we saw each other often in passing. After—" She hugged herself. "After you helped me reconnect with my own daughter, I told Taya to swallow her pride. But then when Merrily returned, I just…"

"Oh, Sally. It's okay. We all overreact sometimes." As I had been accused of doing more than once. "Especially when it comes to protecting what we love."

I stepped forward, rested my hands on her back, and held her as close as I dared. After a long moment, she patted my shoulder blades, then stepped back. She kept her eyes on the snow bank separating street and sidewalk, embarrassed by even that show of emotion.

"Sally." *Not quizzing her, Mom,* I told myself. *Just talking.* "Did it ever occur to you that Merrily might not have stolen from you after all?"

Sally gasped and took a step back. "She pled guilty. She went to prison."

"I know, I know. But she was eighteen. She only worked for you a few months." I called up facts culled from the newspaper archives. "The bulk of the money came from accounts connected to other businesses your husband ran for you. Merrily wouldn't have had access to those accounts, would she? And I think the judge had the same questions."

"I don't know, and I don't care."

"I don't believe you. I think you're a softie who's pretended to be tough for so long, you've almost convinced yourself you don't care. But you do." I paused, not sure I should take the next step. "Sally, what if Merrily pled guilty for another reason? To protect someone else?"

Her jaw quivered and I felt like a total rat. "You mean that baby."

"You knew? You knew about Ashley?"

"Not at first. Years later. After Cliff died, the prison sent me his things. We were divorced, but I was listed as his outside contact, since our daughter was a minor. What possessed me, I don't know, but I read the legal papers he'd saved." She wrapped her arms around herself, shivering in her black-and-white tunic. "The pre-sentence report was— illuminating."

"In what way?"

"The investigator recommended the stiffest sentence possible, because of the position of trust he'd occupied as my husband, the amount of money taken, and his refusal to admit his guilt, despite all the evidence. And there was something else." She swallowed hard. "The same investigator had been involved in Merrily Thornton's case and it was his opinion that Cliff had taken advantage of her. In the worst way. At least, that's how I read it. That's why she got such a light sentence."

"Oh, Sally. I'm so sorry." What a crappy way to learn a crappy thing—that her husband had fathered a teenager's baby. No wonder Sally was bitter.

"I threw the papers in the fireplace."

I couldn't blame her. "I don't know if it's any consolation, but Merrily adored Ashley. So does her husband."

Her eyes softened and she gave me a weak smile, then turned and disappeared into her shop.

I felt like we'd made some peace, Sally and I. And that was a good thing.

Nineteen

hanks, Lou Mary." I wrapped my fingers around the keys she handed me, as eager to get going as any sixteen-year-old borrowing Mom's car on a Saturday night.

"You kids," she said. "You're lost without your phones."

After a consult with Jason, who thought we might be able to salvage the thing, I'd put off running to Pondera for a new one. But Lou Mary had bought the excuse. I owed her.

As I adjusted the seat and mirrors in the small SUV, I felt a twinge of regret over bringing up the subject of Ashley Larson with Sally. My mother would be furious.

Of course, she'd be even more irritated that I'd fibbed to Lou Mary to borrow her car. Fingers crossed that we could keep that a secret.

To solve the mystery of Merrily Thornton's death, I needed more details about her life. I drove up the Stage Road to Granny G's house, hoping to catch Brad Larson. Hers was the third in a row of older cottages that had always looked so sweet, so charming. But as I approached, my heart sped up. What if his dark pickup was the one that had run me off the road? What if I'd dismissed him as a suspect too soon, not yet aware of some secret resentment? What if he'd been so outraged by her leaving him, at her leaving home and family and business to come back to Jewel Bay for—what? Did he think she'd used him to raise Ashley, and now sought revenge?

But if he'd been that angry, wouldn't he have acted sooner? Unless her return to her childhood home had been the last straw.

My mouth went dry. *So if it's his truck, don't stop,* I told myself, gripping the steering wheel so tight my hands hurt. But how would I know? *I would know.*

I slowed the car. Like the other houses in this stretch, Granny G's had no garage.

And no pickup parked in the narrow drive.

My hands loosened their grip. My mouth went dry. I stopped the car and forced myself to breathe slowly. The living room curtains were open, the basket I'd left on the porch gone. Someone had shoveled the steps and walkway, though not the drive. In last night's new snow, tire tracks backed out, but once the rig had reached the Stage Road, I couldn't see which way it had gone.

I felt a little foolish as I continued driving up the curvy, snow-packed road. I'd jacked myself up for nothing, letting questions about Brad Larson rattle around in my head until they'd knocked my common sense loose.

And I still needed information.

Tracy had said Holly Muir was taking a few days off to "deal with" her sister's death. What did that mean, exactly? Write an obituary and a eulogy? Call out-of-town relatives?

Sit home and warm herself with memories?

I'd been to the Muirs' house once, fetching Landon from a birthday party last spring. No phone meant no map and Lou Mary's car had no GPS, but I thought I could find the place.

A few miles up the highway, my heart sped up. This time, though, I knew why. Completely natural to feel anxious at the scene of one's own near-tragedy.

The only signs of any trouble were the bent reflector pole, and the muddy ruts in the ditch where I'd gone in, and where the tow truck had pulled out my once-trusty Subaru. I was going to miss that car.

A mile later, I turned onto a road leading to Shining Waters, an older development of two- and three-acre parcels, hilly and heavily wooded, clustered around pot-hole ponds left by giant boulders an ice age or two ago. This time of year, you could actually see the houses, unlike in summer, when thick brush and foliage obscured them.

At the first fork, I made a right, staying right past two more narrow roads, then left. The gravel roads were almost nicer in winter thanks to snow filling the ruts and plows scraping them smooth.

A red roof glinted through the lodgepole pine. One more house.

I slowed at the next drive and was about to turn in when a dark pickup emerged from behind a giant snow bank. I gasped before spotting Brad Larson at the wheel. I let out my breath, rolled down the window, and stuck out my hand.

But either he didn't recognize me, or he wasn't in a chatty mood. The truck turned and roared down the hill. I continued on.

Holly Thornton Muir stood in front of her open garage, staring through the trees to the tiny pond and the mountains beyond. I parked in the drive behind a small white SUV, its hatch open. Bags of groceries filled the back end.

She whipped her head around, her black-gloved hands rising as if to ward off another visitor. Another intruder.

I got out, careful of my ankle. Not too bad—the remedies were working. "So cold, and so pretty."

"I heard you went off the road. You okay?"

"Stiff and sore, but alive. Thanks. I wanted to check on you. Losing a sister ..." Heat flooded my chest at the thought, and my breath stopped for a moment. "If something happened to Chiara, I'd be a wreck."

"I am a wreck," Holly said, wrapping her arms around herself. "Not working doesn't help. I'll be back in the clinic tomorrow."

"At least you did your part, trying to get Merrily and your parents back together."

She let her arms drop, making a raspy sound. "Merrily was never the problem. She tried for years, but my parents couldn't forgive her."

"For letting herself be used?"

Holly snapped her head toward me. "How did you know? Who told you?"

"Not hard to figure out. Merrily was good with numbers and details, but how could she have gotten access to all the accounts the stolen money came from? And she wouldn't have had any reason to lie for Cliff Grimes. So she had to have had another motive." To protect her unborn daughter.

Holly crossed her arms again, her mouth a line, eyes straight ahead. "You know how big sisters are."

"Was that Brad Larson I saw leaving?"

"He was waiting for me when I got home. He's upset that the sheriff won't tell him when they'll release the body, so he can schedule a service."

"He seems like a nice guy." I gestured toward her groceries. "Sorry. I'd help if I could, but my ankle's kinda messed up."

"It's okay, thanks. Brad is nice," she said, though from her tone, I couldn't tell whether she appreciated that trait or found it annoying. "That's why my family baffles him. Why won't my parents see him, why couldn't I get them to forgive her while she was still alive, blah blah blah. As if it was all my fault."

Ah, so there was a hint of her mother's bitterness in Holly after all. Not surprising, after growing up with Taya. I leaned against my borrowed car.

"Did you know back then that Merrily went to prison pregnant?"

"No. Not until after she was out and married. I took an internship in Billings, not knowing she'd stayed there. She and Ashley came into the clinic with a kitten they'd found. We couldn't save it—it had feline leukemia—and Ashley cried and cried."

"How old was she? That had to have been a shock. To you, I mean."

"Not quite six. Yeah, but I understood why Merrily kept the baby a secret," Holly said, her tone pensive.

"I've been wondering. What about Ashley? Was she born in prison?"

"The prison system's quite enlightened about that. They let the women go to the hospital for births, and newborns can stay with their mothers up to six months. Merrily was about to be released when she had the baby—she served less than a year on a two-year sentence—so Ashley never had to go into foster care."

The explanation was a relief. "Brad says she wants to be a vet. Inspired by you?"

"Brad's a dweeb, but he's been a good father."

Thank God for dweebs. "What does Ashley know about the feud between her mom and her grandparents?"

"I don't know. I never thought it my place to tell her." Holly gazed off into the distance. "For a tiny woman, my mother is one big contradiction. Adored every five-year-old she ever taught, and refused to acknowledge her own flesh and blood."

Part of becoming an adult is realizing that the adults you knew when you were a kid were as flawed and human as you are now. And like Taya Thornton, some are contradictory in ways they don't see.

"I get that Merrily stealing from Sally mortified your folks. But surely, once they knew the real reason she kept quiet, they would have understood. She wasn't the first girl to keep a pregnancy to herself as long as she could."

"There was more to it than that." Holly's voice rose, thin, strained.

Meaning, who the father was. But they had known, eventually. Or figured it out.

Holly's eyes had gone wide and wild, and I feared she was on the verge of panic. I switched gears. "Well, thank goodness you two reconnected. And that Ashley got to know you."

Her breath grew rapid. "I only wish they'd have been willing to talk. For us all to talk. To explain. It was such a confusing time. I never should have ..."

But instead of telling me what she never should have done, Holly marched to the back of her car. Grabbed her bags and rushed inside without saying goodbye.

What had I said? What regret had I triggered?

∞

On the way back to town, I must have seen half a dozen dark pickups. Plus three more in the Building Supply parking lot. They popped up everywhere, like mushrooms after rain.

I found Jason in the office with the forensic accountant.

"You learn something new on every investigation," the man was saying. "The days when an embezzler could rely on the judicious use of Wite-Out are gone. I'll admit, I don't get why an employer hires someone with a financial felony in their background, no matter how good or sympathetic their excuse. Repeat offenses are just too common."

"Greg knew her," I said from the doorway. "He believed it was a one-time thing." If it had been a thing at all, but I wasn't going to share my doubts. This guy wouldn't believe me.

"That's what they want you to think. 'Bad luck, my ex ran off with the rent, I needed the cash to tide me over, I'd have paid it back when I got back on my feet.' BS like that." He slipped a note pad and calculator into his briefcase and snapped it shut.

That pattern everyone kept talking about. But Merrily had never made excuses for herself. When she came job hunting at the Merc, she'd been straightforward, telling me she'd been convicted of embezzlement twenty years earlier but that I wouldn't regret hiring her.

"I suppose you'll have to look at her daughter's finances, to see if that's where she put the money," I said.

He shook his head. "That's up to the cops. But I've worked on a lot of embezzlement cases, and I can tell you, we never find all the money. They drive it, they eat and drink it, they piddle it away."

As I'd read. But not being able to find the money might also mean Merrily hadn't taken it.

"So, I'm off to the bank. Good to work with you—you know your stuff." He shook Jason's hand, nodded at me, and left.

"The bank?" I perched on the corner of the desk, easing my weight off my sore ankle.

Jason leaned back in Cary's chair, hands clasped behind his head. "Looks like she was making payments to suppliers who didn't exist, creating false commercial customer accounts to explain orders for products that were never actually ordered or sold."

My heart sank.

"Next step is to track down where those payments actually went," he continued. "Maybe they can get some of it back."

"What about the missing cash? Was that a pattern, too?"

"A little bit here, a little bit there."

In retail, shortages happen. You give a customer ten bucks more in change than you should have, and they don't notice. (They always notice if you short them.) You miscount the till. You ring up a sale as credit instead of cash, and things don't balance.

And from time to time, someone has sticky fingers.

Oh, Merrily. Was I that wrong about you?

∞

Rolling River Farm showed none of its magic today, the road barely distinguishable from the fields, under a sky as bleak as the land. But I thought the place held the secret to Merrily's death, and to the crimes of the past.

Near the turnoff to the Thorntons' house and barn, a black cow poked her nose at the base of a fencepost, in search of something fresh and green. I drove on and parked alongside the schoolhouse.

Last night's snow had filled in all the footprints. Three days since the body had been found, and the crime scene tape was down. Nothing hinted at death or danger.

Nothing, except the cold and the quiet. And the pounding in my chest as I stood beside my borrowed car.

A single fawn had crossed the yard since the snow stopped, and I marveled at the tiny, heart-shaped hoof prints. Whitetails are said to spend most of their lives within one mile of their birthplace. A few humans do the same—I'd gone to school with the Easter sisters, Bunny and Polly, who'd married local men and stayed put. They seemed content. Others take different paths. My mother had dropped out of college and left the Sonoma Valley to travel, then met my father in Italy and, as she says, followed him home like a love-sick puppy. He'd always believed himself meant to settle in Jewel Bay, and that decided the matter of place for her.

The fawn's companions had beaten a path around the side of the schoolhouse and into the woodland. Spruce and fir branches bent under the weight of snow. The birches extended their gnarled white fingers, knuckles black, stark against the flat, gray sky.

My sister, brother, and I had each created a mix-and-match of our parents' routes, leaving but returning, though whether Nick would stay was anybody's guess.

If Merrily Thornton hadn't found herself in prison in Billings, if she hadn't found a father for Ashley there, would she have come back to Jewel Bay to raise her daughter? Like her sister, Holly, who'd brought a husband home from veterinary school.

I crossed behind the schoolhouse and reached the far side, not sure what I was hoping to see. The snow was extra deep, and the deer had not yet blazed a trail back here. Thankful for my snow boots, I ignored the twinge in my ankle and picked my way through the fluffy stuff, arms out like airplane wings. From here, I caught a glimpse of the Thorntons' big house and the edge of the barn. The cow had moseyed on. It was past noon, but thick clouds kept the sunlight away, and it felt much later. The Christmas lights in the windows of the house must have been on a sensor, the tiny white fairy lights coming to life as I watched.

I am not sure whether I heard the crying first, or sensed the presence of a person in pain. I peered around the front corner of the school-house. The same sensors must have been at work here, too, because the white lights that trimmed the front windows had switched themselves on while I was prowling around.

And in one of the white wooden rockers on the wide front porch sat Taya Thornton in her fur-trimmed parka, rocking and sobbing, rocking and sobbing.

I knocked lightly on the railing as I rounded the corner, not wanting to frighten her. "Taya? Mrs. Thornton?" I called.

Her head jerked up and snapped toward me. "Erin, you startled me. What are you doing here?"

She must have walked down from the big house, meaning my car would have been out of sight. I climbed the steps and swept a dusting of snow off the seat of the other rocker, then sat. "Passing by. I thought I'd stop to look around. It's a special place."

"Even as teenagers, the girls preferred the schoolhouse to the rec room in the house. They'd hang out with their friends all hours of the night, blasting music from their boom boxes. We never worried, with them so close to home." The memory softened her features, reminding me of the teacher I'd loved.

"So you came here to remember."

She nodded. "Merrily was named for Christmas, of course, but the name suited her as a child. She was pure joy. And when Holly came along, Merrily adored her. Tucked her in the stroller and pushed her around the house. She'd have done anything for her little sister. I thought we were the perfect family."

As if there were such a thing.

"God gets you for that kind of thinking," she said, her tone taking on an edge. "He smacks you down for your pride. Destroys what you thought you had."

170

Had that been how she'd seen it when Merrily was charged? Had she felt betrayed, or had the sense that Merrily's crimes were crimes against her crept up over time?

"What if ..." I said. "What if it didn't happen quite like that? What if Merrily was protecting someone then—and now? Would that change how you feel?"

She faced me, lips tight, eyes hollow. "Oh, Erin. Just like your mother, aren't you? Always looking for the bright side. Wanting to fix things." She gazed back at the snow-covered fields in front of us, the shadows flat and ominous. "Some of us are too broken."

"No, Mrs. Thornton—Taya." I held out a hand. "I can understand you might feel that way, but—"

She snapped her head toward me. "You don't understand a thing."

I sat back, every bone in my body stiffening. Was she more than a bad mother? Was she a killer?

As I drove away a few minutes later, I glanced up the hill to the big house, lights twinkling around every window.

In the Thorntons' driveway stood a big black pickup.

Twenty

One of the joint tasks on the wedding to-do list was to finish writing our marriage vows. We'd pored over dozens of samples online and in the marriage prep materials Anne had given us. Love and honor were easy, and "until death do us part" was a no-brainer. The rest, we were still puzzling out.

But one thing no spouse could do, I thought as I turned Lou Mary's car onto the highway and back toward town, was protect the other from grief. Clearly Walt Thornton had tried, and he'd just as clearly failed. When I'd asked Taya if I could do anything for her—call Walt or Holly—she'd simply shaken her head and gone back to rocking.

The truck had been too far away for a good look, and I hadn't wanted to venture up the Thorntons' driveway under Taya's watchful eye. Later.

All was well at the Merc, but my tummy was talking tough, so I limped next door to Red's. Old Ned had my Pellegrino with a lemon wedge waiting before I sat down.

"Girlie, you gotta stop living so dangerously," he said, his gruff voice soft with worry. "Why would someone want to run you off the road?"

"Wish I knew, Ned. Can I get a cheeseburger? And waffle fries?" Dress be darned, I needed comfort food.

"You bet." He clipped the order slip to the wire that ran across the bar and sent it flying to the kitchen. "From what I hear, half the town thinks Merrily Thornton is a two-time thief, and half the town thinks they don't know what to think."

"Yeah. It's crazy." The evidence Jason had found seemed so damning. But it made no sense. Why steal again after her old friend gave her a second chance?

It was clear to me now that Merrily Thornton's biggest sin all those years ago was to violate the family vow to maintain appearances at all costs. From what she'd told me and what Brad had said, I was convinced she'd come back here to repent.

So who had killed her?

Ned had run Red's for decades and knew everybody in town. He held as a matter of faith that anything he told me wasn't gossip.

"Walt pops in for a whisky now and then, but he don't talk much about family. Don't talk much, period, unlike his wife."

"Some couples are like that." I sipped my Pellegrino and shushed my noisy tummy.

"They're funny people, him and Taya. I don't judge folks by what their kids do, and I don't hold with turning your back on blood." Ned rubbed an invisible spot on the counter, and I knew he was thinking of his own son. "Say, I tell you I bought me an RV? Heading south for a few weeks. Not till January—I gotta stick around for some big wedding." He winked.

"That's great, Ned. You can count on J.D." Ned's grandson, a burly redhead like all the Redaway men, had joined the family biz last winter and taken to it like the proverbial duck.

"Yeah, guy I bought it from made me an offer I couldn't refuse. He's pushing me to buy his truck, to pull it. But I got a perfectly good truck. Sunshine and seventy degrees sounds good, don't it?"

Someone selling a truck? Coincidence, for sure. In Northwest Montana, there are pickups and Subarus everywhere. Well, make that one less Subaru.

"Sure does. I think Adam's taking me somewhere warm, but he won't say." I like winter, and winter sports, but a break would be nice.

The twinkle in Ned's eye hinted that he knew Adam's plan. Before I could ask, the kitchen runner slid my burger and fries in front of me, the hot salty aroma enticing. Ned conjured up a bottle of mustard and put his face back in neutral.

Ned checked on other patrons while I ate. By the time he got back to me, I was feeling quite human. Mess with blood sugar, and it messes with you.

"Dang, I've missed your fries," I said. "After the wedding, and this mystery trip, we're rejoining the pool league. Though we'll have to find Nick a new partner."

"Oh, I don't think you need to worry about that."

I cocked my head. What was he talking about? All last winter, Adam and I had teamed up against Nick and Christine until her death. The Caldwell cousins usually beat us all, though.

Oh. Last Monday, when I'd seen Kim in this very bar, she'd been waiting for someone but hadn't said who. As I headed up to Dragonfly for my dress fitting, I'd seen Nick drive into town, looking like a man on a mission. And in the ER—gad, was that only last night?—Nick had been standing behind Kim in the doorway. I'd assumed my mother had called him.

When I was otherwise occupied, had my brother and my childhood best friend found each other? How had I not noticed? Some investigator I am.

"Ned, you sly fox."

The twinkle returned. If it weren't for the small matter of an unsolved embezzlement and murder, and my hit-and-run, all would be well.

$$\infty$$

Lou Mary insisted I rest in the office with my feet up, and I didn't protest. My ankle was throbbing, my bruised cheekbone ached, and I could feel where the shoulder belt had held me. Thank goodness I always wear it.

But I am a Murphy girl. I can't sit still for long. I stared at the timeline and Spreadsheet of Suspicion, wondering what I was missing.

Greg's weekend whereabouts could be key. He hadn't worked Saturday. He and his family had come downtown for the Art Walk, and we'd stood behind them at the tree lighting. He'd been chatting with another couple about the grade school kids' basketball tournament that weekend. The tournament his son's team had played in.

In winter, the Building Supply closes on Sundays. I knew from Wendy that the extended family usually attended church together—part of Reverend Anne's flock—then gathered at the farmhouse for brunch. Aside from that and the tournament, I had no idea where Greg might have been until Monday morning, when Merrily turned up missing and the cigar box surfaced.

That box bugged me. I understood keeping a few photos and tokens at work. Since I'd taken over the Merc and claimed the office for myself, a handful of mementos had crept in, taking up precious space on the small desktop and the single bookshelf. But my personal touches were all plainly visible. Why had Merrily kept hers in a box in a drawer?

Unless she'd wanted them close, but didn't want them to be seen. Why keep Ashley a secret?

Everybody who loved me had warned me that all this running around would only make me hurt worse, and they were right. I reached in my pocket for the bottle of arnica pills. Gone.

I'd emptied out my leather bag before leaving it with April, and now I tore through the pile of junk on my desk. Not there, either. I grabbed my coat from its hook in the hallway and checked the pockets. Nope.

I slipped out the back door, the quickest route to Bill's hole-in-the-wall herb shop. Which reminded me of the air leak under the door. If I didn't find a handyman soon, I'd try replacing the seal myself. I couldn't make things worse, could I?

Tracy had cleared a path the width of the snow shovel through the courtyard we'd worked so hard to reclaim. Soon it would be time to plan our outdoor summer events. In retail, you've always got to think a couple of seasons ahead.

I unlatched the gate in the six-foot-high wooden fence and pushed it. It opened a few inches, then stopped. I tried a second time, and pain shot through my shoulder. Still no give. I peeked through a knothole and saw the problem: A plow had trucked down the alley, clearing the driving lane but creating a berm of snow that was blocking my gate.

I was preparing for a good shove, despite the promise of pain, when I heard the back door to the bistro and bakery next door open.

"You have to tell them," Wendy said, her voice firm, her words clipped. "Everything. No more secrets."

"Not my secret to tell," Greg replied.

"If you don't tell the truth, that Detective What's-his-name will slam you in jail. You're worried about the Building Supply. What do you think will happen to it then? And to your family?"

I eased up on the gate, but the dry, cold wood gave a loud creak. I kept the pressure steady and my ears on alert.

"Merrily went to prison to keep the secret. I can keep it, too."

"Merrily was wrong," Wendy replied. "And she's probably dead because of it. You can't protect other people from their sins forever. There are children involved."

The way she said it, something clicked into place. I knew the connection between Greg and Merrily. And so did Wendy.

"If Holly Muir can stick her arm upside a cow and yank out a stuck calf, she can deal with her own past. If not for her, none of this would have happened."

I leaned into the gate, both to keep it from squeaking and to keep my head from snapping off.

Next door, Greg made an exasperated noise. "You win. But don't say a word to anyone. Not yet."

I stayed put until I heard a truck start up. Though I wanted to peek out to make sure Greg's passenger door was intact, I didn't dare. It was clear Greg Taylor had done a lot I hadn't known about. Even if he said it was for "other people."

He had to mean Holly. But why?

I peered through the knothole to watch the truck head down Back Alley, and when I couldn't see it anymore, I squeezed out the narrow opening.

Bill's clinic and herb shop is a cozy two-room wreck that should have been torn down ages ago, but any replacement would have to meet current county building codes, including setbacks and parking requirements. The result would leave about enough room for a dog-house, so the clinic stayed put.

The sharp tang of incense greeted me, and the Tibetan bell that hangs over the door announced my presence. Bill stepped out of the back room, closing the door quietly. Tall and slightly stooped, he practices acupuncture, dispenses herbs and homeopathic remedies, and leads herb walks on the Nature Trail above the river. Better for the soul, he says, than practicing law, as he did for years.

"If you're here for acupuncture on that ankle," he said, "you'll need to wait. I've got a case of back pain on my treatment table."

"Thanks." That was a relief. I'm not afraid of needles, exactly, but ... well, okay, I'm afraid of needles. Easy for him to say they don't hurt. "Lost my arnica."

While he made up a fresh supply of the remedy, I sat in a time-burnished oak armchair in front of his ancient black lacquered desk, a piece he'd bought from one of his teachers. The conversation in the alley rattled in my head.

"Bill, when you practiced law, did you ever handle adoptions?"

"A few. Why?"

"When an unmarried woman has a baby, does she have to name the father on the birth certificate?"

"No. Some women have good reason for not identifying the father." He sat, a small brown vial in his hand. "But if they go to court for child support, they have to prove paternity. Or if they apply for assistance, the state will insist on going after the father for support, if they can."

"What if he's in prison?"

"Doesn't mean he lacks assets. He'll also get notice if there's ever a step-parent adoption."

My assumptions about Merrily Thornton had just gone all cattywampus. Brad Larson had described her as a young women determined to get back on her feet after a big mistake. To find a job as soon as she got out of prison, and a father for her daughter. I'd assumed he'd adopted Ashley. But an adoption, like going on public assistance, would have triggered notice to Cliff Grimes—notice Sally would have found in his papers. Had Merrily feared Cliff's response? Been determined to keep him from Ashley? Or had she feared that years down the road, Ashley would discover that her biological father was a dirty rotten rat who'd cheated on his wife, stolen from her, and planned to run?

Now I was more puzzled than ever.

It all came back to the sisters, didn't it?

Whatever Holly Thornton Muir had done, her big sister had loved her very, very much.

Twenty-One

*W*ithout my phone, I couldn't tell time. But the clock tower at the library was chiming the hour, and I was late for my appointment at the bank.

I limped up Front and turned onto Hill. If ice heals a bruise, shouldn't walking in the cold do the same?

Apparently not.

I limped into the bank lobby, stood on the state seal in the middle of the marble floor of the original structure, and scanned the place. Peered through the giant artificial Christmas tree to the glass-walled conference room. Pamela Barber leaned forward, hands on the table, facing an employee and a man and woman I didn't know, both wearing dark suits and darker expressions.

My appointment had obviously come at a bad time.

The employee spotted me and spoke to Pamela. She glanced out, then down at her watch. Which reminded me that I had one, somewhere. She opened the door and I heard her say, "Back in fifteen. Carolyn, pull up all their records. Even the closed accounts. Eagle eyes."

Her heels rat-tatted on the marble floor, her suit the same not-quite-navy, not-quite-purple as the circle blooming around my eye.

"Thank goodness you're all right." After a quick, careful embrace, Pamela led the way to her office. "I wish these icy roads weren't so good for business. And I'm sorry I need to make this quick. Something's come up."

I sat across from her while she scrolled through screens showing the financial info Adam and I had submitted for our remodel loan. That paperwork had included the contract for deed with my mother, so Pamela knew what we made and what we owed.

She swiveled her chair to face me and folded her hands on top of the desk in a way that telegraphed bad news.

"I'm sorry, Erin. You've got a good credit rating—you both do—but with the debt to your mother and the loan from us, you're over-stretched. A dealer could probably give you financing, but the rates will be higher."

"You can't give me a car loan?"

She pressed her lips together. "I'm afraid not."

"Even for a used car? I don't need a new one." I'd never had a new car. I'd also never had trouble borrowing money. We'd gotten a good deal from my mother, but forty acres with an orchard, a house, and a view hadn't come cheap. And neither had bringing the place into the twenty-first century.

"I wish I could. You and your family have been good customers for ages, but your debt-to-income ratio is at our limit. A little above it, actually."

I caught my lower lip in my teeth and blinked back tears of disappointment. Working retail, even when you're your own boss, doesn't bring in the big bucks. Neither did Adam's job. The price of doing what we love.

But that wasn't Pamela's fault, and I wasn't going to let it interfere with finding out the truth about Merrily.

"Nice to see you've got your office back," I said, fighting to regain control over my emotions. It was only a car and money, after all. We'd figure out something. "And I hear your staff is in the clear. Not that I had any doubt. But you're still stressed."

Her shoulders sagged. "You've talked with your brother-in-law. We're following up on what he found."

My brow furrowed. "False invoices. Oh. She set up automatic payments to accounts for vendors who didn't actually exist. But she wouldn't have set up those accounts here, would she?"

"The accounts receiving the funds aren't in our system. We can tell by the numbers. But we've got to analyze all disbursements made from the Building Supply's accounts and weed out the improper payments. That means gathering our internal documentation, then calling in the regulators." Pamela caught one lip between her teeth, the fuchsia lipstick that matched her silk blouse nearly worn off. "I hate calling the regulators."

"Surely they can't blame you. Or the bank. You're not responsible for what account holders do."

"In some cases, we are," she said. "Regulators are perfectly nice people, trained to question every detail. I just don't like screw-ups on my watch."

Which was one reason I liked her so much. Her smile as we parted looked as forced as mine felt, and I bundled up to head back outside.

At the corner of Hill and Front, I detoured into Dragonfly Dry Goods. The amazing collection of fabric and yarn is a magnet for a certain kind of shopper, along with Kitchenalia, Food for Thought Bookstore, and if I'm not being modest, the Merc. I have no needlework skills—Chiara got all the artistic talent in the family—but the colors and soft pettable yarns do tempt me.

"You got my message," Kathy said. "I wasn't sure it was going through—it cut me off short."

I hadn't gotten her message, but I didn't bother trying to explain being phoneless in the modern world.

"Your wrap is finished," she said, sounding satisfied. "That yarn has an incredible halo. Come see." She gestured and I followed her into the workroom where my dress hung on a form. Around its shoulders lay a swath of red angora, softer and more beautiful than I could ever have imagined.

My sister the artist would know exactly what to call that color red. I called it perfect.

And burst into tears.

No way would Kathy let me get tear-snot on a custom-made dress and hand-knit shawl, though. She held out a box of tissues. I sat and sniffed, aware that I was over-reacting, the emotion of the accident finally catching up with me.

"Kathy, you worked with Taya Thornton, right, when you taught art in the grade school?" I blew my nose again and fired the crumpled tissue at the waste basket. "She ever talk about Merrily? Her plans? Any concerns?"

"All I remember about Merrily was that she'd registered for a business and accounting degree at UM. Taya wasn't all that happy. She'd hoped Merrily would follow her footsteps and become a teacher." Kathy reached for a pile of cotton scraps and started flattening them out on the work table. "But Holly was the one who kept them up at night."

"Holly was a problem kid?" News to me. "Not in the classroom, if she got into veterinary college."

"Oh, both those girls aced school." Kathy's capable hands made quick work of the fabric, folding the pieces into neat stacks. "Though they were different in other ways. According to her mother, Holly didn't choose the best friends. But after her sister went to prison, Holly saw the light. Never one more lick of trouble. Valedictorian, I think."

Merrily had just graduated that fateful summer, making Holly a sophomore. My brother or sister—a class ahead and a class behind—might remember the details. Or at least the talk.

Kathy stood in the doorway, hands full of fabric, ready to get back to work. I gave my dress and the magnificent red shawl one last look.

"Soon, my lovelies," I said. "Soon."

∞

"Where have you been? I've been calling and calling," my mother said when I walked into the Merc's back door a few minutes later.

"Long story. Dead phone. I'm pooped." And my head was spinning. Loan denials, fake invoices and fraudulent bank accounts, the sobbing mother of a murder victim, a romance hiding in plain sight, and a wayward kid turned trusted vet. All less than a day after being run off the road.

I'd come back to Jewel Bay after ten years in Seattle, drawn to the serenity of my hometown. Apparently serenity had been an illusion.

"Are you cooking today?" I said, puzzled. This time of year, our commercial kitchen sits idle a few days a week. Summer's fresh berries are already jammed, its cucumbers pickled, its tomatoes sauced. We'd blended our herbal teas and packed up our spice mixes for the Christmas season. Only the items with short shelf lives—truffles and fresh pasta chief among them—kept it busy. And my personal fave: chocolate-Cabernet sauce.

"I came in to check on you. And to give you a piece of my mind."

Uh-oh.

"I am so disappointed in you."

Sometimes I wish my mother were a screamer. That might be easier. *Disappointed* made me feel three inches tall. But though she's calm about it, you always know where you stand with Francesca Conti Murphy Schmidt.

"You promised me you wouldn't upset Sally over this murder business."

"I asked her a few questions. If she got upset, that's her doing."

"Don't get all technical on me. You know what I'm talking about."

For reasons I have never fully understood, my mother's sympathy bone goes into overdrive when it comes to Sally Sourpuss Grimes. Mom always says that she's been so blessed in her own life, despite the loss of my father, that Sally's misfortunes pain her deeply. That Sally had brought some of them on herself—mainly her estrangement from her daughter, now resolved—made no difference. My mother seemed to understand that Sally sometimes spoke without thinking, and that, as Lou Mary had said, we all get thrown off center once in a while. And those to whom an easier road is given need to lend a hand to others on their journey.

But she wasn't being so philosophical at the moment. Her eyes burned into me. "And then you conned Lou Mary into lending you her car so you could drive all over kingdom come on a sprained ankle."

"It's a strain, Mom, not a sprain. Plus it's my left—"

"Sprain, shmain. You were told to take it easy. Is that so hard to understand?"

I gave her the look she deserved. *She* never took it easy. She'd taught by example that work heals all wounds. It doesn't, but all three of her kids had become workaholics before we figured that out.

I hated to tell her the latest, but I had to. "The bank won't give me a car loan. Debt-to-income ratios and other jabber."

"Are you sure your car can't be fixed?"

She hadn't seen it. I prayed she never did. "Pretty sure. And it's so old, when I do get a check from the insurance company, it will barely be enough to buy a bicycle."

"You'll work it out. Meanwhile, there's someone here to see you. He seems quite anxious. I gave him a mug of chai."

Inwardly, I groaned. If it were someone we knew well, she would have just said who it was. I was not in the mood to spar with Oliver Bello.

But to my surprise, the man sitting on one of the red-topped stools, cradling a heavy white mug, wasn't the feisty detective, but the grieving widower.

"Brad. Sorry I was out. How are you?"

The sunken eyes and pale skin said he wasn't good. And while I hated to see his pain, I also felt a surge of relief that Merrily Thornton was so deeply missed. Wherever she was, in whatever the afterlife is, I hoped she was feeling the love.

"Sorry I didn't recognize you on the road today until too late," he said. "I was upset. Thank you for the gift basket, by the way."

"You're welcome." I sat next to him. "Mind if I ask what was so upsetting?"

"I went in to introduce myself to Walt and Taya, and to let them know Ashley will be here this weekend. I know it's rough on them, but for Pete's sake. What Merrily did was twenty years ago, and none of it was Ashley's fault."

I poured myself some Cowboy Roast and refilled his chai, then sat once again beside him. "They've had a bad shock. They'll change their minds." They had to.

"When you meet Ashley—" He shook his head. "She's more than a star student and standout athlete—did I tell you she's on a soccer scholarship?—she is a genuinely nice kid. Beautiful ... not sweet-pretty like her mom, but a real head-turner."

I knew. I'd seen the pictures. "And dark-haired, instead of blond. So she looks like her biological father?"

He jerked his head back, then recovered his composure. "I imagine so. I never asked."

"And you never adopted her?"

"Merrily didn't want to hassle with the paperwork. Said it wasn't necessary."

But that wasn't the real reason. She didn't want to be forced to let the biological father know.

"We've been so busy, I shouldn't be out of town this long," Brad said. His barstool squeaked. "But Merrily deserves a decent funeral. I know she never loved me the way I loved her, but I want to give her that."

"December is our busy time," I said, gesturing to the shop, "but I wouldn't have thought that about plumbers."

"Ice dams. Frozen pipes. Cold water can be pretty dangerous."

I shivered. I knew.

"We had more calls than we could handle, all weekend. I musta worked sixteen hours on Sunday. But I had to come up, as soon as I heard. My dad's filling in for me now."

If I'd had any lingering doubts whether Brad Larson had killed his not-yet-ex-wife, the woman he admitted loved him less than he loved her, the woman who left him to reclaim her past, he'd just given me the alibi that washed those doubts away.

We sipped in silence for a moment or two, then I asked if he knew whether Merrily had been ordered to pay restitution twenty years ago.

"Court fines. And she paid every penny out of her own salary—she took nothing from me."

"When did you last talk to her?"

He squinted, thinking. "About two weeks ago. She called me. She had questions about some vendors."

"Why call you?"

"I run a plumbing company. I know all the suppliers in this part of the country. She'd found invoices for names she didn't recognize—not all plumbing companies, but a few."

I reached over the counter for a pen and the yellow pad my mother uses for notes when she's cooking.

"Write them down," I instructed. "Every name you remember."

The dead can't answer questions, but the living can.

Twenty-Two

After Tracy and Lou Mary left, my mother emerged from her Merc's basement refuge, an *I'm not done talking with you* look on her face.

A knock on the front door saved me. I hustled to open it, ignoring my strain-shmain.

My hands shook as I fumbled with the catch on the antique brass lock. I hated disappointing my mother. And facing my sister wasn't going to be any easier.

Chiara entered, swaddled in an ancient wool cape, Landon and Jason in her wake. Ever-intuitive, she sized up the situation in a glance, but before she could open her mouth, Landon piped up.

"Auntie, Mommy says I upset you and I have to apologize I'm sorry I learned a new song to cheer you up." No breath, no pauses, no hesitation. "*On the first day of Christmas, my tulip gave to me ...*"

My mother slipped her arm around my waist.

Sometimes a Christmas carol is all it takes to mend a breach.

While my mother and sister reveled in Landon's Christmas spirit, I led Jason into the back hall and handed him Brad Larson's list. The light in the hall isn't that great, and he adjusted his rimless glasses. He read it twice.

"Where did you get this?"

I explained.

He gestured with the list. "If Merrily was making up invoices for suppliers that sounded like the actual companies, a word off or some other tiny difference, why would she call him?"

"Exactly."

"They installed a new system right about the time Merrily came. I haven't been able to search back further, to see when these invoices were created. They have a backup, but the old programs aren't installed on the new machines. So I've got to get the programs, install them, and run a check."

"If it wasn't Merrily, then somebody wants us to think it was her. Cary Lenhardt? But why?" Bello had said they were watching him, but they hadn't made an arrest. Would this list convince him?

"There's another option," Jason said, his face grim.

"No. Not Greg. Why would he steal from his own company? And kill to cover it up?"

"He doesn't own the Building Supply."

"Not even a percentage?" That shouldn't have surprised me. I didn't have a share in the Merc, officially. My mother owns building and business. But I'd only been running the place a year and a half. Greg had managed the Building Supply for ages.

"So he—whoever—could have been using these fraudulent accounts to siphon off money for years," I said, and Jason nodded. "How long will it take to check the backups?"

"Twenty-four hours, maybe forty-eight."

Which didn't give me long. But it might be long enough.

∞

"You scared her," Adam said. "It's not about protecting Sally. Your mother over-reacted to your accident because that's how she lost your father. Doesn't matter how much time passes or how happy she is with Bill. That wound will never fully heal."

"I know that. And I will always be her baby." I reached for a pre-dinner cookie, one of the privileges of adulthood, then put my feet on the coffee table, another privilege. Sandburg settled in next to me. "And she's super emotional about me right now because of the wedding. By the way, Heidi wants us to pick out a few new things for the gift registry."

"I haven't tried those yet." He pointed at the cookie tray, and I threw him a bourbon ball.

"Good arm," he said. "So, what's the problem with the registry?"

"First someone from Minnesota splurged on us. Then someone else called and bought up the rest of the list. We know it's not Tanner. Your brothers?"

He sank into the brown leather chair, mouth hanging open. "What are they up to?"

"Being nice? Making up for your childhood?"

"I suppose." He gave out a half laugh. "But they're up to something."

Another pleasure of adulthood is eating dinner in the living room when you've pushed yourself too hard and your ankle is swollen and your ego dented. Adam, bless the man, said nothing about my aches and pains. He kept my wineglass full, tossed a salad, and cooked up the pasta I'd brought home, served with my mother's basil pesto. (*The taste of summer*, the label proclaimed, and I agreed.)

We were just finishing the pasta when Nick called Adam's phone and asked for me.

"Hey, sis. Your phone's not working."

"I know. But getting a new one means making a trip to Pondera, and no one will lend me a car. Or the money. Though we kept Mom's landline; you could have called that." Adam had promised to take me to the phone store in Pondera Saturday "if necessary."

It was definitely necessary.

"Hey, sorry I let you down about the building. But I called to make you an offer you can't refuse."

"I'm all ears."

"Christine's SUV is still sitting at my house. Consider it a wedding present."

In the background, a woman spoke, but I couldn't make out Nick's response. Like he'd covered the receiver with his hand. Who was it? Where was he?

"Seriously, Nick? That would be great." Bittersweet—I'd loved Christine, and I'd loved my Subaru—but great.

"You can have the keys and the title next week."

"Ha. Part of Mom's conspiracy to keep me on the couch."

He didn't deny it, though he claimed the vehicle needed a mechanic's once-over first.

That voice in the background piped up again, and this time I recognized it.

"Gotta go, sis." Nick hung up before I could say another word.

"My brother's giving us a car. Can you believe that?" I set the phone on the coffee table. "Hey, have you heard, is Nick dating anyone?"

Adam stood and picked up my plate. "Not that I've asked, but I kinda thought he and Kim ... Not from anything specific, but they give off that vibe."

"What? And you never said?"

"I don't share every passing thought," he said, his tone teasing, and headed for the kitchen.

"That one's kind of important, don't you think?" I called after him.

"Not our business," he called back.

I grunted. That never stopped me.

But the conversation did prick my conscience. When Adam came back, I pulled him down on to the couch next to me and showed him the spreadsheet. "I started it the other night when you were out. It's how I organize my investigations."

He studied it, scrolling up and down and all around. "Do the cops know about this?"

"No."

"You might want to tell them, little darlin'. Because it's brilliant."

Would I never learn? There was no reason to hide the truth from this guy. He was on my side. I promised to stay put while Adam went downstairs to hook up the TV. Going wireless involves a lot of cables.

"What do you think, Sandy?" I asked my feline consultant. I'd started today convinced Merrily was innocent of both the new crime and the old, then wavered. "How do the two thefts relate to Merrily's murder?"

As for Cary Lenhardt and Greg Taylor, you couldn't investigate embezzlement without considering everyone who had access to the money—or the computers that track it.

They run our lives, those things. God help us if they turn on us.

In a way, they had. Not on me, but on the thief—who might also be the killer. That's why I'd been run off the road, and why I'd warned Jason.

And why Detective Bello thought killer and thief one and the same, and that "the one" might be Greg. Just because I didn't want to believe it didn't mean it wasn't true. I added my questions to the spreadsheet.

Those fraudulent invoices might be the key. They'd led Merrily Thornton to call Brad and ask if he recognized the suppliers' names. They'd sent the forensic accountant to the bank, where Pamela Barber and her staff were sniffing their own records for the stink of fraud.

Greg was hiding something. But I still couldn't believe he would steal or kill. Unless he had some addiction I didn't know about. Gambling and drugs can turn an otherwise law-abiding citizen into a rabid rat in search of free money.

I replayed my mental audio files of every conversation I'd had about the murder and the thefts the last few days. No one had said anything about drugs.

No. But Kathy Jensen *had* said Holly Thornton was a wild child who straightened out the moment Merrily pled guilty.

I've watched a lot of old movies, late at night. That's my only excuse for my next thought: "The plot thickens."

Adam's phone lay on the table. I called my brother back, not at all sure he'd pick up. But he did.

"Hey, Nick, indulge me in a bit of time-travel. In high school, did you ever hear that Merrily Thornton used or sold drugs? Used regularly, I mean—not pot or an experiment or two."

The line was quiet for a moment. "As in, that's why she needed the money?" he said.

"Yeah."

Another silence.

"Nick, you still there?"

"Yeah. No. It never made any sense. Holly, on the other hand…" He hesitated, as if deciding what to say. "You're too young to have known, but there was a group of kids—"

"There's always a group of kids," I interrupted. "In every class. Since Grog and Grunt first sniffed glue from the hoof of a wooly mammoth."

"I guess. But these kids were my friends. We used to hang out, play music, goof off. And yeah, smoke a joint or two. But then some of them got deeper into the drugs, and the group split up. After that, I stuck with my crowd—the science geeks and hiking nerds—and I didn't see much of them outside of school."

"Including Holly and Merrily Thornton?"

"Not Merrily," he said quickly. "She stayed straight. But Holly and a few others went after the drugs pretty hard."

"Who else? Names, Nick."

"Greg Taylor."

I felt a chill, afraid I knew the answer to my next question before it left my lips. "Where did you hang out?"

"The schoolhouse at the Thorntons' place."

My heart sank. "Thanks, brother," I said. "And tell Kim I said hi."

Twenty-Three

With December so busy, I'd been tempted to cancel the usual Friday-morning meeting of the Village Merchants' Association. I was so not in the mood for a gripe-and-groan session about parking, snow removal, and absent merchants who didn't do enough to promote the community. Since I'd taken over, I'd worked hard to keep us on target and on time, and a certain amount of air-clearing is inevitable, but some people grind the same ax over and over.

I grabbed a cup of coffee and an apple turnover from the mini buffet inside Ray's back dining room and sat at the end of the long table, my sister on one side and April on the other.

"How you doin'?" I said around a mouth full of fruit and pastry.

"I am so fat," Chiara said. "I have been pregnant for fourteen months."

"At least you're not an elephant," I said. "They're preggers for two years."

She shot me a look as dark as the deepest jungle.

"Any luck with my bag?" I asked April.

"Not yet. I might need to send it to a professional cleaner."

Uggh. "My car got totaled and my phone's a goner, so fingers crossed that we can salvage something."

"Welcome to the Bayside Grille." Ray stood, his white T-shirt blindingly bright. "First, I can't thank you enough for the Yelp campaign. The Grille's ratings are better than ever. Yesterday, we sold more Reubens than anything else on the menu, and I'm baking extra bread and cooking up more kraut for the weekend."

"Great," someone said. "The whole town will smell like rotten cabbage." But it was said with a laugh, and we all joined in.

My turn. Small group today, about fifteen. "Thanks, Ray. That illustrates how we can help each other, honestly, with immediate results. Not much to discuss this morning. Decorating Day went smoothly, and the town is sparkling like a true gem."

"When is Undecorating Day?" Ray asked.

I spread my hands. "Can't tell you—my calendar's on my phone, and it died in my accident."

"Better it than you," he replied, and others murmured agreement.

"January twentieth," Heidi said, glancing up from her iPad. "You'll be on your honeymoon, you lucky girl."

"Now that's pushing things a bit far, ain't it?" Ned asked. "Planning a wedding so you don't have to take down your lights and bows yourself."

I felt myself blush. One more thing to add to the procedures manual.

"Our ad ran in the regional newspapers last Sunday," I said, my face still hot, "and the follow-up is scheduled for the next two weekends. At the Merc, we offered a free jar of jam with a fifty-dollar purchase, and traffic is definitely up."

We talked for a few minutes about the ad and the responses to the trip starters and other promotions merchants were running. Sally tried

197

twice to complain about the size and placement of her ad, but Kathy shushed her and we stayed on track.

One more item on my agenda. "A curious thing happened after the Art Walk," I said, and told them about the cash and note left at our back door. "Any theories?"

All down the table, frowns and shaking heads.

"You expect a certain amount of shoplifting," Heidi said. "And I've had people try to return things I'd swear they stole to get the cash. But nothing like you described."

"A scam of some kind?" another merchant asked, but no one could figure out what it might be. "Could it have been Merrily? Although I agree, the note sounds like a kid."

"Speaking of theft," the manager of the rental cottages by the bay said, "and Merrily Thornton, can you believe what happened at the Building Supply?"

"He never should have hired her," one of the real estate agents said. "I saw him at the grade school basketball tournament last Saturday, after we finished up downtown. Nice guy. I can imagine him angry, but not enough to kill."

He was clearly Greg Taylor.

"If not him, then who?" the cottage manager said. "There's a killer among us, and I'm telling guests to lock their doors until he's caught. I'm not shopping at the Building Supply until then, either."

Ouch. Though, I had to admit, it was a natural reaction.

The shift in the conversation signaled an end to the meeting, and we all drained our coffee and pushed back our chairs.

"Come over and update the registry soon," Heidi said. "I'm getting calls for gifts and I have nothing left to suggest."

"I wanted to wait for Adam."

She rolled her eyes, and I promised to come over after we opened.

I hobbled out behind Chiara and April and tossed a five in the stainless-steel bowl to cover the coffee and pastry. I might have let Ray buy my lunch the other day, but he didn't have to buy my breakfast, too.

∞

Nothing like butter and sugar to soothe one's aches and pains. Upstairs in my office, I counted out the till, then scanned the inventory and vendor list.

"Criminy. Why didn't I think of him sooner?" I asked the walls. They didn't answer, thank goodness.

Like a lot of people in the valley, Jimmy Vang makes a living with a little of this and a little of that. In season, he forages, like others in the Hmong community—he has a nose for tender nettles and a knack for finding morels. But in the off season, he often picks up work as a handyman. I called and left a message about my sad soffit.

As soon as Tracy and Lou Mary arrived and we'd flipped the sign to OPEN, I crossed the street to Kitchenalia. Our gift list didn't say who'd bought what—gifts are meant to be surprises, after all—but it did show me that our family and friends were generous, and that I'd be roping my honey into writing his share of the thank-you notes.

While Heidi helped a customer, I found a heavy pan perfect for Adam's lasagna. With Le Panier right next door, I don't bake much bread, but every kitchen needs loaf pans and muffin tins, and they matched the lasagna pan. Plus a springform pan might entice me to make cheesecake more than once a year.

"Here you go." Heidi placed an exquisitely wrapped box on the counter, then reached for a shopping bag emblazoned with a big *K* shaped from a spoon and two forks.

"Oh, no bag," the customer, a man in his fifties, protested. "Your bags are too nice." She ignored him and slipped the box inside. When he tried to refuse his credit card receipt, too, she tucked it in the bag and handed him the package with her trademark brilliant smile.

The door closed behind him and our eyes met. "Men," she said. "Skip the receipt and bag and he might not remember where this fabulous gift came from!"

"Speaking of men, what's your take on Walt Thornton? He's so protective. Is Taya really such a fragile flower?"

She poured herself a fresh cup of coffee from the urn she keeps full for customers and gestured toward me. I held up a hand. Caffeine had been adding to my post-accident jitters, an unfortunate side effect I hoped would fade with my bruises.

"Opposites can make a great match. Taya is as protective of Walt as he is of her." She told me about Walt's battle with diabetes and the neuropathy that had left him barely able to walk. To get him off insulin, Taya had trained a hawk's eye on every bite he ate, walking him around the village twice a day, even getting him in to see Bill for acupuncture and other treatment. And it had worked. I'd seen Walt bounce around the barn at the Lodge like a kid, petting his oversized Christmas treasures.

"And I thought she was just a hypochondriac, always acting like you're sneezing on purpose to infect her," I said.

"Oh, she is a paranoid hypochondriac," Heidi said. "But she's putting it to good use." She printed out the additions we'd made to the registry, and I thanked her for both the gift guidance and the town talk.

Outside, I squeezed between a Cadillac SUV and a Prius, and crossed the street to the Merc.

Tracy and Lou Mary stood by the meat cooler, talking intently in low tones.

"What's up?" I asked, and they flew apart like I'd thrown a fire-cracker between them.

"Just chatting about cheese." Lou Mary's cheeks flushed a lovely peach. They matched the silk scarf tucked into the upturned collar of her loose-cut chocolate-brown blouse.

"Right." My two professional and trustworthy clerks looked like kids who'd been caught snooping in Santa's workshop. But it was the time of year for secrets, so I let it go.

Ten days to Christmas. I rubbed my lucky stars. This should be our busiest weekend. We had quite a few last-minute orders, so I headed downstairs. Now more than ever, I wished we had a better location for the shipping station, but I gritted my teeth and gripped the stair rail.

Boxes packed, I stuck out my lower lip. How was I going to get them to the post office? I dragged myself upstairs, then snuck out the back and into Red's Bar through the courtyard.

Five minutes later, I had the keys to Ned's truck, and his promise to never breathe a word to my mother. "Lie to my landlord?" he'd said, but his eyes had sparkled like the tiny white lights in my shop window.

Twenty-Four

While I had wheels, and enough sugar on board for courage, I decided to sneak in another stop.

One look at the object hanging from the chain around Holly Thornton Muir's neck, and I knew I'd figured right.

She slipped it back inside the vee neck of her tunic. "Erin, thank you for comforting my mother at the schoolhouse the other day. This has been a rough time for her."

"For you, too, imagine."

Her lips quivered and she touched a finger to the corner of one blue eye.

"Brave of you to stay in touch," I continued, "after your parents cut Merrily off. And to give her a temporary job."

The muscles in her jaw moved and she breathed out heavily through her nose before changing the subject with a lightness that didn't reach her eyes. "So Miss Pumpkin is still aptly named?"

"Sorry to say, yes, though the low-carb food you suggested has made a difference." I wasn't worried about the cat's weight, now that she had another cat to chase her, and a human who didn't let her eat all the oil-packed tuna she wanted. Although I did occasionally let her lick my yogurt bowl. But I'd bluffed my way past the receptionist by saying I was passing by and had a quick question about Pumpkin's weight, so I kept up the charade.

"You might try another brand." She slid behind her desk and dug a small pad out of a pile of paper. Tried two pens, tossed them aside, then found one that worked. Scribbled a note and handed it to me. "Try her on this—the pet shop in Pondera carries it. If she's still tipping the scales in a month, we'll check her A-1C, and look at other options."

For a fat cat? "What other options? And what's an A-1—what did you call it? The only A.1. I know is steak sauce."

"A-1C. It's the primary test for diabetes. We do put cats on insulin, although I'm out right now." She gestured toward a cabinet along one wall, bottles and vials of drugs visible behind the thick glass. "But diet and exercise is the best method, like with humans."

She stood, but I wasn't done. "Your pendant," I said. "It's your talisman, the way an ex-drinker keeps a token from AA in his pocket. Or a woman uses a Weight Watchers' key ring to remind her that being watchful is key to keeping the pounds off."

In another room, a patient barked. Holly studied me, wordless.

"Your sister kept one of those tokens from the old movie theater in a cigar box in her desk," I went on. "Your crowd in high school used them to send messages to each other, to meet at the usual place." A secret code had sounded so cool—I'd filched my brother's token eons ago.

She just blinked. "Lots of people kept those tokens. The Bijou handed them out for decades."

"But you carry yours around your neck. To remind you what your sister did for you."

Holly's gaze drifted away, the tip of her tongue slipping out between her lips, like a cat's. "She gave me back the life I nearly threw away. I owe all this to her."

"Juvenile convictions wouldn't have kept you out of vet school, but if you'd stayed on that path ..."

"Then I'd have been the one in prison. Sometimes I think I should have been." She perched on the edge of her desk, her small fingers pulling out the chain and working the token. "It wasn't just drugs. I was the youngest in the group, the sweet-faced kid who could pocket packages of Sudafed without being noticed. The boys cooked meth in an old shed on the back of my parents' property, past the schoolhouse. Mom and Dad never went down there. They had no idea."

Meth? "And Merrily? Was she involved, too?" Nick had said she wasn't, but I wanted Holly's confirmation.

"No. Funny thing is, it was her crowd to start with. She and Greg Taylor, your brother, Anne Christopherson, a few others. All good kids who might spike a bottle of Hawaiian punch with vodka or pour rum in their Coke cans. They played guitars and sang along with CDs, passing the same joint around all night, pairing off to make out in the teacher's apartment in back."

"And Greg?" I had to ask.

"Start of sophomore year, a couple of older guys started hanging out with the group. They were pretty hard-core. I never knew what drew them to us, except maybe to take advantage of us. And I gave them access to the shed. My sister tried to stop me, but I wasn't having any of it. She and I fought a lot that year, always about the drugs and my 'bad crowd.'" She wrapped her arms around herself, remembering. "And about Greg."

"He was Merrily's boyfriend, right? How did she feel about his drug use?"

"She hated it. He was torn. He liked the excitement, the feeling that we were daring to do what other people never would. We were brave. We were bad. And that was good."

"You said he was torn," I prompted.

"Greg is not bad. He isn't even all that brave," she said wryly. "And he was crazy about my sister, even after she broke up with him."

A mental slide show began flashing through my mind. PowerPoint brain. Greg's insistence that Merrily would not harm anyone. His visible pain at the thought of her betrayal, and the terror in his voice when he called to say he'd found her in the schoolhouse. The place they'd both loved. The place forever associated with her.

What had he said? Something about no one trusting him anymore. So teenage drug use was what he hadn't wanted the police, or anyone else, to know. Or had he been involved in the dirty work?

"She didn't come back here to pick up with him, did she?"

"No, he's happily married. But he was afraid of what she would say. That's why he killed her."

"What? Because he used drugs twenty years ago? Had a kid he didn't know about? That's not so bad." Unless you accepted Walt and Taya's worldview. "Oh. Are you saying he doesn't know he's Ashley's father?"

Holly bit her lip. "I don't think he does. But either way, it all comes back to Cliff Grimes. He figured out that I was 'the blond bandit,' as the newspaper called me. I never looked like a meth-head—no one would have suspected, if he hadn't seen me."

"Seen you where?"

"In Pondera, doing a drug deal in a sleazy bar. It was right when news of the embezzlement broke. Cliff tried to leave the country, but he got caught."

"So he blackmailed Merrily to take the fall for his schemes. By threatening to expose you." The creep, the absolute creep. How could anyone do that to a teenage girl, especially a man with a daughter of his own? My throat ached with sympathy for Merrily and Sally.

"I couldn't let my parents find out," Holly said. "They'd have never forgiven me."

That, I believed. Their self-righteousness had been a heavy burden on both their daughters.

"They don't know what Grimes did, do they? You kept your position in the family and let her take the blame."

"No. No, it wasn't like that, Erin, I swear." Holly pushed herself off the desk, her hands in fists, ready to plead or fight. "I thought what everyone thought—that my sister stole from our mother's best friend. I didn't find out the truth until we reconnected in Billings. I forced it out of her. I begged my parents then to change their minds..."

"But they wouldn't relent," I said.

"My father's always been a softie when it came to his girls. But he wouldn't stand up to my mother. He wouldn't push her to take Merrily back into the family."

"Not even when you told her about Ashley?"

Holly shook her head. "Ashley would always have reminded her of Merrily's sins. Remember, she thought Cliff Grimes was the father. We all did."

"And they blamed the teenager, not the man old enough to have been her own father?"

She shrugged. Of course. If your view of the world was black-and-white, it was all too easy to see a pretty young girl as a seductress, instead of a fully grown man as a manipulative slime-ball.

Careful, Erin. Your own self-righteousness is showing.

"Do you know anything about the embezzlement at the Building Supply? That may be what got your sister killed," I said.

206

"No, I don't," Holly replied, her eyes wet, her whole body shaking. "What are you going to do?"

Well, I wasn't going to slap her for her foolishness, though I wanted to. At least she'd tried to persuade her parents, though the task rivaled that of Sisyphus, the mythic Greek doomed to keep pushing a rock uphill no matter how often it rolled back down. "I'll keep asking questions. Make sure Brad and Greg know the truth, and urge them to tell Ashley everything. But that's their decision, not mine."

On my way out, I spotted the box of Christmas decorations sitting outside the front door. Jack Muir, in a short-sleeved blue tunic like his wife's, leaned a ladder against the building.

"Kinda late, I know." He gestured to the box and the heap of lights on the sidewalk. A too-small wreath hung on the door, decorated with plastic dogs and cats and topped with a crooked red bow that resisted my efforts to straighten it.

"I'm sure your in-laws would be happy to help," I said, but the look on his face said he doubted it.

Twenty-Five

I drove past the turnoff to the sheriff's office. I needed to tell Detective Bello what I'd learned, but the facts were still sorting themselves out in my brain. And I had to get my customers' packages in the mail.

P.O. first, I decided, *then pee-oh the detective.*

The Thorntons' view of love and loyalty looked seriously skewed to me. Sure, bad choices are scary, and they upend hopes and dreams. But aren't we meant to help those we love change their ways and live their best lives?

Not if they don't want to.

But who doesn't want to? What kind of person chooses a gulf—a canyon, a breach—over a bridge? What kind of parent?

Just before the bridge over the place where Jewel Bay meets Eagle Lake, I turned right. My heart ached for all the loss and pain in this precious corner of the world.

I steered into the post office parking lot, wondering how Sally had ever fallen for a scumbag like Cliff Grimes. Smart women, bad choices—happens every day.

I parked Ned's big, dark truck next to one much like it, and opened the door. I swung my left foot out, but the truck was higher than I was used to and I half stepped, half slipped toward the ground.

"Ye-owww!" Pain tore up my tender ankle. I screeched like a wounded cat, grabbing the inside door handle to catch myself. After a long moment, my breath, ragged with pain, returned to normal, and I pulled myself up, looking through the driver's side window to the truck parked next to me.

In a flash, I was back on the highway from Pondera to Jewel Bay, the too-bright headlights too close behind me. And then the metallic scrape of the side of the truck along my door, the panic in my throat as my car left the road, as it slid into the ice-filled ditch, as I fought to gain control, to keep the car right-side up. As I struggled, and lost.

Breathless, I shut my eyes. Told myself it was my imagination, triggered by the sudden flash of pain.

And then I saw—really saw—the passenger-side door of the other truck.

Long, deep scratches ran across the door and back panel, almost to the wheel well. The truck was newly washed, despite the frigid temperatures, and that alone made it stand out. But when I stepped away from the safety of Ned's truck and looked closer, I detected bits of sage green paint.

My guts cramped like someone had wrapped baling twine around them.

The electric door to the post office opened and I raised my head at the sound of footsteps pounding on the pavement. A woman I'd seen around town but didn't know stalked toward me, her cheeks flushed, her jaw clenched. The red-orange Coach bag she gripped looked genuine.

No, not toward me. Toward the truck next to mine. As she neared, I could hear her muttering sounds of fury signifying—what? And who was she? Why would she have driven me off the road?

The woman noticed me standing between our nearly identical trucks. "At least you don't seem to mind driving a big old tub. My husband took my Volvo in for service and sold it. Too bad he didn't sell this dented piece of garbage instead."

I couldn't form an answer. She climbed in and started the engine. I flattened myself against Ned's truck as she zoomed away, barely glancing at traffic.

I watched her go, trying to steady my pounding heart long enough to get the plate number, but she was moving too fast. A basic Montana plate, deep blue with the numbers and outline of the state in reflective white. Same as the witness had seen the other night. With so many specialty plates—more than a hundred, fundraisers for organizations from Spay and Neuter to the University alumni association—the basic blue weren't everywhere, but they weren't scarce, either.

I caught my breath and dragged myself inside.

You can feel sometimes, when you walk into a place, that there's just been an incident. Liz says it's a disruption of the flow of energy a space holds, a principle of feng shui. I doubt anyone's ever feng shui'd a post office, except maybe in Hong Kong or parts of California, but it was clear that there had been a disturbance in the Force here.

Another customer held the door for me as I lugged in my first tub of packages, a bemused look on her face. As I approached the counter, Rosemary, my favorite clerk, called to me, "I can help you, Erin."

I bent down to pick up an envelope lying on the floor. Turned it over as I straightened. Addressed to *Cary and Marla Lenhardt*, and to the left, in red, *PAST DUE*.

"Someone dropped this," I said and handed it to Rosemary.

"After all that commotion," Rosemary quietly said to the other clerk, turning to place the envelope with a few others behind the counter, "Marla Lenhardt dropped half her mail. As if her bills were our fault."

"Sure," the other woman replied in an equally low voice. I held my breath to catch her words. "She wouldn't owe anybody any money if we didn't deliver them."

Rosemary huffed a small laugh and turned back to my tub of packages as the pixels jumping around on my mental screen slid into place, and the picture became more clear.

∞

"So, I know you've been checking out everybody in the bank and the Building Supply, including Cary Lenhardt. Once Jason hacks into the old computer system, I'm sure you'll find Lenhardt's been using phony invoices and fraudulent bank accounts to siphon off money for years, so he could live above his means. That list"—I gestured to the list Brad Larson had made, now on Detective Bello's desk—"clinches it. The closer Merrily came to the truth, the more desperate Lenhardt got, selling off his toys and his wife's fancy car. I'm sure that's who Ned Redaway bought his new RV from. From his wife's reaction to the past due notices, I suspect she didn't know what he was up to. But Merrily did, and he had to silence her."

Bello listened without comment, sucking away on another of those miniature candy canes.

"And from the damaged truck, we can guess he wanted to keep me quiet," I continued. "Which means Jason and the forensic accountant might be at risk, too. And maybe Greg Taylor."

I'd rushed over to the sheriff's office as soon as my packages were safely in the mail, actually eager to see Bello. He knew some of the financial details already, but what I'd learned might give him enough evidence to prove that Cary Lenhardt not only stole money from the Building Supply for years, but had also run me off the road and killed Merrily Thornton.

My tale finished, I sat back in the vinyl chair, feeling pounds lighter. Merrily and Greg weren't thieves. Greg wasn't a killer.

Bello was quiet. "That explains a lot," he finally said, taking the candy cane out of his mouth. "And it's good work. But Lenhardt's not the killer."

"What?" I sat up fast. "How do you know? Who is?"

"Medical examiner's report came back. Time of death isn't easy to determine, given that the body was found in winter in an unheated building, but he's pretty certain that Merrily Thornton died between twelve and three Sunday afternoon."

Exactly when she should have been at my house, or on her way. I was right. The cookies proved it.

"Cary Lenhardt coaches the sixth-grade boys' basketball team. They were in Pondera for the annual holiday tournament last weekend. He was there the whole time. We have eyewitnesses and photos."

"Greg Taylor's son is on that team, isn't he?"

Bello nodded slowly. "According to everyone I've talked with, Greg Taylor missed the first half of Sunday's afternoon game."

And for that, I had no explanation. Only deep, deep sadness.

∞

"Third time this week," the cashier at the Building Supply said with a smart-aleck grin. *Judy?* That didn't sound right. "The joys of home

212

ownership, huh? Though I'm glad to see you. Things have been so quiet, I'm afraid people are taking their business elsewhere. With all the talk, you know."

I knew. "Sorry to hear that."

She lowered her voice. "I'd quit in a minute if I thought Greg Taylor was a killer. I'm glad you're investigating."

"Thanks. Your daughter home for break yet?"

Her eyes lit up, then turned sad as she spoke. "She'll be home this afternoon. I didn't know she was planning to give Ashley a ride up here to spend Christmas break with her mom. Ashley's coming anyway, since her father's here."

Both fathers, though she didn't know that yet.

"That's great. Your daughter will have company on the drive, and Ashley will have a friend while she's here." Time to clear up the matter of the cash in the cigar box. "Hey, last Saturday, did Merrily come back in later?"

"Not that I saw, and I was right here all day."

Merrily hadn't come back to hide the stolen cash in her cigar box. So how had it gotten there? Maybe Lenhardt had snuck the money out of the bag to cast suspicion on her, then snuck it into the cigar box Monday morning, when her absence gave him the opportunity.

That would explain what had bothered me. If a woman kept her daughter's picture in a keepsake box, it would be on top where she could see it, not hidden by a dirty wad of bills.

"I still can't believe it," the cashier continued, and I racked my brain for her name. *Not Judy, and not Julie* ... "So hopeful when she walked out of here, and I never saw her again. Stinks."

"That it does." I paused. "Greg in?"

"No. He's meeting a contractor on a job site, working up a materials estimate. Not sure when he'll be back."

Well, pooh.

Which meant it was back to minding my own business.

∞

It's Christmas-time in the village.

That's not the way the song goes, but you couldn't persuade me otherwise—not with every parking spot full.

A few of my neighbor merchants like to gripe about parking, and I've certainly felt the flush of annoyance on summer days when I've been forced to circle through our one-lane village, eyes peeled—days when even the secret spaces only the locals know were occupied.

My poor car. Though I was grateful for Nick's generosity, I doubted I'd love the new rig like I had the Subaru. The first car I'd chosen myself, it had shuttled me safely all around the Northwest for years.

I slowed and turned into Back Alley a second time. Truth is, a village wants a parking problem. It signifies busy sidewalks and shoppers searching for treasures.

Delivery trucks aren't supposed to block traffic or parking spaces, but it happens from time to time. One August morning before our annual art and food festival, a beer truck driver ignored the No Access signs, and while he was unloading cases at Red's, vendors started setting up their booths at the intersection of Back and Front. He was trapped. I hope he enjoyed himself at the festival, because it was probably his last day on the job.

Finally, I scored a space wide enough for Ned's pickup. Got out carefully, remembering the jolt on my ankle an hour ago, and pocketed the keys.

Three steps inside the Merc's back door, I could tell we were hopping. I detoured to the office and called Wendy to order three Caprese panini.

The Holidaze were in full swing. Lunch was on me.

I changed into dry shoes, swapped my coat and gloves for an apron, and joined my staff on the shop floor. Behind the chocolate counter, Tracy chatted up three customers at a time, talking flavors and nuts and cocoa solids while filling boxes with truffles.

At the cash register, Lou Mary had a line of her own.

I threw them each a happy smile they were too busy to catch, and made for the meat cooler, where a couple were debating options. "The beef is raised a few miles north of town," I said. "Grass-fed, organic, no hormones. Same with the pork, though it comes from south of town."

"And the chicken?" the woman asked.

"East." I helped them pick a few cuts and took their order for a Christmas turkey. Then it was on to a customer filling her shopping basket with jams and jellies as gifts for her office staff. Two younger women, one with a baby cradled in a cloth carrier, were testing Luci's lotions, and as I answered their questions, I made a mental note to suggest a line of baby products.

And so it went. Village retail is a low-tech, high-touch business. I sent Tracy next door to pick up our sandwiches, and we took turns sitting at the counter to eat. The creamy mozzarella, ripe tomatoes, and spicy-green basil tasted like heaven on grilled bread.

Tracy popped open a Diet Coke and I looked at her in alarm. "What about Polka? Don't you need to run home and check on him?"

"No." Her eyes lit up. "Rick's here. He surprised me a day early."

Her boyfriend, Rick, traveled the state selling products from his family's grain business, Montana Gold. He'd tripled sales in less than two years, and I liked to think I'd had a hand in that—not because we were good customers, though we were, but because I'd convinced him that small markets like the Merc could play a big part in feeding our communities.

During the mid-afternoon lull, I limped upstairs for a breather. The updated gift registry lay where I'd tossed it earlier. I reached for my phone before remembering it didn't work. I sighed again. But I hated to buy a new one, if there was a chance the old one could be saved.

I made another call instead. Texting is so easy. But with only the Merc's landline, I had to do things the old-fashioned way.

Tanner answered on the first ring. I'd finally met Adam's childhood sidekick this past summer, when he came out to meet me and ask Adam for a very big favor. Since then, I'd served as an informal business consultant for his sustainable active wear company, and we chatted briefly about an equipment upgrade he was considering.

Business done, I dove in to the personal stuff. "What's the story with Adam's brothers? He always calls them Cain and Abel, but that's a joke, right? I mean, they run a business together."

"Think Fred and George Weasley in Slytherin instead of Gryffindor. Though without the wizarding cloaks. They've grown out of the worst of it. Mostly."

That made the point. I wriggled in my chair, stretching out a sore hip. "I can't believe we're using Hogwarts dorms as family metaphors."

Far away in Minnesota, Tanner snorted. "When we were in grade school, Z and I fantasized that we were real brothers who get left on the wrong doorsteps. Major stork screw-up. I don't have any sibs, but—well, you've seen pictures, right? As soon as we learned about genetics, we saw the flaw in our theory. The Zimmerman boys are all peas in a pod."

We signed off and I returned to my Spreadsheet of Suspicion. The mystery of the theft at the Building Supply was solved, in my mind, but a murderer was still loose. In the list of suspects, I wrote in Cary Lenhardt's name for my attacker, then struck it out as the killer. I'd already eliminated Brad Larson, so that left me with Greg, Walt, and Taya.

Heidi had said the Thorntons would do anything for each other. Did she mean that literally? Even kill? I couldn't believe it. If Merrily going to prison shamed Taya enough to shun her, surely she would never do anything that might land her in prison herself.

But we all have our breaking points, the things we simply can't see logically.

I switched screens to update the Merc's social media. Added a few new holiday photos of the shop and updated the Merchants' Association accounts as well.

As I scrolled through my feed, pics from the grade-school basketball tournament popped up. There was Holly Muir on Saturday, cheering on the fourth graders. She wore a puffy coat like Merrily's, although hers was black, and a pair of those same super-cute red-and-black plaid gloves. Merrily had said they were a gift—from Holly?

The image of Merrily lying on the schoolhouse floor came into my head. No blood, no weapon. How had she been killed?

I tried to push the image away, but something about it called to me. As if Merrily herself were asking me to find her killer.

Twenty-Six

The Merc. This is Erin," I said into the shop phone.

"Darling, family dinner tonight, your house," my mother said. "I'll bring dessert."

"At your service." What else could I say? A mother retains lifelong rights to invite herself over for dinner, even after she sells her kid the house.

We were a few minutes from closing, so I had just enough time to pick up the liqueur Mom had asked for. When I reached the shop floor, Tracy and Lou Mary were behind the chocolate counter, working and chatting.

At my approach, Tracy slid the small chalkboard with today's truffle menu across the counter, blocking my view.

"What are two you up to?" I said.

"Nothing," they replied in unison.

I flicked my eyes from one employee to the other. "Ri-i-ight. Hey, I've got an errand to run, but I should be back before Adam gets here to pick me up."

In the liquor store, Greg Taylor stood in the far aisle, a large bottle of Bombay Sapphire gin in one hand.

"Hey," I said, and he jerked his head toward me, obviously startled.

"Hey—Erin." He waved his empty hand toward the colorful bottles on the shelf. "You know about these fancy drinks, don't you? I need something for my wife."

"Better to ask your sister, not me. What does she like?"

"Sweet things."

"How about a sparkling wine? A rosé cava would be nice. Celebrating?" I barely knew the woman, and I wondered what she had thought about Greg hiring Merrily. And what she would think when she found out about Ashley.

"Not exactly." He drew the words out.

Oh. So this needed to be a special gift, for a very serious conversation.

"Greg," I said quietly. "How long have you known you were Ashley's biological father?"

He exhaled slowly. "Merrily was holding the picture, the one in the frame, when I walked into the bookkeeping office about two weeks ago. She stuck it back in her desk like she hadn't wanted me to see it." He poked his tongue into his cheek and gave a slight shake of the head. "The picture bugged me. You know my family—we all look alike. The girl looked like Wendy, or how I think my daughter will look when she's a teenager."

He shifted his weight slightly, as if he felt boxed in. Good. That might keep him honest.

"After she was killed," Greg continued, "I had to get her personnel file for the cops. I found the forms designating the beneficiary of her life insurance policy, part of our benefits plan. It's supposed to be confidential—I'd never seen it. Her sole beneficiary was Ashley Larson, also known as Ashley Thornton. I counted back from the date of birth. It works. I have a daughter I didn't know about."

I'd guessed right, both about paternity and about the reason for the gift for his wife.

"Did you tell Bello?" I asked.

"Are you kidding? That will clinch it for him. He'll be convinced I killed Merrily to keep her quiet. That she was stealing to put pressure on me, get back child support—I don't know what else."

"You didn't know you were the girl's father before Merrily died."

"No," Greg said. "But I'd started to think I might be."

"A gift might help you break the news to your wife," I said, "but you're going to have to tell the detectives, too. And Ashley. She's on her way here, to join her father."

"Brad Larson may have raised her," Greg said swiftly, "but he couldn't have adopted her. I would not have given up my parental rights. If I'd known..." He trailed off.

I had no doubt that Brad viewed Ashley as his daughter, legally adopted or not.

"I never did believe Merrily stole Sally's money," Greg said. "But I'm having a hard time understanding why going to prison pregnant was better than telling me."

"I suspect that she believed her parents would have insisted she either get married or give the baby up. Despite all her plans for college and a career, she was willing to keep the truth from you so she could keep the baby. We may never know for sure."

But I did know she'd received a short sentence, allowing her to protect her sister from Cliff Grimes's threats and keep her baby with her. Though her actions had protected Greg, too, from both a high school marriage and criminal accusations for drug manufacturing.

"One more thing," I said. "Where were you Sunday afternoon? Not at the basketball tournament."

His cheeks pinked. He opened his mouth, but we were interrupted before he could speak.

"Hey, you two." Donna, the owner, bustled out of the back room. "Last call. Need any help?"

I stifled my usual reply—*No, thanks, I'm beyond help*—and grabbed a bottle of Grand Marnier from the shelf.

"Greg needs a gift to butter up his wife," I said, a playful tone in my voice. As if anything could ease the pain of telling her he had another child, one he hadn't known about.

∞

"That is one giant mound of tomatoes," Adam said as I chopped a fat red slicer from the winter greenhouse at Rainbow Lake Gardens. "What army is going to eat them all?"

"Mom said 'family dinner.' Your guess is as good as mine."

"She does remember that this is our house now, right?"

"Are we too close for you? My family, I mean?" A far cry from his—too far? "Could you please scrub those cucumbers? We need a green salad."

"No." He reached for the cuke. "About the family, I mean. Well, maybe. I like the Sunday-afternoon tradition, and you did the cookie party last Sunday. This month is messed up by the wedding and you working extra hours. But twice in one weekend is a bit much, as a regular thing. In the future, I'd like Friday nights to be ours."

"It's a date." I reached for another tomato. "Hey, I talked with Tanner today. He sounds great. Says his blood counts are good and he's got lots of energy. I'm eager to see him."

You can tell when someone's gone still, even without looking.

"Sometimes, I can't believe you love me." Adam's dark eyes filled, and he waved the cucumber at the kitchen we'd designed ourselves. "I can't believe all this is real."

"What?" I put down my knife and turned to him. "I am the luckiest girl alive. This smart, gorgeous, funny guy got a thing for me fifteen years ago, and gave me another chance."

"If you'd actually paid any attention to me back then, I'd have freaked out and run for the hills. You were so out of my league. You still are."

"Adam, no." I put one hand on his arm, the other on his chest. "I mean, it's sweet of you to say that, but I've never met anyone as strong and honest and loyal as you. You grew up with nothing, and look what you've made of yourself."

"Right," he said, in a sarcastic tone. "I'm so loyal, I didn't want my own brothers to come to our wedding."

"They're probably not going to put an M-80 in the toilet at the reception." Tanner had told me a few tales of the twins' boyhood pranks. The tomatoes done, I dug out the garlic press and a few cloves. "You left home at eighteen. You've changed. Sounds like they have, too."

"You asked if I think your family is too close. And no, I don't. I admire it. I see how you became who you are, because of them. But…" His voice trailed off. "Sometimes, I feel such a sense of loss when I see what you grew up with. And I wonder if I can be a decent husband, and a decent dad."

My eyes teared up. I felt a little selfish, not having grasped what he was feeling, and I took his hands. "Adam, you might doubt yourself, but I don't doubt you, not for one minute. I know the love and commitment in your heart from the way you treat me, and my family. And Tanner. That's proof enough."

222

I gazed up into those beautiful black-coffee eyes, capable of so much compassion, and my throat went dry. I could never find the words. Adam pulled me close and our arms wrapped around each other and our lips touched, deeply, there in the new-old kitchen that had served up so many meals, so many memories, and if the stars shone, would serve up many more.

"*Ciao, bella!*" my mother called from the front entry. "We're here!"

Adam ran his fingers over my bruised face. "Even with a black eye, you are the most beautiful woman I have ever known. And I will do everything I can to make you happy, always."

"Me, too," I whispered.

"Oh, we're intruding," my mother said from the kitchen door, a mischievous lilt in her voice.

"It is their house, my dear," Bill said, teasing.

Adam laughed. "Let me take that, Fresca." She handed him a tray with something wrapped in dish towels. Bill set a galvanized bucket filled with snow and bottles of white wine on the counter. My mother might send me to the liquor store for emergency after-dinner drinks to go with her dessert, but she chooses the wine herself.

Chiara and her family arrived just as we finished tossing the salad.

A few minutes later, I set a platter of shrimp Florentine over rotilli on the dining room table, next to a giant bowl of green salad. A pair of headlights caught my eye, winding up the long drive from the highway. *Not the sheriff*, I pleaded silently.

It was, and it wasn't. It was obvious the moment Kim stood in our doorway, Nick grinning behind her, that Sheriff's Detective Kim Caldwell was not here on official business. She scanned our faces with a tremulous smile, and I realized how intimidating we might seem, the extended Murphy clan seeing her not as my best friend, the girl they'd known since she and I were ten, or even as a deputy sheriff, but as Nick's girlfriend. As part of the family in a whole new way.

At least now I knew why Nick had been too busy to help me with the building.

Nick put a hand on the small of Kim's back and nudged her forward. I threw my arms around her, then him, and led them to the dining room.

My mother reached for the chair at one end of the table and Bill quietly said her name. She slipped into the chair he held out for her instead, leaving the end seats for Adam and me.

We poured wine and passed around the food. As we ate and talked, Landon filled my mother in on the first grade doings. Chiara didn't eat much, her skin clammy and pale. Kim glowed, and Nick looked, finally, content.

The clink and clatter of silver on plates died down, and my mother cleared her throat. "Erin, darling, Adam, you've done wonders with this house. I was a bit concerned about some of the changes—these windows, for example." She crooked a finger toward the double windows we'd installed at the end of the dining room, framing a section of wall where our Christmas tree stood. "But they're perfect."

"They look like they've always been there," Bill added.

"And I owe you an apology," she said.

"No, you don't, Mom," I said.

"I've been a hair too possessive about the place." She spread her hands. "Such as inviting you all to have dinner here. But we'll have plenty of gatherings at the River House, and I wanted to see all three of you here, in this house, before the big day."

Her voice trembled, and her gaze settled briefly on Kim, in a welcoming way, before circling around the table. Bill took her hand, and Chiara let out a soft moan and patted her belly.

I glanced at Adam, who gave me that crooked grin I love. Despite her words, my mother would never not see this place as home to the whole family. And why not? We were the third generation to live here. Three makes a tradition.

"Adam, when do I get to call you Uncle?" Landon asked.

"Any time you like, little buddy."

I started to clear the table, and Kim joined me in the kitchen.

"You okay with this?" she said. "Nick and me, I mean."

I set the empty salad bowl on the counter. "Are you kidding? I'm thrilled. I wish I could say I saw it coming, but I didn't, even though I always knew you liked him."

"Yeah." Her cheeks reddened. "But then about a month ago, everything changed between us, you know?"

"I know." We hugged, and I wiped a tear from my eye. "By the way, I hope you have a great dress for the wedding, because I might need a stand-in for my stand-up."

"Now you know why I didn't want to investigate your crash," she said. "That, and the Santa suit thefts turned out to be a front for a drug smuggling ring across three states and two provinces. They hid cocaine in the costumes."

I gasped. "And I gave you a hard time about it. I'm so sorry."

"No worries."

"But about this case. Has Nick told you—" I stopped at the sound of someone in the doorway.

My mother. "Kim, I can't tell you how happy I am." They hugged, and the tears ran down my cheeks. "Darling," Mom said to me. "May I use your broiler?"

I laughed. "*Mi casa è tu casa.*" That might not be good Italian, but it made the point.

A few minutes later, we were all back at the table with freshly heated lemon-almond tart on our plates. Some of us poured small glasses of Grand Marnier. Chiara had fled to the bathroom—again.

"You made that?" Kim said. "It's gorgeous."

"I wanted something besides cookies," Fresca replied.

"I can never get enough cookies," Adam said.

My mother gave me a wink. There was one Italian wedding tradition we hadn't mentioned.

"Erin, I followed up on that list you gave me," Jason said, changing the subject. "Every supplier Merrily asked Brad about had a name close to that of a company the Building Supply bought from, but not quite the same. And the payments were sent automatically to bank accounts with a routing number I don't recognize—not a bank around here. It goes back years."

"Did they all go to the same account?" I asked.

"No. Multiple banks, too."

Kim's brow furrowed, her dessert fork hovering midair. "What are you talking about?"

I filled her in. "Merrily figured out that Cary Lenhardt had created false suppliers to redirect money from the Building Supply to himself. He also created fake invoices to account for the purchases."

She flicked her eyes between us. "You tell Bello?"

"Yeah," I said, "and he's on it, but he's convinced Lenhardt didn't kill Merrily."

What if, when Merrily called to ask Brad if he recognized the names of the suppliers she was questioning, he'd spotted a prime reason the thief might kill her—and he'd taken the opportunity, knowing Greg or Lenhardt would be blamed?

But—why? Fear that his wife had left him for her teenage sweetheart seemed far-fetched. A reason to finalize that divorce, sure, but not a reason to kill. I couldn't fathom a credible motive for Brad Larson. And if his alibi—a weekend of ice dams and burst pipes—didn't hold water, pun intended, Bello would find out.

You never know, I thought, seeing my brother and my BFF. Some things can be plain as day, right before your eyes, and you never know.

Chiara returned, yellow-green around the gills, and sat down heavily. "This baby can't come too soon."

After dessert, Adam invited the guys to head downstairs and check out the new tech set-up. Jason rose to follow him, Landon already out of the room. Nick pushed his chair back.

"Brother, would you stay a moment?" I said, and he stayed put, a question on his face. I refreshed his wineglass. "You and Chiara were good friends in high school with Greg and Wendy Taylor. Holly Thornton was a year behind you, and Merrily a year ahead."

Nick nodded, long fingers loose around the stem of his glass. "Yeah, we talked about this yesterday."

"Yes, but Holly told me things today that I'd never heard before. You figure on the edge of them." Would he want Mom to hear this? I couldn't help it. Plus, I'd seen how toxic family secrets can be.

I fished the Bijou movie token out of my pocket and pushed it toward him.

After a long moment, in which he had to be very conscious of the deputy sheriff sitting next to him, Nick spoke. "Holly was headed down a dangerous road, with nothing to stop her. It was self-destruction. But then, almost overnight, she changed. After Merrily pled guilty and went to prison."

"This is what you didn't want to tell me the other night?" Kim asked. "When Erin called back while I was out of the room, and you said she had questions about the car?"

Nick studied the table, his lips tight. They were going to have to work that one out themselves.

"But that's all in the past," I said. "No point bringing it up now. I don't think it has anything to do with the murder."

Chiara picked up her water goblet. "Isn't it strange how different Holly and Merrily were? Both desperately trying to get their parents' attention, in completely opposite ways."

"I never thought of it that way," my mother said. "I figured they were one of those families where one kid follows the rules and the other tests the limits."

"Have Walt and Taya always been so close?" I asked. "You hardly ever see one without the other."

"Living in each other's back pockets," Bill said. "As the saying goes."

"Exactly," I said. "Heidi told me you treated Walt for diabetes. She thinks he wouldn't be alive if not for you."

"Acupuncture was a big part of his treatment, for sure," Bill said. "Taya wanted him off the drugs, and she got her way."

"Mom knows," I said, "but did the rest of you know Merrily went to prison pregnant?"

"What? No." My brother and sister spoke in unison.

Chiara asked my mom, "How did you know?"

"A few years ago, while we were working on a fundraiser, Taya let it slip. I'm sure she thinks of that as her moment of weakness. Holly found out somehow, and thought it would change their minds about writing off Merrily. It was the only time I know of that Walt and Taya disagreed."

"Who wanted to do what?" Kim asked.

"Walt wanted to reconcile with Merrily and be part of their grand-daughter's life. But Taya insisted she made her own bed, she had to lie in it." My mother's jaw tightened. "I told her to stop being so proud."

"Did she think Cliff Grimes was the father?"

"Yes, of course," Mom said. "Are you suggesting he isn't? Wasn't?"

"Greg Taylor," Chiara said.

"You knew?" I said. "He swears he never guessed until last week."

"Not until right now." Her eyes met mine. "It makes perfect sense, doesn't it? Merrily came back to Jewel Bay to reconcile with the past. All of it."

"Now the question is, who should tell Sally that Cliff Grimes didn't have an affair with a teenager?" I asked. "Ashley is coming to town tonight."

"That man," my mother said. "If he weren't already dead, I'd kill him."

I choked back a laugh.

"We can talk to Sally," she continued, taking Bill's hand. "I would be happy to ease that woman's burden."

We fell silent, and I sipped my wine, relieved, even though we still didn't know who had killed Merrily Thornton.

Nick reached for the token and played it in his fingers. "Where did you get this?"

"I found it in your secret stash forever ago, up in the homesteader's shack." The migrant workers' shack from the 1930s, when this place had been a bustling cherry orchard. Nick's hideout. "It made me feel like one of the big kids. It's time I gave it back."

He closed it in his palm. "Thanks."

Twenty-Seven

Bells, bells, bells. The ringing and the singing of the bells.

Why was I dreaming an Edgar Allan Poe poem?

More bells rang, and I emerged from sleep to realize that the first set of bells had been the landline upstairs. The second came from Adam's cell.

He sat up, groggy, and reached for it. I'd fallen asleep against his chest on the new couch in our basement, the two cats each claiming a cushion on the other couch. The sky was dark outside the small windows high on the wall. But someone wanted us awake.

"Hello?" He listened. "Now? You are? We'll be right up." He stood. "Chiara's water broke and they're on their way to the hospital. They're outside with Landon."

We rushed upstairs. Through the living room window, I could see Jason's SUV in the driveway, motor running. Adam opened the door and Jason handed him the sleeping boy. "Erin, call your mom when you think she'll be up." He gave me a small bag of Landon's clothes, then hurried down the walkway.

"Tell Chiara we love her," I called after him. She'd been anxious about going to the hospital, but her miscarriages prevented another home birth with a midwife, as she'd had with Landon.

"What time is it?" In sweatpants and no shirt, his curls a mess and a child in his arms, Adam looked adorable.

I peered into the kitchen and squinted at the stove clock. "Five thirty. Why don't you put him on our bed and let him sleep? I think I'll stay up."

He nodded and padded down the hall. While I waited for the coffee, I stared out the window into the dark, dark night. I'd been hoping the baby would arrive in time for the wedding. A double celebration.

The wedding. Nine days.

∞

Adam had the day off, and while he could have dropped Landon at Mom and Bill's house on the river, he knew Mom would want to be able to get to the hospital the moment Jason summoned her.

"We'll have a boys' day," he said as the three of us drove down the hill. "We'll go out for chocolate chip pancakes and cocoa, and be back in the village in time for the snowman contest."

In the backseat, Landon was just awake enough to clap and shout, "Yay!"

"Sounds fun," I said. "The Merc will be super busy. I'll call you when I hear about the baby." I missed texting.

"I'm going to be a big brother," Landon sang out.

We were early arrivals in the village, but I didn't mind. With an extra hour or two in the office, I might even catch up.

The guys dropped me off out front, and I sent the droopy garland a mental message to hang tight.

No sign of Wendy in Le Panier, which was good for her. I had a lot of questions that she wouldn't want to answer—about her brother, Holly, and the conversation in the alley. And why she hadn't wanted to tell me what she'd known.

Michelle bustled out of the back room with a fresh tray of rolls, hot and yeasty. I am usually faithful to the French pastries, but the heady fragrance of sugar and cinnamon got to me.

"Double shot, skinny, and a cinnamon roll," I said, blindly trusting that my caffeine sensitivity was over. And that my dress would still fit.

She spoke over her shoulder as she fired up my latte. "I'm so excited about this project, Erin. I've started the groundwork." She paused while the espresso machine hissed. "By the way, I think I know who your thief is. I talked to Mimi George at the Inn. We think she's one of her part-timers. Works weekends."

Which would have put her in the village the day of the theft. But what project was Michelle talking about?

"Thanks. I'll talk to Mimi. I don't want to get the girl in trouble."

"No, it's fine. Mimi loves the idea. She wants to help."

"Help with what?"

"Your thief made me see that this community needs a place where kids can get socks or a decent shirt, free, without being embarrassed."

I was embarrassed, realizing I'd almost forgotten about the paper bag left outside the Merc's back door a week ago. But as she described the need and her vision, I knew Michelle was right. A town where lakefront houses sell for millions and people drop buckets of dough for dinner, wine, and art shouldn't have kids who pretend to be tough because they don't actually own a coat or boots that fit.

"Try the community center first," I said. "But if space is too tight there, ask Kathy about her work room. She doesn't use it much, now that she's given up dress-making, and it's close to the school."

"That's brilliant." Michelle set my latte on the counter and reached for my cinnamon roll. "Who should we ask for donations?"

The *we* worried me. My plate was already overflowing. "Ask Donna at the liquor store to help you work up a campaign. She'll know who's most likely to donate. Get Kathy's knitters and quilters involved. They're mothers and grandmothers—they'll love it. You might also ask a few of the merchants to contribute unsold items—scarves, inexpensive jewelry. The Merc will kick in soap and lotion." Only fair, since soap had started this train.

"Oh, Erin, thank you!"

"Got a name for this project?"

She smiled. "The Jewel Bay Treasure Chest."

Bingo, as Old Ned would say. I smiled as I spun around.

"Erin, hi." Brad Larson held the door and I paused, uncertain whether he was holding the door for me to leave or for the striking young woman with him to enter. "Ashley and I were on our way to see you. I'd offer to buy you coffee, but you beat me to it."

"Ashley." I shifted my coffee to my other hand so I could take hers. "I'm Erin Murphy. I'm so sorry about your mother."

"Thank you," Ashley said in a small voice. I led them to a table in the corner. We had the place to ourselves for a few minutes, anyway. Brad ordered for them and Michelle hustled, as she always did. But I saw her sneaking glances at Ashley. In person, her resemblance to Wendy was unmistakable.

"I hear you got a ride up with a classmate. Her mother works in the Building Supply."

"Jasmine's mom?" Ashley said. "Jane. I met her last night."

Jane! How could I forget that?

"I've never been to Jewel Bay before," Ashley continued, one long, athletic leg wound around the other. "My mom didn't get along with my grandparents. I hope I get to meet them before the funeral."

Wild horses couldn't keep my own mother from a grandchild. I popped the lid off my coffee. "So the service has been scheduled?"

"Yes, finally," Brad said. He shot the girl a protective look.

"It's okay, Dad. You don't have to shield me anymore. I want to know who killed my mother, and how, and why."

Brave kid. Braver than I'd been when my father died.

"I told her everything last night," he said. "About her mother and prison, and her grandparents. And that I'm not her real father."

She reached out a hand and covered his. "Yes, you are. Maybe not by blood, but by everything that matters. You will always be my dad."

My throat tightened and my eyes got hot and misty.

He turned his hand over to squeeze hers. Then he looked at me. "They're waiting on the toxicology results. Merrily wasn't strangled after all. Something in her blood ..."

Michelle approached and they sat back, letting her place their drinks and breakfast on the table.

As I'd guessed, but I sure as butter wasn't going to say so. I picked up the paper bag with my rapidly cooling cinnamon roll and scooted back my chair. "Again, I'm so sorry for your loss. If there's anything I can do to help either of you—"

"Don't go yet, Erin." Ashley laid her hand on my sleeve. "Please."

I stayed put.

"Last Saturday, Mom sent me a care package. Truffles and jam and some great scented soap, from your shop. She said—you can read her note." Ashley's voice broke, but she swallowed and gathered her strength. "She said you were a friend, and that if anything happened to her, I should give this to you. And I knew she was right, when I got your sympathy card."

She slid an envelope out of a quilted faux leather handbag and laid two sheets of yellow paper, folded in thirds, on the table. As she did, a familiar glove fell on the floor.

I bent and picked it up. "These are really cute."

"Aren't they? I worked in a shop last summer that carried them, and I used my discount to splurge. I bought a pair for my mom and for Aunt Holly, and for me."

Ah. So that's why the memory of the gift had given Merrily such a glow.

"Anyway," Ashley continued, "I didn't get her package until Thursday. Campus mail is kinda wonky sometimes. So last night, when I showed the note to Dad—"

The bakery door opened and a trio of women came in, ready to fuel themselves for a day of shopping.

I set down my cup and bag, and reached for the first page. Pressed it flat with one hand. *My darling daughter*, it began, and quickly moved from expressions of pride in Ashley and anticipation of seeing her soon, to the comments about me and her request.

Names and numbers filled the second page. Dates, names I recognized from the list of possible fraudulent accounts, strings of numbers in columns labeled *INV* and *ACCTS*—invoice and account numbers? And dollar figures, all in the same careful handwriting as in Merrily's note.

The part of me that adores spreadsheets knew Merrily had loved them, too. But this was information she couldn't entrust to the computer. To anyone who had access to the system. So she'd entrusted it to her daughter.

And to me.

These were originals. Had she kept a copy of the list? Was that what Cary Lenhardt had been searching for when he found the cigar box, the perfect place to hide the cash and misdirect investigators?

"As soon as I saw this," Brad said, "I knew it was important, because of all the questions Detective Bello's been asking about Merrily and the missing money. I didn't know how to reach you, so I called Reverend Christopherson. She gave me your cell number, but no answer."

"My phone got soaked when I got run off the road Wednesday night." I gestured to the bruises and my rainbow eye. "Did you call the detective? This will make his embezzlement case against Lenhardt stick."

"He doesn't trust me," Brad replied.

"It's not personal. He doesn't trust anyone." I turned to the girl. "Ashley, did your mother send you any cash?"

"A ten. She sent me one every week, to buy myself a latte and a bagel, or lunch that wasn't from the school cafeteria."

As my mother had, though back then a five would do the job. Merrily had not sent her daughter a wad of stolen cash.

I studied the figures in my hand. They were the nails in Cary Lenhardt's coffin.

But they didn't tell us who had put Merrily in hers.

Twenty-Eight

*I*n groceries, the busiest days tend to be the Thursdays before July Fourth and Labor Day, and the weeks before Thanksgiving and Christmas. In Jewel Bay's peculiar blend of retail, those days are important, but in winter, we live and die on the second and third Saturdays in December.

Weather is the key. We need enough white stuff to get people in the spirit, but not enough to keep them home, where they can shop online. I was sitting at the counter, finishing my coffee and finally starting my cinnamon roll when outside there arose a clatter. Ignoring my ankle, I sprang from my stool to see what was the matter.

A happy sight: A man with a ladder.

Not just any man, but Jimmy Vang, a leather tool belt around his hips, a hammer hanging from the loop in the sideseam of his worn brown Carhartts.

I pushed the door open. "Jimmy, I am so happy to see you, I could kiss you."

"Miss Erin." The Hmong man bent his head, his shaggy black hair falling over his eyes like a curtain. He flicked it back and began chattering and gesturing. His English wasn't great, but somehow, we always under-stood each other. I scurried inside for my coat and joined him on the sidewalk.

We quickly developed a rhythm. Jimmy charged up the ladder, un-hooked a section of garland into my waiting arms, dropped down the ladder, and scooted it down the sidewalk to the next hook. Shoppers veered around us. When he got to the spot where I'd wired the gar-land to the gutter, he peered down at me. "You do this?"

I nodded, chagrined.

"Very bad." He unwound the wires and descended the ladder, then pointed at the damaged gutter and splintered soffit. "Too much weight. Lucky it didn't break. I rip out old wood, nail up new. New hooks, too. In spring, I paint it for you."

"Perfect," I said, but I wasn't looking where he was pointing. I couldn't take my eyes off the lights tied to the long strand of garland in my hands.

I knew who the killer was.

∞

By ten thirty, I also knew this would be our best sales day ever. Luci the Splash Artist joined us, wearing a frilly white Mrs. Claus apron, to talk with customers about her soaps and lotions. "Baby products," I whis-pered, and her eyes lit up like—well, like Christmas.

Tracy had charge of the chocolates and Lou Mary ran the cash reg-ister, leaving me to roam, restocking, straightening, and answering questions.

At ten thirty, Oliver Bello strolled in. To my surprise, the Cuban heels were gone, and he wore a shiny new pair of Sorels with fleece cuffs, perfect for a Montana winter. I led him to the back hall, out of shoppers' earshot.

"I've interviewed the Larsons," he said. "Thank you for urging them to call me."

"I'm sure you can understand Brad's reluctance. He thinks you're eying him as a murder suspect."

Bello didn't admit or deny it.

"Did they tell you who Ashley's father is?" I asked. "Her biological father, I mean."

"Yes. And that keeps your friend Mr. Taylor first on my list."

"Not if he didn't figure it out until after Merrily's death."

"According to him," Bello replied. "Maybe she told him before that. Maybe she wanted money."

"Maybe so." I couldn't deny the possibility, much as I wanted to. On our way back through the shop, I plucked one of Candy's canes out of the display and offered it to him. "Try one of these. To sweeten your mood."

He pointed the end at me like a sword and winked.

Maybe I should have told him my theory about the killer, I reflected as the door clanged shut behind him. But I wasn't sure yet of all the details. Better to logic out the steps first. All the ways the killer had tricked Merrily into coming to the schoolhouse, appealing to her deepest desires and fooling the rest of us.

"Ready!" a customer called, the front counter piled high with her choices.

I limped to the counter. "Looks like you're doing all your shopping in one place. We appreciate it."

"Oh, honey, I'm just getting started," she said, her Texas twang music to my ears. "From here, it's on to the kitchen shop and the bookstore. Then we'll see what damage I can do after lunch."

I love retail.

Next came a couple bearing three "Christmas in the Village" baskets—Montana Gold pancake mix, huckleberry syrup, and Cowboy Roast coffee. A pair of Reg's handmade ceramic mugs is extra, but worth it.

The man spotted my bruised cheek. "What happened to the other guy?"

"You don't want to know," I replied, and he cackled as he scooped up the baskets and followed his wife out the door.

No word yet on Chiara and the baby. All would be well, I knew, grateful for the busy spells that kept me from worrying.

I refilled the sample pots of coffee and chai, and joined Tracy behind the chocolate counter.

A woman bent down to study the truffles displayed behind temperature-controlled glass. "Do you have sugar-free? I adore chocolate, but I'm diabetic."

"I wish we did," Tracy said. "I've experimented with a few non-sugar sweeteners, but I haven't found the right combination yet."

"Better be careful," the diabetic's shopping companion said. "You tick off your hubby, he might do a Claus von Bulow on you." She gestured as if poking the other woman in the arm, and they drifted off, laughing.

"Claus von Bulow," Tracy said in a low voice. "The guy who shot up his wife with insulin and put her in a coma for what, twenty years? Why would you even joke about that?"

That was a question I couldn't answer, but I finally knew how Merrily Thornton had died.

∞

"I can still catch the snowman contest if I hurry," I told my staff. "Do you mind?"

"Nooo, go, go," Lou Mary said, and off I went, moving down Front Street as quickly as my ankle would allow. Between the community center slash library and the bridge sit what everyone calls "the cottages." Sweet one- and two-bedroom bungalows, immaculately landscaped, they're where I'd stay if I came to Jewel Bay on vacation. In front of the office stood a jaunty snow gentleman sporting a top hat and a wooden cane, branches for arms, with striped mittens stuck on the ends. I waved hello to him as I passed by.

The steel truss bridge has guarded the south entrance of town since 1912. Every decade or two, the highway department makes noises about replacing it, but after the locals remind them that its charm brings tourist dollars our way, they pony up for repairs instead. And every December, Elves drape the trusses with garland and lash saplings trimmed with red bows to every pillar and post.

On the other side of the bridge, a mountain range of snow towered over the entrance to the park. Plow crews had been building the pile since the first flakes fell in November, so the kids would have enough of the white stuff to make snowmen and other statuary. A few ambitious adults had hauled in ice and snow sculptures made elsewhere, the figures now positioned like a welcoming committee: Mickey Mouse, Dumbledore, and Shrek. A twelve-foot tall grizzly, catching a fish. A howling wolf that Nick would appreciate. A trio of singing ice angels.

But the last in the lineup was easily the winner: a ten-foot-long ice-breathing dragon, its wings spread, serpentine tail coiled and ready to strike.

"Must have taken a crew to build it, let alone get it here safely," a woman said, and I turned to see Holly Muir. She tucked her hands in her armpits. "Brrr. At least it's cold enough. The sculptures should last through Christmas."

"Fun event," I said. "Nothing like it when we were kids."

"Jewel Bay's a lot livelier now than it was back then." Her voice held a note of resentment.

"But you never had any doubts about coming back here."

She grunted. "I had plenty of doubts."

Whoa.

We stopped in front of what I guessed was meant to be a polar bear. It slumped heavily to one side, as if the maker hadn't quite been able to hoist the midsection into its proper place. Some adult assistance was allowed in the children's categories, but this one looked entirely the work of the ten-and-under set.

"Must be hard for your folks right now," I said, "dealing with tragedy during the holidays."

"They're so wrapped up in each other, they barely notice anyone else," Holly said. "My nine-year-old played in his first basketball tournament last weekend, and they skipped it."

That surprised me. "Did they come Sunday?"

"No. The fourth graders played Saturday. I'm not sure who played Sunday."

I thought back to the photographs I'd seen, with her in the same black coat, clapping her plaid gloves.

Not the black gloves she wore now. The black gloves she'd been wearing when she unloaded the groceries earlier this week.

"Which kids are yours?" I asked.

"There. The ones making the snow cat." She pointed to a boy and girl thirty feet away, working on a giant, lopsided cat under Jack Muir's watchful eye. "You can tell they're vets' kids."

"Cute." Another twenty feet past them, Landon smoothed a snow penguin's belly while Adam shaped the beak. My guy looked up and smiled, and I waved. "I didn't realize your father had been ill. The stresses with your sister must have aggravated the problem. That explains why your mother is so protective of him. And a teeny bit of why she was so hard on your sister."

Holly's laugh was bitter, and she shot me a harsh look before strolling on to inspect the next snow sculpture.

In a flash, the pixels in my brain rearranged themselves again. I'd been wrong about the lights. Walt and Taya decorated everything— their shop, their home, the schoolhouse—with tiny white lights. But the string around Merrily's neck bore old-fashioned colored bulbs.

Walt had told me, down at the barn, that his purchase of leftover Christmas decorations included tubs full of lights, and that he'd donated them all to the village. I'd thought he'd had wrapped a stray string around his daughter's neck, to divert attention from the tiny puncture wound in her skin. Her neck, I'd guessed, or maybe he'd stuck the old syringe full of insulin straight through her red coat.

"It was you," I said, stepping into Holly's path. "Not your dad. Detective Bello was right about the summons, but wrong about the person. He's convinced Merrily got a call from someone who knew her secret. I'm sure he checked her phone records, but a call from you wouldn't raise any suspicions."

Holly clenched her fists, a muscle in her cheek twitching. "Even my darling sister wasn't suspicious of me. She should have been."

"It was the other way around, wasn't it? She knew *your* secret. And you were afraid she'd tell your parents why she pled guilty all those years ago. To protect you, the child they thought so perfect."

"I hate Christmas," Holly Thornton Muir said.

"What you told her, I don't know. Maybe you claimed your mother was having a change of heart. Or that she wanted to meet Ashley. You needed a powerful hook, to lure Merrily to the schoolhouse."

"What if I don't want to have a holly, jolly Christmas?" she said in a mocking tone, as if she hadn't heard me.

"When I stopped at the clinic, to break the news about Merrily, I saw a box of decorations inside the front door. You hadn't put anything up yet. You must have had the box in your car when you asked Merrily to meet you at the schoolhouse. Then, later in the week, your husband was decorating. I bet he was short a string of lights. The string you used on your sister, to make everyone think she'd been strangled. A sweet bit of revenge."

"That's plain silly, Erin." She shot a look past me to her family and mine, busy with their snow sculptures, then her eyes darted toward the park entrance.

"What about the insulin? Is that silly, too? You told me you'd have to order insulin for my cat because you'd run out. You ran out because you used the clinic's supply on your sister."

Her eyes turned shiny-bright and her hands twitched, her face a picture of desperation. The last face Merrily Thornton had ever seen.

I pointed at Holly's black-gloved hand. "The red-and-black plaid glove under her body was yours. You lost it at the scene. Merrily left hers in her kitchen."

Maybe she had, maybe she hadn't. All I'd seen on the kitchen chair was her bag. But why else had Holly Thornton Muir changed from the super-cute plaid gloves just like her sister's to the basic black pair she'd worn the rest of the week, if she hadn't lost one?

"I hate Christmas," she repeated. "I hate my name, and I hated my sister. She was going to ruin everything. I stopped her, and I am not going to let you pick up where she left off."

She shoved me and I staggered backward. She turned and sprinted toward the park entrance. I reached instinctively for my phone. My pocket was empty. I glanced over my shoulder, but in the time it would take me to reach Adam and get his phone, Holly would get away.

I pushed after her, ignoring the barking in my ankle and the voices in my head telling me to stop. Outside the park, Holly headed for the bridge, and I followed.

I couldn't lose her. I had to catch her. For Merrily, and for Ashley. Even for Walt and Taya. For Jewel Bay.

For justice.

She stopped for breath by the cottages, and I caught up with her. She snatched the jaunty snowman's heavy oak cane and raised it.

"Give yourself up, Holly. It's for the best."

She took a swing and I ducked. She swung again, but I wasn't quick enough and the cane grazed my shoulder. I darted behind the gentleman snowman, pain shooting up my left leg.

Where had she gone? I peeked around, only to see Holly searching for me.

Surely someone would see what was happening and call the sheriff. But all the shoppers were up in the village, and the families were down in the park.

I bent and grabbed a handful of snow. Pressed it into a ball, stepped out from behind my guardian, and pelted Holly. Scooped up another handful and aimed. Backed away as she attempted to move in on me.

She swung once more and once more I ducked. She pivoted and ran up Front Street.

I couldn't run anymore. I glanced around, desperately hoping for a passerby or a cottage guest who could catch her. But it was just me and the snow gent. I grabbed one of his rock eyes and packed it in a snowball. Fired. Hit Holly in the upper back and she stumbled. I grabbed the other eye. By the time she righted herself, I was closing in on her. I fired again.

Down she went, hard, arms and legs splayed. She didn't get up.

And then I saw what I had not wanted to see: That it had been easier for me to imagine a husband loving his wife too much than a woman not loving her sister the way I loved mine. And I saw, too, that I wanted Adam's relationship with his brothers to be like mine with my sibs, to be as close as I'd thought Holly and Merrily.

I stood in the icy street, panting, watching Holly Muir rant and writhe.

So that's what they mean by a snow job.

Twenty-Nine

The dapper snowman had given his eyes and accessories in the service of a good cause. After Bello and Oakland arrived, I'd told them my story and hobbled to the Merc to warm up and smear a fresh dose of arnica gel on my swollen ankle. Then Adam, Landon, and I strolled back to the cottages to spruce him up. His cane had been taken into evidence, and one mitten was missing. But with his top hat back in place, a sprig of cedar tucked into the red-and-green plaid hatband, and two new eyes, he looked quite the gentleman again.

Bello had confirmed my insulin theory. The string of lights had not distracted the pathologist. The tox screens, as Bello called them, had detected low blood sugar but elevated levels of sugar in Merrily's heart. She wasn't a diabetic, and they'd ruled out an insulin-producing tumor. That left an injection as the most likely cause of death. Deputies had begun executing search warrants that morning, and they'd found a used syringe in the trash at Holly's home, along with Merrily's phone.

Holly hadn't been seriously hurt by my illicit snowball, thank goodness, and no one said I should have let her go and called for help, but I could tell that's what they were thinking. That's what I was thinking.

Still, I had a talent for this investigating thing. Consider it a form of community service.

Cary Lenhardt had also been arrested. He admitted to running me off the road. Deputies had found a map in his truck showing Jason and Chiara's house, confirming my suspicion that Lenhardt had intended to warn him off, too. They'd also found boxes full of unpaid bills and collection notices. The small amounts he'd stolen from the Building Supply had grown over the years, to the point where he considered himself entitled. He'd gotten in over his head with the expensive toys, like the RV he'd sold Ned, and a mortgage he couldn't afford with a balloon he couldn't meet. Cash had never been his principal means of theft, but as I'd guessed, he'd seen the opportunity to sneak the cash out of the deposit bag before Merrily took it last Saturday. Then he'd snuck it into the cigar box in her desk. I felt bad for his wife, but Bello dismissed that as "sympathetic drivel," saying she should have realized they were living beyond their means ages ago.

As for Greg Taylor's mysterious absence from the basketball tournament Sunday afternoon, when Merrily was killed, he'd been on a top-secret mission in his uncle's barn, working with his French chef brother-in-law and other friends. He'd been about to tell me in the liquor store when we were interrupted.

They'd been carving the ice dragon and he hadn't wanted his son to find out. The boy adored dragons, so the father had kept on working to finish the sculpture by the entry deadline, even though it had meant getting to the basketball game late.

I reported all this to Tracy and Lou Mary from the safety of the Merc, in between customers.

Then Oliver Bello returned. "I've just come from the Thorntons' shop," he said. "They want to see you and the Larsons. They are some seriously strange people."

"Because they want to see me?"

He laughed and offered me a baby candy cane. I took it.

First, I stopped in Le Panier for a tray full of hot drinks. Wendy took me aside to say that Greg had told the family about Ashley, and though they were astonished, they would welcome her.

"Even Greg's wife?" I asked.

She nodded. "I suggested he put diamonds in her Christmas stocking."

I laughed out loud.

Then it was on to the antique store, where the shock of Holly's actions and arrest had not yet set in. I'd asked Bello if the Thorntons had said anything about hiring a lawyer or putting up bail, and he said he'd made the suggestion but they hadn't responded. Shock, he thought.

Shock, or lost in their obsession with Christmas. I couldn't tell. Walt and Taya's transformation into soft-hearted Mr. and Mrs. Claus was going to take time. Gaining a granddaughter did not make up for the loss of both daughters, or the realization that they had punished the wrong one. Learning that Merrily had gone to prison to protect Holly and spur her into turning her life around, because she'd adored her little sister and feared that the truth would devastate their parents, had them stunned. Holly, it seemed, had not actually been a force for reconciliation. Instead, she'd nursed her parents' grudge, reveling in being the good daughter.

"One question, though, Taya," I said, as I sat in the Thorntons' back room, the shop closed for the day. "At the schoolhouse, when you heard that Merrily was dead, you slapped Greg Taylor. You didn't know he was Ashley's father, did you?"

"No." Taya shook her head, her cap of silvery-blond hair moving furiously. "I thought—I thought that if he hadn't given her a job, she'd have gone back to Billings. To safety."

Walt spoke for the first time. "And she would still have been alive."

No hot cocoa could have stopped the shiver that ran through me. "You knew. You knew it was Holly. Did you see her car drive in Sunday afternoon? Or recognize the glove she dropped?"

The puzzled look on Taya's face cleared. "No. No, we weren't home. We'd gotten a call about a collection of Putz houses up in Eureka. The owner's daughter wanted to find out if they were valuable."

"Putz houses?"

"Sometimes called Glitter Houses," she said. "They're cardboard, covered with glitter or white flocking. They originated in Germany in the 1800s, and whole villages were made from them, though cottages and chapels were the most popular. They were quite the rage in the 1940s and '50s. Both our parents collected them, and we've always adored them."

I felt like I'd dropped down the Christmas rabbit hole. What had Heidi said? *There's passion, and there's obsession.*

"Anyway," Walt said, "we drove up for a look-see, and bought the lot." He pointed at several cartons stacked along one wall. "Go ahead. The top box is open."

I reached in and lifted out a small, light object wrapped in tissue. I peeled back the paper to reveal a white cottage that fit in the palm of my hand. Yellow cellophane windows peeked out from under a red roof, and flocking covered the bottle-brush trees in the yard. Charming and curious, I couldn't help thinking they'd be delightful under the tree in the Merc's front window. I put it back, reluctantly.

"So if you weren't home, and you didn't see Holly drive to the schoolhouse Sunday afternoon, how did you know she'd been there?"

"Because of the lights," Taya said.

"You don't see that style much anymore," Walt said. "When we saw Merrily—when we saw her body, we knew right away that they came from a batch we'd given Holly and Jack years ago, when we upgraded. It's the shape of the cup that holds the bulb, and the way it clips onto a tree or a garland."

Only someone as obsessed with Christmas as these two would ever notice such detail. I understood now that they had responded to Merrily's death so oddly because they'd spotted Holly's involvement, but had been too tortured to say so.

Would they still relish the season, after all this was done?

When I'd found Taya on the schoolhouse porch, a place her daughters had loved as much as she did, she'd been crying for both of them. For the whole family.

I wanted to do the same, but I had a shop to run.

Brad and Ashley Larson arrived as I was leaving. "They've had quite a shock, but I think they will welcome you," I said, smiling at Ashley. "As long as you love Christmas."

Though her eyes still grieved her mother, she brightened. "It's my favorite holiday."

Out on the sidewalk, I rubbed my lucky stars. Brad would always be on Ashley's side, I knew. As my mother had said, you can't protect your children from life's ups and downs, no matter how hard you try. But I thought Ashley would be okay.

The Thorntons were another story. If they couldn't forgive themselves or Holly, as they hadn't forgiven Merrily, they might be too mortified to stay in Jewel Bay.

I glanced up Front Street to the Jewel Inn, the chalet-style building across the tiny square from Dragonfly. *Oh, heck, as long as you're meddling. Just be quick.*

Mimi George, co-owner of the Inn, stood at the reservation desk. "Ah, Erin. I think I know why you're here." She held up a finger, then beckoned to a short girl with light brown hair clearing a table.

"I'm Erin Murphy," I told the girl. "I run the Merc. I want to thank you for your honesty."

"Being honest about being a thief isn't exactly gold-star stuff," she said, her hazel eyes flicking nervously between Mimi, the floor, and me. "But you're welcome."

"You've heard about the Treasure Chest project, to give hard-working kids a chance to pick out clothes and some basics their families can't provide?"

She bit her lip. "I think it's really great."

"Maybe you can be an advisor," I said. "Listen, I know you work here all weekend. Once or twice a week, after school, you could come to the Merc and help me pack orders for shipping. It'll only be an hour or two, so it won't interfere with your homework. We'll have more hours for you in the summer."

Her face lit up as if a switch had flicked on behind eyes too young to be so wary, and she glanced at Mimi, who nodded, then back at me. "Yes. Yes. Thank you."

I wasn't the only employer in town who believed in second chances.

I made my way back to the Merc slowly, admiring the window displays. Contest or no, the other merchants had taken the Thorntons' window as a challenge to up their game. The sculptor had filled his front window with bronze animals decked out for the season. In a clothing shop, headless mannequins wore red and green scarves draped across their torsos and cedar bough skirts. And in Food for Thought, a stack of books in the shape of a Christmas tree glowed with tiny lights, a star on top.

The holiday surprises didn't stop there. Inside the Merc, on the steps to my office, sat a basket filled with boxes of truffles. Each three-pack had been tied with ribbon—silver, dark red, and forest green. My wedding colors.

I carried one to the front of the shop where I found Tracy, tiny red chili peppers dangling from her ears.

"You needed wedding favors," she said. "We've been packing them up whenever we had a chance."

No matter that we had customers waiting, that I was a wet, soppy mess. I threw my arms around her and kissed her.

The front door chimed and Candy Divine waltzed in, holding a small cardboard box. "This got delivered to Puddle Jumpers by mistake. It's for you, Erin."

I was in such a good mood, I didn't even mind her squeaky voice. "What? Did the phone company take pity and send me a replacement after all?" I'd gone more than forty-eight hours without a phone, and that was about forty-seven too many.

I grabbed a knife and cut the clear tape, then tore into the box, tossing bubble wrap aside, eager to see my new magic electronic whizbang.

My brow furrowed. No magic, no electronics. Inside the box lay three brass nametags in the shape of the state of Montana. *The Merc*, they said, followed by our names, one each for Tracy, Lou Mary, and me.

I'd forgotten I'd ordered them early in the week, after my frustration at never being able to remember the name of the cashier at the Building Supply. *Jane* was now permanently etched in my brain. I hoped.

"You don't need a new phone," Candy said. She reached into the pocket of her pink tulle ballet skirt and pulled out a battery. "I have an extra battery, from when I dropped hot syrup on the screen of mine and it cracked and—well, you can have it."

I retrieved my poor phone from my desk upstairs and handed it over. She popped off the back like an expert and snapped the battery in. One push of a button and it sparked into life.

And then I surprised even myself. I hugged Candy Divine.

Thirty

"Relax, Erin," Chef Kyle Caldwell said. "This isn't the first rehearsal dinner we've ever hosted. It isn't even a particularly big one."

Maybe not, but it was *my* rehearsal dinner. The long pine tables were set with the Lodge's best plates and gleaming silver. Fresh green boughs dotted with pine cones graced the center of the table, white pillar candles in canning jars ready to light.

Another table held the tins of cookies my great-aunts Sophia and Carla had carried on the plane, for an Italian wedding tradition I knew Adam would love.

And yes, there were biscotti.

As was the custom, our out-of-town guests would be joining the wedding party for dinner—my uncles, aunts, and cousins from California, a few friends from Seattle and Missoula, and Adam's family.

I had laughed till I cried when I met the twins—two tall, dark-haired men with curls and dancing eyes and dimples just like Adam's. Calvin had been the first to wrap me in a bear hug—or had it been Alan? I threatened to make them wear name tags, but one of the wives—May or June, cousins who could easily have been twins—said they'd probably just switch and confuse everyone, even themselves. They'd hugged Adam, clapping him on the back, and though I knew he kept expecting them to shake hands with a buzzer hidden in their palms or sneak in the house and short-sheet our bed, they'd proven themselves excellent guests. They'd charmed my mother, played endless hours of games with Landon, and completely behaved themselves.

And when I took May and June into the kitchen shop, they confessed that the boys, as they called their husbands, had finished their big construction project early and earned a bonus, so they splurged on us. Which, in my experience, was a very brotherly thing.

"They went a little overboard," May had said, and June chimed in, "As they always do."

"Erin, got a minute?" Now Alan, or Calvin, stuck his head in the dining room.

I didn't—it was nearly time to get dressed—but I walked over anyway. "What's up?"

"Our numbnuts brother has run off, and we need your help finding him."

For a nanosecond, I almost believed him, then I remembered who I was talking to. The twin who'd summoned me opened the door and tugged me out in to the cool, dark evening. The other twin wrapped a swath of soft fabric—a scarf I thought I recognized as Adam's—over my eyes and tied it behind my head.

"Oh, no. No, guys. No." I reached up with my free arm but a hand grabbed mine before I could tug the scarf loose. "What are you doing? I have places to go and people to see. A wedding to rehearse."

"Oh, we'll get you to the altar on time," one of my soon-to-be brothers-in-law said. "Our dear brother didn't trust us with a bachelor party, and while snowshoeing through forty feet of snow was fun, in a perverse sort of way, we have something else in mind."

With me as the bait.

They wrapped another scarf around my hands and loaded me into the back seat of their rental car. *Just track the turns they make and figure the distance. You'll be fine,* I told myself. *You'll be back in no time.*

The driver—I had no idea which one it was—pulled out of the parking lot and made a hard left, the back end of the car sliding to the right. I breathed in sharply.

"You idiot. Have you never driven on ice before?" the passenger brother said.

"What are you talking about? We don't have ice in Minnesota," the driver twin replied.

We drove up the hill on the main road a quarter mile. Turned right.

"Not that way, you goofball." Backed up and went the other way. We turned left, the sound of the tires on pavement telling me we'd reached the highway. We crossed the big bridge over the bay, and stopped for the town's single stoplight.

"Where are we going?" I said.

"It's a surprise," came the unsurprising answer. We circled round, me doing my best to figure out where we were, then I realized we were back on Lodge property.

"Long way 'round Robin Hood's barn," I said.

One twin chuckled. "What does that mean, anyway?"

We hit a rut and the car lurched to the left, then leveled out and I knew we were on one of the service roads.

"We've been exploring," one of them said. "This place is amazing."

Trust them to have found every secret nook and cranny.

The car slowed to a stop, and the driver shut off the engine. The doors opened, and one of them helped me out, quite gently. A barn door on wheels slid open and the familiar smells of horses and hay hit my nostrils.

I sneezed, doubling over with the force of it.

"Good gravy, girl. That would blow a man back to the Midwest," one of my captors said.

"I can't help it. I always sneeze at the first smell of hay and the first taste of champagne."

"Very romantic," he replied.

A horse whinnied. "Ribbons," I called. "Good girl." She neighed back in response. I hadn't seen the chestnut mare since she'd gone to winter pasture, but she'd been brought back to pull the wedding sleigh. She'd be paired with Kintla, a big Appaloosa I was equally fond of.

We were deep inside the barn now, one brother on each side.

"Here we are. You're going to go up the ladder, one step at a time," one said. "I'll be right behind you."

Climbing a ladder with a blindfold and your hands tied behind your back, even if with a cashmere muffler, is unnerving. Alan—or Calvin—talked me up the steps, with encouraging murmurs from his brother on the ground.

"Now, I'm going to help you," my guide said, one hand on my shoulder, then other on my back. "Sit, then swing your legs over the side. I'm right here with you."

"Careful if she sneezes again," his brother called. "You'll be flat on your back on the barn floor."

I smelled horse blankets. I knew where I was, and I wasn't afraid. I let them lower me into the box, one of Walt Thornton's unsold prizes— an oversized Christmas package. My feet found the small steps inside. The twins hoisted the lid into place, and left me alone in the dark.

I probably could have gotten out, if I'd been willing to stand and rock the box onto its side. But after what I'd been through this week—

getting run off the road into an icy ditch, then whacked in the back by a mad woman yielding a snowman's cane—I decided to sit and wait. To be part of the joke, whatever it was. This was not just a practical joke on their brother—it was my initiation into the Zimmerman family. And I was determined to pass the test.

But I didn't have to huddle in the corner, blind and helpless. I was able to snag the knit scarf binding my hands on the edge of a step and loosen it enough to slip off. Then I untied my cashmere blindfold, wrapped it around my neck, and leaned against the pile of blankets. A few air holes let in barn light, and after the craziness of the last week, it felt good to rest.

I woke to the sound of urgent voices.

"What did you do with her?" Adam asked. "First you send me all over the place on a scavenger hunt. Then you kidnap my fiancée—"

"We haven't done anything, man," one twin said.

The other added, "Smart girl like that, she musta run off. Did you think she would marry a goon like you?"

"But don't worry, brother," the first one said. "We brought you a very special gift, all the way from the North Pole."

Tanner howled. "Now you're in for it, Z. You really should have let them throw you a bachelor party. What did you think they would do? Hire a stripper to jump out of a cake?"

Ah, my good buddy, throwing me a clue. Or cue. Or whatever.

Something thunked against the side of the box. The ladder. The lid rose a few inches, then slid off and landed on the barn floor with a thud. I climbed the tiny steps, threw up my arms, and yelled, "Ta-da!"

Adam punched the nearest twin, and the other jumped on his back. Tanner reached in to separate them and found himself sitting on the barn floor, laughing. From my perch atop the box, I rubbed the stars on my wrist and watched, eyes wide, one hand over my mouth. My black eye was barely noticeable now; I didn't need anyone else sporting one on our big day.

∞

The sleigh driver, Kim's father in a sheepskin coat and a cowboy hat trimmed with a red silk poinsettia, pulled on the reins gently. Ribbons and Kintla slowed and the sleigh slid to a stop. Ribbons tossed her mane and turned her head toward me, big eyes shining, as if she knew this ride was special.

I took Nick's hand and stepped down, my ankle perfectly sound in my red cowboy boots. My mother adjusted the red angora wrap around my shoulders. Then Kim, wearing the first dress I'd seen her in since our high school graduation, handed me my bouquet, and led the way. My mother and I took my brother's arms. Tanner met us at the carriage house door and he and Kim began the procession.

Everyone stood, except my sister, sitting in the front row with my new baby niece in her arms. Beside her, Landon clutched the ring bearer's pillow, ready to leap into action when called upon.

In front of the lectern, in her angelic white robes, Reverend Anne beamed.

I took a deep breath, and we started up the aisle. At the front of the room, Nick and my mother kissed me, and stepped back to find their seats.

And there stood my beloved, my knight in a blue suit.

Adam took my hand and I knew, without a doubt, that we would live happily ever after.

THE END

Cooking Up Trouble with the Murphy Clan

The Christmas Cookie Exchange

Cookie exchanges are a great way to fill your holiday cookie jar without spending days baking. Each participant brings enough of one cookie or candy for other participants to take home a half or full dozen, plus a few to sample. Choose sturdy cookies that pack and keep well. Pack offerings in advance, or at the gathering. And bring recipes!

Almond Bianchi aka Almond Cloud Cookies
These gluten-free delights are light and meringue-like, with a magical almond flavor. Perfect with espresso or a strong cup of tea.

8–10 ounces almond paste (package sizes vary)
1 cup sugar
¼ teaspoon salt
2 large egg whites, lightly beaten
⅜–½ teaspoon almond extract
Powdered sugar, aka confectioners' sugar, for topping

Heat the oven to 325 degrees. Line two baking sheets with parchment paper or silicone liners.

In a stand mixer, blend the almond paste, sugar, and salt until the mixture becomes uniformly crumbly. Gradually add the egg whites while mixing, to make a smooth paste. Stir in the extract.

Scoop the dough by heaping tablespoons onto the prepared pans. (You won't think you have enough for 2 dozen cookies, but you will!) Sprinkle the cookies with the powdered sugar—they will expand as they bake, so be very generous. Use three fingers to press an indentation into the center of each cookie.

Bake 22–25 minutes, until they're brown around the edges. Remove from the oven, and let the cookies cool right in the pan.

Makes 2 dozen.

Merrily's Russian Teacakes

So good, they could be deadly. A classic, also known as Snowballs, Mexican Wedding Cakes, and Pecan Sandies.

1 cup butter (2 sticks), softened
½ cup powdered or confectioners' sugar
1 teaspoon vanilla extract
2¼ cups all-purpose flour
¼ teaspoon salt
¾ cup finely chopped pecans
About ½ cup additional powdered sugar, for rolling baked cookies

Preheat oven to 350 degrees.

In a mixing bowl, cream the butter, sugar, and vanilla. Combine the flour and salt and stir into the creamed mixture. Stir in pecans. Chill up to an hour.

Roll dough into 1-inch balls and bake on an ungreased cookie sheet for 10–12 minutes. Pour the additional powdered sugar into a flat bowl or on a plate. When cool enough to touch but still warm, roll cookies in the powdered sugar. Cool, then roll in sugar again if you'd like.

Makes 4 dozen.

Molly's Six-Ingredient Peanut Butter Cookies

Okay, so they're not a traditional Christmas cookie, but when they're this tasty, who cares?

These cookies are gluten-free and freeze nicely. Spritz your measuring cup with cooking spray—one quick burst will do—before scooping up the peanut butter, and it will slip right out and clean up easily. Adams' No-Stir Chunky peanut butter is perfect for this recipe—and not just because of the name!

2 cups peanut butter
2 cups white sugar (scant)
1 teaspoon vanilla extract
2 eggs
2 teaspoons baking soda
1 pinch salt

Heat oven to 350 degrees.

In a medium bowl, cream together peanut butter and sugar. Beat in the vanilla and eggs, one at a time. Stir in baking soda and salt. Roll dough into 1-inch balls and place on a cookie sheet 2 inches apart. Press a fork into the top to make a criss-cross pattern. Bake 10–12 minutes. Cool on baking sheet 5 minutes before removing to wire rack to cool completely.

Makes 4 dozen.

Fudge Ecstasies

Adding half the chocolate chips just before baking gives these crackle-topped cookies a soft, fudgy interior. And mixing the batter in the sauce pan makes clean up easy!

1 12-ounce package (2 cups) semi-sweet chocolate chips, divided

2 ounces unsweetened chocolate

2 tablespoons butter

¼ cup all-purpose flour, heaping

¼ teaspoon baking powder

2 eggs

⅔ cup sugar

1 teaspoon vanilla

1 cup chopped walnuts or pecans

Heat oven to 350 degrees.

In a heavy medium saucepan, melt 1 cup of the chocolate chips, the unsweetened chocolate, and the butter, stirring constantly until melted. Remove from heat and allow to cool slightly.

In a small bowl, stir together the flour, baking powder, and a dash of salt.

Add the eggs, sugar, and vanilla to the chocolate mixture, in the saucepan but off the heat; mix well. Add the flour mixture and mix well. Stir in the remaining one cup of chocolate chips and the nuts.

Drop by teaspoons onto a baking sheet. Bake 8–10 minutes, or until the edges are firm and the surface dull and cracked. Allow to cool on the baking sheet for a minute or two, then transfer to a rack to cool completely.

Makes about 3 dozen.

At Home with the Murphy Clan

Classic Italian Lasagna

"Oven ready" (no boil) noodles make this dish easy-peasy! Perfect with a green salad dressed with Basil Vinaigrette.

1 pound ground beef or sirloin
½ cup chopped onion
2 cloves garlic, minced
3 cups (25-ounce jar) spaghetti sauce
1 cup chopped tomatoes, with the liquid (fresh or canned work equally well)
1¾ cups (15-ounce container) ricotta
1 egg, slightly beaten
1 teaspoon dried basil
1 teaspoon dried oregano
9–12 oven-ready lasagna noodles, uncooked
3 cups (12 ounces) shredded mozzarella
½ cup grated Parmesan

Heat oven to 350 degrees and spray or lightly grease a 13x9-inch pan.

Brown the ground beef and add the onions and garlic, cooking until onions are translucent. Add the tomato sauce and tomatoes, and mix.

In a small bowl, mix the ricotta, egg, basil, and oregano.

Spread ½ cup of the beef and tomato mixture into the prepared pan. Top with three noodles, making sure the noodles do not touch. Spread ⅔ cup of the ricotta mixture on top of the noodles. Add another layer of beef and tomatoes, and 1 cup mozzarella. Repeat, layering noodles, ricotta, beef and tomatoes, and mozzarella, until done. Top with the Parmesan.

Cover with foil and bake 35 minutes. Remove foil and bake another 10–15 minutes, until hot and bubbly. Allow to rest 5 minutes before cutting and serving.

This dish can be assembled and frozen without baking. Cover tightly and refrigerate up to two days, or freeze up to two months. Bake the refrigerated dish 40 minutes, then 10–15 minutes uncovered; bake the frozen dish 1 hour 30 minutes, then 10–15 minutes uncovered, or thaw and bake as if refrigerated.

Basil Vinaigrette
A lively vinaigrette to give your salads the taste of summer all year-round.

½ cup extra virgin olive oil
1½ tablespoons red or white wine vinegar
1 tablespoon water
1 small shallot, peeled and sliced
1 scant teaspoon Dijon mustard
¾ teaspoon kosher or flaky sea salt
2 cups loosely packed fresh basil leaves

Put the olive oil, vinegar, water, shallot, mustard, and salt in a blender or the container for an immersion blender. Coarsely chop the basil leaves and add them immediately. Blend until the vinaigrette is smooth. Thin if you'd like by adding a little more water or olive oil.

Serve at room temperature. Store in a covered jar up to a week in the refrigerator. Makes about ¾ cup.

Erin's Spur-of-the-Moment Shrimp Florentine
Florentine means "with spinach." Alternate translation? Quick and yummy! Erin used a blend with sundried tomatoes, parsley, horseradish, lemon, and other herbs and spices. Try an Italian blend, an herbed salt, or a Cajun spice blend for a different flavor punch!

1–2 tablespoons olive oil
1 teaspoon or 1 clove minced garlic
2 slicing tomatoes or 2–3 Roma tomatoes, chopped
1 tablespoon of your favorite spice blend
2–3 cups (or handfuls!) fresh spinach
20–24 medium shrimp, cooked
Cooked jasmine rice or a short, sturdy pasta, such as penne or rotilli

Heat the oil in a large skillet. Saute the garlic until fragrant, about 2 minutes. Add the tomatoes and cook over medium-low heat until soft, 3–5 minutes. Toss in the seasoning and stir well to blend. Add the spinach and cover for 2–3 minutes, until spinach is soft. Toss in the shrimp and stir; cover and cook until shrimp are heated, another 2–3 minutes. Serve over rice or pasta.

This recipe is flexible and easily increased. Serve with a green salad. It pairs well with red or white wine.

Serves 2.

Pan-Baked Lemon-Almond Tart

Because you can't eat cookies all the time! This gluten-free treat is perfect with vanilla ice cream or a tiny glass of Grand Marnier, for dessert or a special brunch.

2 tablespoons sliced almonds, toasted, for garnish
4 eggs
¾ cup sugar
Pinch of salt
½ cup ground almonds
½ cup cream
½ cup sliced almonds
1 lemon, zest and juice
2 tablespoons butter
3–4 tablespoons powdered sugar, for garnish

Heat oven to 300 degrees. Toast 2 tablespoons sliced almonds for about 10 minutes. (Remember, they will continue to darken as they cool.)

Raise oven temperature to 400 degrees.

In a bowl, combine eggs, sugar, salt, ground almonds, cream, sliced almonds, and lemon zest and juice.

In an 8-inch oven-proof skillet over low heat, melt the butter. When the foam subsides, add the almond mixture, tilting the pan to distribute batter evenly. Cook tart until the edges just begin to set, about 3 minutes, then put the pan in the oven and finish cooking, about 10–15 minutes.

When tart is done, broil for about a minute, until just golden on top. Sprinkle with powdered sugar and sliced toasted almonds. Cool slightly before cutting and serve.

Serves 6–8.

The Perfect Lunch Break

Grilled Caprese Sandwiches

Nothing is quite so comforting as grilled cheese, as this variation of the famous Caprese salad demonstrates. A sturdy bread will grill nicely with oil, but you can use the more typical butter if you prefer. If you've got a panini press, press away!

4 slices rustic sourdough or Italian country bread
1 large garlic clove, peeled and halved
½ tablespoon olive oil
3 tablespoons basil pesto
3 ounces fresh mozzarella cheese, sliced
1 ripe heirloom tomato, thinly sliced
Kosher salt
Freshly ground black pepper
4 large basil leaves

Lay the bread on a flat surface. Rub one side of each slice with the cut side of a garlic clove and brush with oil. Turn over. Spread basil pesto on the unoiled side of two slices, then layer with cheese and tomatoes, dividing evenly. Season to taste with salt and pepper. Top with remaining slices of bread, garlic side up.

Heat a large frying pan over medium heat and butter or spray with cooking spray. Place sandwiches in pan. Cover and cook 2–3 minutes, until golden on the bottom. Flip and cook 2–4 minutes, until the other side of the bread is golden. Remove from heat and place on serving plates. Garnish with fresh basil leaves or carefully open and insert the basil. Cut in half with a sharp knife and serve.

Makes 2 people very happy.

Treats Too Good to Save for Weddings!

Herbed Squash Toasts

An appetizer that will make your guests swoon. The diced butternut squash available in many grocery stores is perfect; pumpkin or other winter squash would work nicely, as well. This spread is best made a day ahead.

2 pounds butternut squash, peeled and seeded, and cut in cubes or
    large pieces (about 4 cups)
3 tablespoons extra virgin olive oil, divided
½ medium onion, finely chopped
2 tablespoons finely chopped fresh mint
⅛ teaspoon freshly grated nutmeg
¼ cup walnuts or pistachios, lightly toasted and finely chopped
⅓ cup grated Parmesan
Salt and freshly ground pepper
Baguette, sliced about ½ inch thick, about 16 slices
Additional mint and nuts, for garnish

Heat the oven to 425 degrees. Line a baking sheet with foil and oil or spray it.

Place the squash on the baking sheet and rub or toss with 1 tablespoon of the olive oil. Bake until tender, 40–60 minutes depending on the type of squash and the size of the pieces. Turn the pieces two or three times, using a spatula or tongs, so they cook and brown evenly. When tender, remove from oven and allow to cool a few minutes.

Place cooked squash in a food processor bowl. Pulse, scraping the sides of the bowl, and purée until smooth. Add a little broth or water if needed, to get a smooth puree.

Heat 1 tablespoon oil over medium heat in a large, heavy skillet. Add the onion and a generous pinch of salt, reduce the heat to medium low, and cook, stirring often, until very tender, sweet, and lightly cara-melized, about 20 minutes. Remove from the heat and add to the squash in the food processor bowl.

Add the mint, nutmeg, walnuts or pistachios, Parmesan, and 1 table-spoon olive oil, and pulse together. Season to taste with salt and pepper.

Oil and toast the baguette slices in the oven, 3–5 minutes or until lightly crisped. Spread a tablespoon of the mixture on each slice. Gar-nish with a sprinkling of crushed nuts and a small mint leaf. Additional mint leaves and nuts make a nice decoration on the serving platter.

Makes about 2 cups, or 16 toasts. Spread keeps several days in the refrigerator and freezes well.

Tanner's Life's-Too-Short-For-Rehearsals Champagne Cocktail
As readers of *Treble at the Jam Fest* remember, Tanner loves creating special cocktails. This drink honors the bride: classic, with just the right balance of sweet and tart!

For each drink:
1 sugar cube
5–6 drops Angostura bitters
½ ounce St. Germain (elderflower liqueur)
5½ ounces champagne
Lemon twist, cut with a channel knife or paring knife

In a champagne flute, soak the sugar cube with the bitters. Add the li-queur, and slowly pour in the champagne. Add the lemon twist.
Salut!

∞

Readers, it's a thrill to hear from you. Drop me a line at Leslie@
LeslieBudewitz.com, connect with me on Facebook at LeslieBudewitz-
Author, or join my seasonal mailing list for book news and more. Sign
up on my website, www.LeslieBudewitz.com. Reader reviews and rec-
ommendations are a big boost to authors; if you've enjoyed my books,
please tell your friends. A book is but marks on paper until you read those
pages and make the story yours.

Thank you.

About the Author

Leslie Budewitz is passionate about food, great mysteries, and her native Montana, the setting for her national-bestselling Food Lovers' Village Mysteries. The first, *Death al Dente*, won the 2013 Agatha Award for Best First Novel. She also writes the Spice Shop Mysteries, set in Seattle's Pike Place Market. A practicing lawyer, Leslie is the first author to win Agatha Awards for both fiction and nonfiction. A past president of Sisters in Crime, Leslie loves to cook, eat, hike, travel, garden, and paint—not necessarily in that order. She lives in Northwest Montana with her husband, Don Beans, a doctor of natural medicine and musician, and their cat, an avid bird-watcher.

Visit her online at www.LeslieBudewitz.com, where you can find maps of Jewel Bay and the surrounding area, recipes, and more.